G000037349

THE LIES WE WERE PROMISED

A novel by Rachel Ivan

THE LIES WE WERE PROMISED

TRUST CAN BE A KILLER...

To Mandie, I hope you enjoy this!

Rachel xx

RACHEL IVAN

Copyright © 2021 by Rachel Ivan All rights reserved.

No part of this publication may be reproduced, distributed or transmitted in any form or by any means, including photocopying, recording, or other electronic or mechanical methods, without the prior written permission of the publisher, except in the case of brief quotations embodied in critical reviews and certain other non-commercial uses permitted by copyright law.

*Dedicated to all the lost children around the world
and the mothers who are so desperately searching for them.*

*'The trust of the innocent is
the liar's most useful tool.'*
— Stephen King

'In India, a child is taken every eight minutes.'
— BBC News report, 2020

CHAPTER

1

Southern India, monsoon season.

It took just a few seconds on a sweltering afternoon for everything to change for Preeti. A brief glimpse of a snake tattoo on the stranger's arm was the last thing she could see before a hessian covering was pulled roughly over her head, plunging her into blackness.

"Please let me go." she cried, desperately.

As the van door slammed shut with an almighty shudder, a damp cloth pressed close caused everything to spin. Hearing the blaring wail of police sirens as they raced past made the dazed child wonder why she had been forgotten.

As Preeti clung desperately to the sides, the fast-moving van weaved its way through the bustling traffic. The usual afternoon street noises were coming from outside, somewhat muffled through her hood. An eclectic mix of horn-honking from irritated car drivers and wobbling, three-wheeled autorickshaws impatiently caught up in the traffic alongside the bellowing grunts of skinny cows, bony ribs protruding sharply through translucent leathery hide as they wandered aimlessly from one end of the road to another. The sounds came crashing through all at once, a deafening crescendo to overwhelm her senses.

Suddenly, the van swerved sharply, and she found herself thrown sideways.

'Slow down idiot! You will get us all killed!' an angry male voice screamed, spewing a tirade of curses from somewhere in the back.

Preeti could hear frantic voices arguing loudly, but her whimpering cries were ignored. The grainy coarseness of the hood material clung too close, making it hard to breathe. Its rough texture and musky scent reminded her of *amma's* overflowing rice sack, bulging out of the narrow kitchen larder.

She did not know that a crowd of horrified onlookers had gathered outside the school, both children and parents, witnesses to her abduction. The humid air was abuzz with mutters of shock and speculation.

Everything had happened in just seconds.

Until then, it had been a regular school day, no different to any other. Preeti had hopped up and down excitedly, balancing on one leg chatting to her best friend Anita, by the entrance gates. She could see Anita's mother, Hema Chandran, standing nearby talking to a friend whilst small circles of women animatedly exchanged juicy titbits of their daily gossip. Loud peals from the school bell announced that the day was over as the crowd of senior students piled eagerly down the steps, weighed down by overstuffed rucksacks.

The following weekend was all Preeti could think about. Bongo, the juggling circus clown, famous for his jaw-dropping magic tricks would be at Anita's seventh birthday party and she couldn't wait. Only a few more sleeps.

With her short mane of shiny, bobbed hair and trusting, doe-like eyes, little Preeti was adorable. Her dazzling, shy smile was enough to melt even the hardest of hearts. Harry Potter was her world, and a day would not go by when she did not pin back her dark hair with rainbow-coloured hair grips, the letters 'HP' inscribed boldly in the middle.

Amma always came late for collecting her. Preeti never understood why and fervently wished she was like the other mothers who always showed up on time, showering their children with wide smiles, hugs and candies when they saw them. She once overheard Hema aunty describe *amma* as 'more in love with sticky *halwa* sweets, than her own daughter.' Luckily, aunty always patiently kept a watchful eye on her, lingering protectively after school to make sure she wasn't left alone.

Preeti turned, eyes wide with delight, as she heard the ice cream vendor Vellu, enthusiastically pressing the rusty bell on his cycle handlebars, over and over, attracting the children who would gather around him like fluttering night moths inextricably drawn to the flickering light of a candle stub. Sweat encased his faded white vest, causing it to stick in damp patches to his lanky frame, and his bright blue *lungi* was pulled up above his knees. Vellu's hair was peppered generously with flecks of dull grey, and deep lines crinkled his eyes, but he had been doing the school circuit faithfully for nearly twenty years without fail. He knew the children needed him.

Each day he parked his old black cycle faithfully in the same spot at three pm precisely, like clockwork. Attached behind the bicycle was a rectangular trailer, and no sooner had he lifted the lid, then swarms of excited children pushed and jostled each other, vying for the best place near the front.

Preeti glanced shyly as Mrs Chandran reached in her purse, and handed a shiny rupee coin to each girl, to buy ice cream. 'Don't forget the change!' she smiled.

Standing alongside her best friend in the queue on the pavement waiting for their impending treat Preeti felt happy, pushing both her thumbs into her mouth, an oddly comforting habit since babyhood. Luckily, *amma* wasn't around to stop her. She knew how much her mother hated her doing that.

It was whilst waiting for the ice-cream that Preeti spotted her father in the distance, running toward her along the edge of the road in order to avoid the throngs of noisy schoolchildren spilling out of the narrow pavement. She was surprised, papa never usually picked her up after school. He looked agitated, and was waving his arms frantically in the air, shouting something but she couldn't hear what he was saying.

The screech of sharp brakes was deafening. She felt herself suddenly being pulled from behind, so quickly that she didn't have time to register what was happening except to glimpse Anita's horrified expression, watching helplessly as her friend was pulled head-first into the unknown vehicle.

As the van hurtled down the road through a cloud of dust, all that remained were the high-pitched screams of Hema aunty exploding hysterically into the balmy afternoon air.

CHAPTER

2

The Olive Tree bar, Central Croydon, Surrey, UK.
Three days before India.

As she slouched against the bar, Kerensa Oldfield was sure she could sense his presence – the masculine odour of cheap Brut cologne intermingled with woody undertones of Mysore sandalwood soap was unmistakable. She could even imagine the familiar oval-shaped soap, damply covered in lathery bubbles, left carelessly in a warm, sludgy mess on the side of the bath. A faint childhood memory indelibly imprinted that refused to leave.

The smell of Kaian. Her father.

The man who had shattered her entire world at just five years old when he walked out without so much as a backward glance.

"A double Baileys, with extra ice, please?" Kerensa raised her voice, hoping to grab the bartender's attention as her words echoed harshly in the confined space. She noticed a shiny badge imprinted with the name 'Ben' pinned lopsided on the front of his shirt.

The Olive Tree bar, wedged between a bustling Tesco Express and a bespoke antiques shop was inconspicuous, seamlessly blending into obscurity on the busy Croydon street. Inside, gaudy yellow and red chaser lights flashed sequentially along a worn 1950's jukebox that stood lonely in the corner surrounded by clusters of dark, chipped wooden tables and chairs that had seen much better days. It was the ideal hideaway into which Kerensa could disappear when she desperately needed space just to think. Reflect.

She would be meeting Kaian for the first time since childhood. On his home turf, the town in which he lived, grew up. What words could be said to the father who chose to leave his own child heartlessly at just five years old? What if he refused to have anything more to do with her?

Her anxiety suffocated, all-consuming as it tightened its grip. Ruminating thoughts had been persistently reliving the countless possibilities of their first meeting in her mind, like a groundhog-day, endlessly repeating itself over and over.

Years of curious questions had accumulated in her mind, questions only he could answer. The thought that her father could choose to leave them so heartlessly, disappearing into the night without a word, was unbelievable. The more time she spent thinking of him, the angrier she found herself. One thing Kerensa had learnt effectively over the years if nothing else, was to swallow any pent-up emotions relating to her father.

Work was Kerensa's main priority. Based with the prestigious Travers & Haines in the heart of Croydon, her hard-earned position as a senior accountant at twenty-seven guaranteed security and a steady income. The years devoted to studying had paid off. Security made her feel cosseted, a buffer against the emotional problems that life had thrown her way.

Perched on the edge of the chipped wooden stool, legs dangling, Kerensa took a lingering sip from the glass, smiling contentedly to herself. Catching a fleeting glimpse of her reflection in a glazed mirror mosaic tile on the wall, she glanced critically at the dark tresses that tumbled loosely down her back, and olive skin, usually glowing but had looked tired of late, with tell-tale dark circles crowding the area under her eyes. The heaviness of emotional burdens seemed to have taken its toll she thought to herself with a tinge of regret.

The bartender edged closer to where Kerensa was sitting.

"Hey, just finished work?" he asked gently, vigorously wiping a random glass with imaginary stains. Strands of highlighted blonde hair flopped messily across his forehead, and his piercing blue eyes seemed kind, immersive, the sort that could draw someone in. There was something about him but venturing down that road was something she knew she just couldn't afford to do at the moment.

Kerensa managed a wry smile, not feeling in the mood for small talk.

"Yes, but so tiring, just needed this Baileys desperately!" She sighed.

"I know what you mean!" He laughed heartily. "I'm Ben, by the way, and you are...?"

"Kerensa. Nice to meet you," she replied politely as he flashed a broad smile.

"Gosh, your name is really beautiful! I don't think I have heard it before, where is it from?"

"My mother is Cornish, and I believe it's quite a traditional, old-school name." She reached for her glass - the rich creaminess of the Baileys was comforting.

As they chatted, Ben mentioned he had been offered a much-prized opportunity to undertake work experience at the British Consulate, so was shortly wrapping up bar work to venture eastwards to Singapore.

Before she could mention that she too was on her way to the East, Ben hastily grabbed a colourful leaflet from a neat stack by the till, scribbling something on the back.

"I hope you don't mind, I don't normally do this, but this is my number...do give me a call Kerensa, I would really love to take you for a drink or dinner sometime." he stuttered, embarrassed, offering her an appreciative glance.

It was then that a large group of people walked through the door, appearing to be colleagues for after work drinks. There were eruptions of raucous laughter, much back-slapping and giggling from a few women in the group who huddled together, deep in conversation. Ben smiled apologetically, an unspoken goodbye as work beckoned as he hurried back to the other side of the bar. More customers were coming in, de-manding his undivided attention.

Folding his card, she squeezed it into the side of her purse, making a mental note to look at it later but realistically over the next few days she knew she would be occupied with last minute preparation for her trip to India. She felt relieved to be left alone for a while with just quiet thoughts for company.

The peace didn't last long however, she could feel a squeeze of her right shoulder accompanied by peals of hysterical laughter coming from behind. There was only one person with that distinctive laughter – Emily.

Unceremoniously dropping herself on a nearby stool Emily tossed her tan leather briefcase onto the floor, landing by her feet.

"Kerensa Oldfield! Thought you would be here, I know you wanted to disappear quietly without a fuss, but surely you didn't think that I would let you drink alone in your last week, did you?"

Early thirties, four years older than Kerensa, the two of them had gelled instantly. They had gossiped and laughed, drinking endless glasses of iced peach daiquiris, as they bonded over Thursday evening Pilate sessions.

"Keri, how are you feeling? Not long until India." Emily stared at her expectantly, probing eyes peering into her friend. "Can you imagine meeting your dad after so many years?"

The only one at work who truly understood the reason for Kerensa's work sabbatical was Emily. Everyone else assumed she was languishing, 'finding herself' in the subcontinent, almost like a corporate slave having a premature crisis out in a different world to determine the true mean-ing of life.

"Em, honestly, I have mixed feelings. I feel quite excited at going, but also scared. It's a huge place. What if I travel all the way there, but don't find him?"

"You can only do your best, take it as it comes." Emily's expression was encouraging. "Remember Kerensa, you have spent months making a game plan, so try to make friends who can help you, and make sure you stay safe. I've got to admit, I was feeling worried. India is not the safest place for women travelling alone, but I know you're smart Keri. If you need me, just shout anytime okay, you know I'm always here for you."

Kerensa watched Emily raise an imaginary glass to her lips, indicating it was time to get a drink before disappearing into a crowd at the other end of the bar. She couldn't help but laugh at her friend who always had an uncanny way of making her forget her troubles, if only momentarily.

Kerensa took the large gin and tonic handed to her, as Emily swallowed a big gulp from her own glass, before slamming it down on the table.

"Wow, have you seen the bartender? He's damn cute!" she pointed, rather indiscreetly, to Ben on the other side of the bar.

"We were talking earlier, and he gave me his phone number." Kerensa mumbled, looking down, a little embarrassed.

"Honestly, you always get the good-looking ones interested in you, it's simply not fair!" Emily rolled her eyes dramatically, as she gave her friend a teasing, playful nudge.

With curly strawberry blonde hair wrapped in a neat high bun away from her face, her short skirts accentuated a pair of lithe, slim legs that usually grabbed the attention of most of the red-blooded males in the vicinity. Renowned for her efficiency in producing detailed balance reports at short notice whilst confidently researching systems databases and spreadsheets with little training or supervision, Emily was the capable accounts clerk that the firm desperately needed.

Ed Sheeran's 'Shape of You' came on in the background, its catchy lyrics echoing around the dimly lit room. '*The club isn't the best place to find a lover, so the bar is where I go.*' The all too familiar rhythm felt strangely comforting. Kerensa found herself subconsciously mouthing the words, humming along.

"Hey, how is mum?" Emily asked suddenly, her tone lowered, clearly concerned. Kerensa remembered the traumatic events of a few months before that had almost broken her, a shell of the girl she used to be.

"She's much better than before, thanks. Getting there slowly. The new medication seems to be really helping her slowly back to normality." Kerensa sighed, looking down at her glass, moving it side to side contemplatively as though the answers to her problems lay within. The glacial cubes clinked loudly, hitting the sides, engulfed by the creamy bubbles. "I wish you were coming to India with me, Em." Kerensa felt suddenly wistful, it would have been good to have the company, rather than travelling alone to a strange place.

She knew her friend couldn't afford any long-haul trips at the moment - Emily had recently taken out a mortgage on her brand new two-bedroom flat, a huge commitment, and the timing wasn't right for her to be travelling to any exotic destinations.

Everything Kerensa had done over the past few months had gathered momentum for this moment in time. Hours spent planning the intricacies of her trip, taking time off work to get her visa from the Indian High Commission, learning simple language phrases from Youtube – all led up to answering a much bigger question. Why on earth did her father desert them?

"I know you don't want to go Keri but it's all going to work out, wait and see. Once you find Kaian, you can get all the answers you need and close that chapter of your life completely if you want to." Kerensa felt Emily squeeze her arm supportively, as she continued. "Listen, to take your mind off things I promise that once you are back, we will go away for a nice long weekend okay? Just the two of us. Somewhere cheap and cheerful, a real treat. Maybe Brighton? Some indulgent shopping, a few late nights drinking copious amounts of pink gin, and binging on Netflix!"

"It sounds perfect, can't wait!" Kerensa replied managing a smile, feeling more cheerful.

India suddenly didn't seem as daunting anymore. She could breathe once again.

CHAPTER

3

It started with the small things. Especially the shiny, sparkly ones.

They were what attracted young Samuel de Mello, who, at the tender age of eight loved pretty things.

He used to see them, perched precariously on the top shelf of Tony's convenience store, situated alongside Calangute beach, Northern Goa. Kept far out of the reach of mischievous hands.

Miniature windmills from the Netherlands, a golden Eiffel Tower, that lit up when the small button underneath was pressed. A model of the Orient Express train that had doors that opened, and figures of tiny occupants inside. And, of course, no ornament shelf would be complete without a Taj Mahal. The one there did not disappoint. Its ornate white domes were precise and beautifully carved from stone, and when lifted it emitted dulcet tones of an instrumental sitar. Beautiful.

Mama used to take them down for him while she did her food shopping so that he could be occupied, and she could shop in peace.

"Which one is your favourite Samuel?" old Mr D'Souza used to ask as he shuffled over slowly from his stool behind the ancient till. He was kind, with crinkly dark eyes and a small grey beard.

"I like them all sir." Samuel replied diplomatically. But he knew the Taj was his favourite. He wanted it.

He felt bad because he had no money to buy it. Mama said that five hundred rupees was a ridiculous price for a trinket.

So, when old Mr D'Souza was busy with a foreign tourist, Samuel decided to wrap it in his hanky and put it in his pocket.

CHAPTER

4

Kerensa found she couldn't stop herself from rewinding the fateful events of that day over and over in her mind.

She'd had a sense that something had been terribly wrong the moment she stepped through the front door. It'd been the pills of all shapes and sizes strewn carelessly around the carpet that had caught her attention first. After knocking persistently on the barricaded bedroom door, the eerie silence from within had sent waves of panic through Kerensa until she'd managed to finally prise it open.

The memory of mum lying face down, unconscious, was shocking and would remain imprinted in her mind to return to haunt her over and over. Just like discovering a faded black and white polaroid hidden amongst an old box of treasures a mere glance of which could cause a tucked away, indelible memory to resurface.

Then there'd been the frantic race to the nearest hospital. Sirens wailing furiously. Mum's stomach pumped.

For five days it had been touch-and-go according to the head nurse who kept a watchful eye on Catherine. Thankfully, she had pulled through, but it took time, and many long evenings waiting anxiously at her bedside for both Kerensa and her younger brother, Matt.

Kerensa recalled frantically grabbing packets of crisps from the hospital vending machine to grab a bite to eat after racing over to the hospital from work. Hours were spent at mum's side, hoping and praying she would fully recover. She was really the only parent she and Matt had.

This incident, six months before, had made her realise that she had to find Kaian. It was the right time to track down her father. Before it became too late, and the window of opportunity passed. It was something that she had vowed to herself she would never do. To chase a man who had obviously not been interested in staying around and fulfilling his responsibility as a father. But much to her annoyance, it seemed that there was little alternative. Her mother wanted, and deserved, emotional closure for peace of mind and healing. They all did. There was only one option - to find him and get some answers.

The diagnosis for Catherine had come back as severe bipolar depression, which shook her to the point where she lost herself completely.

Kerensa had watched their beloved mother go downhill gradually, changing from a loving parent to a vulnerable woman with erratic mood swings whose behaviour often frightened them.

Childhood solace existed at granny Rosie's cosy, two-bedroom cottage in St Ives Bay, Cornwall, where the long summers were idyllic and were an avenue for them to temporarily leave the tensions of homelife behind. Long walks on the nearby beaches preceded picnics, sitting barefoot eating granny's home-made scones smothered generously with fresh blackberry jam, as the powdery sand sifted coarsely through their toes. That time had been a time of blissful happiness. They could simply be normal children with no worries or cares, just a limitless imagination and zest for life.

She finally left the bar after an hour and a half, feeling chilled.

Emily had left a little earlier, hugging Kerensa closely wishing her all the best. The bartender, Ben, was nowhere in sight.

There was a lot that needed to be finished, as she was just a few days before setting off on the venture she had waited a lifetime to do. To find Kaian. The father she had not seen for over twenty years.

CHAPTER

5

The faceless clock on the wall had no hands. Time did not exist in that place.

A fly buzzed noisily around the cold, dry slice of toast. A thin sliver of congealed jam had unlovingly been dumped by the side.

Soft sobs came from the little girl sitting on the broken, stained mattress in the corner. She had been weeping endlessly, there was no love or comfort in the place of utter desolation.

The long chain fastened around her small ankle rubbed painfully against her tender skin, the other end secured onto a large bolt on the stone wall nearby.

The room was dingy and small, and a solitary lightbulb swayed low from the ceiling, casting menacing shadows eerily.

The man came only to bring tasteless food and large mugs of tepid water. He even brought a comic book once, with colourful pictures as a treat. He told her to eat and looked at her sympathetically with some kindness in his eyes. He told her she would be leaving the place soon, going to a brand-new home. A new family. Far away.

This made Preeti cry even more.

She was six and didn't understand why mama wasn't coming to take her home.

CHAPTER

6

'*Good afternoon. Emirates Flight EK 404 to Dubai is now boarding at Gate 11C.*

Please proceed as instructed and await further announcements.'

Aruna Pillai, from Manhattan, was a woman who knew how to be difficult. That's how she got results. It took just a pursing together of her signature, blood-red smeared lips coupled with a penetrating glare of utter disgust to send a fully grown man to whimpering.

Sharp heels clicked loudly against the marbled floor of the airport lounge as Aruna strode purposefully towards the departure gate, tablet in one hand, impatiently dragging the bulging Louis Vuitton cabin bag with the other. Terminal four at JFK just seemed to go on forever.

Pausing momentarily to brush an invisible fleck of dust from her paisley Hermes scarf, a kaleidoscope of pastel hues that wrapped loosely around her neck, Aruna remembered that it had been a gift from a grateful client many years before, whose case she had taken on had led to victory. The journey ahead to India would be long, but it would give her a chance to reflect on what needed to be done. There were deals to be finalised and urgent correspondence to be dealt with.

Not many at the Hillsview apartments, Central Park, knew much about the well-dressed Indian lady who lived in the penthouse suite. She preferred to remain private, keeping herself to herself, with a certain aloofness that was not unnoticed by her neighbours, who had all but given up on the pursuit of friendliness.

Mid-forties, slim and of medium height, Aruna did not particularly stand out from the crowd. She always said a routine 'good morning' to the concierge at the front desk, each morning on her way out for her daily stroll around Central Park, fresh coffee balanced in one hand, phone in the other, her short, ebony hair pinned back for comfort, large D&G glasses perched precariously at the end of her long nose.

The joggers always annoyed her the most - inconsiderate to those, like herself, who preferred to take a more leisurely stroll. She kept stopping to let one pass as they brushed past her, muttering a hurried thanks under their breath, oblivious to the angry glare emitted from behind the dark frames, by the tiny woman.

In another life, Aruna had been a first-class lawyer-determined and ruthless, tirelessly fighting for her clients to win. Her icy reputation preceded her in North American legal circles. A New York Times article had described the determined Aruna as 'formidable, a force to be reckoned with.'

That is, until her chance meeting with the Indian billionaire, Suresh Reddy, a friend of a friend whom she'd been introduced to at an elite social gathering - she preferred not to refer to them as parties, as frivolity had no place in her life.

Renowned for his self-made background, Suresh had risen up from the ashes of abject poverty. Growing up in a slum dwelling in Mumbai, where homework was done under the flickering flame of a candle stub, he worked his way up through sheer hard work, rapidly climbing the ranks of the Indian banking sector. His hunger for money was matched only by his love for food and the finer things in life, and his clothes reflected this. Handmade suits tailored in Saville Row, London and lined with spun gold brocade, were flown over especially for his personal use, which sat comfortably over his rotund, heavy built frame.

The business proposition he'd discussed with Aruna was high stakes, lucrative, grabbing her attention immediately. Moral and ethical views didn't interest her but wealth and assets most certainly did.

Aruna's intense work ethic had initiated a death knell for her fifteen-year marriage. Her long-suffering husband had left her for another woman, one who was softer and more attentive to his needs. No children had come from the marriage, thankfully. Aruna had no patience for children.

In the airport lounge, the little brats were everywhere. Why on earth couldn't their parents control them, Aruna thought to herself, bristling with irritation. Running around unsupervised in the lounge, they were ignored by exhausted parents who were absorbed in chatting or looking at magazines, as they snatched a few moments of 'me-time', oblivious to the high-pitched screams.

On boarding, she made her way to the window seat in row one of Business Class. She sat down, balancing her laptop on the open tray table, ready to begin working.

There was a lot that needed to be done, and Aruna Pillai was the woman to ensure that any loose ends were securely tied.

***

As the plane roared ascending up from the Heathrow runway, houses and fields disappeared slowly, folding into one another picture book style, as they became smaller and smaller. Once they were barely visible, obscured by a haze of vaporous cotton clouds, Kerensa sat back in her window seat, pushing on the headset given to her by an air hostess.

A mental list of what needed to be done swirled in her mind. Her passport was tucked safely into the handbag pocket, visa stamped securely for a year. Jabs had all been successfully taken-warned by the nurse at her surgery that typhoid was rampant in the town, she knew that she had to take the correct precautions. A sealed bottle of sun lotion lay in her handbag, picked up last minute from the airport lounge, alongside the light, cool linen outfits, modest and loose, ideal for the tropical weather and the conservative environment, which had been packed neatly with care.

This trip simply had to be done alone, there was no choice. Matt was busy, immersed in his final year project at university and her mother was just not well enough to travel extensively. Granny had come to stay with them, which was a relief and gave Kerensa peace of mind.

She had promised to be in touch often with home. Mum had given her a chunk of her own savings-Kerensa knew India was relatively cheap but was immensely grateful for her generous gift.

Two seats away, an oversized grey-haired man coughed wheezily for what seemed like an eternity. He turned to her, apologetically, covering his mouth with a starched hanky. She waved away his apology with a smile. He continued coughing loudly and reached for a water bottle in the rucksack by his feet, gulping the clear liquid down.

"I'm so sorry," he wheezed, voice husky as he struggled to compose himself. "Is this your first visit to India?"

"Yes, it is," Kerensa replied. She smiled. "Are you okay?"

"Apologies, I have just recovered from a really bad chest infection but had to travel. My wife and I moved to India many years ago, we just love it there. Our home is near Kanyakumari beach, on the southern coast. I shuttle between London and Nagercoil often for work." He sounded proud and happily shrugged. "So, what made you choose India?' he asked pointedly.

Kerensa didn't feel like talking about herself or reasons why she was visiting the sub-continent. Especially to a stranger.

"India has always fascinated me.' she stumbled, 'And I have always wanted to explore the temples in South India." This was partly true- they were on her bucket list of dream destinations to travel to. In particular the Thunamalayan temple was famous, she had read so much about it... over a thousand years old, it was ornate and seeped with religious history. She intended to go there at some stage.

"Ahh you will love them!" The man smiled "I'm David, David Holdsworth by the way." He reached in his top shirt pocket. "This is my

card, my wife is Pat, please don't hesitate to give us a call if you get stuck
or need anything okay? Remember India is different to the west, and
you need to watch your passport and money carefully," he advised gently.
She was sure that if her father had been in her life, this is what he would
have advised too.

"Thank you, you're so kind. I'm Kerensa." It was a relief to have a
contact point, just in case. In case anything went wrong.

An hour into the ten-hour flight, she was already beginning to feel
slightly more at ease.

India beckoned enticingly with an alluring charm.

CHAPTER

7

"Come with me, and I promise you will have the most delicious meal that you have ever tasted!"

These throwaway words were sweet music to the ears of little nine-year old Mano, who had not tasted a hot meal for as long as he could remember.

The foreign looking lady with the dark eyes and light face had been staring at him for some time. He had felt her eyes on him when he was sitting with his metal bowl on the station steps, begging people for coins, tears streaming down his cheeks. The soulful tears of a crocodile, tugging at heart strings; appealing to soft hearted motherly types, elderly grandfathers with generous wallets, and small girls, who would sometimes give him their last rupee coin.

"How old are you, my little friend?" The lady had come in front of him, crouching down to his level. He noticed she had been watching him for a while and seemed to be quite fascinated.

"I don't know ma'am." he replied in broken English, glancing at her shyly. He remembered a few English words picked up from kindergarten school. Another life, a long time ago.

"Don't worry, I will look after you," she smiled at him. "Come with me, and I will buy you your favourite food."

He followed her down the steps and around the corner to a small place called Ram's Hotel. Run down with a cracked sign hanging lopsided on the front, it was packed with ravenous men sitting side by side on narrow wooden benches similar to those in a school canteen, wolfing down large plates piled high with rice and various accompaniments. Mano could see dishes of curry, tandoori chicken, bowls of spicy vegetables and skewered meats. His mouth was watering. The men couldn't stop staring hungrily at the woman. She was beautiful, and the sole woman in the restaurant.

"Let's sit here." She pointed to a small table in the corner, which appeared to be private, away from the staring eyes. She was now conversing in Tamil to him, but it was broken, and it was obvious that she was unfamiliar with the language.

Mano followed her lead and sat facing her, a look of anxious expectation written on his face. The delicious aromas were wafting under his nose and it was almost too much to bear.

"Can we take two plates of mutton biryani with extra salad and chicken-65 please?" She said to the young waiter, who promptly scribbled down the order on a small notepad pulled from his pocket. Mano had not heard of chicken-65, but it sounded wonderful. His stomach was growling in anticipation.

"It won't be long now. You must be hungry." The woman looked at him rather kindly. There was something about her that he was not sure of. Why would a well-dressed stranger like her buy him a hot meal?

He was too hungry to care. The food came quickly, and Mano wolfed it down, he couldn't even remember having a meal as delicious. He spent his days foraging in overflowing dustbins, hoping for even meagre scraps, and hanging around the street food stalls, waiting for half-eaten, discarded leftovers from well-dressed customers, which he would quickly gulp down before the irate stall owners would shout at him and shoo him away.

As he ate, the woman talked to Mano about a new life, opportunities, having a nice place to live. Moving away to a new place, a new country.

He was only half listening, but her talk sounded exciting. He was too engrossed in filling his stomach to rationalise it all.

She walked with him back to the station, and the tiny wooden crate he called home, behind the steps of Platform three, Nagercoil station. She promised to come the next day, to tell him more about his new life.

He was excited, and his belly was full. He would sleep well tonight.

Mano realised suddenly that the pretty lady who was offering so much, had not even once asked him his name.

CHAPTER

8

The darkness covered everything.

Kerensa felt a hand tap her arm as she jolted awake. The air hostess was leaning over, an unspoken apology written on her face.

"We are landing in an hour and a half ma'am. Please return your seat to the upright position. Dinner is being served shortly."

The cabin lights came on, section by section, row by row. People were yawning, stretching. Somewhere, a child started screaming.

She glanced over at David. He was snoring lightly, open mouthed. She smiled at the hostess and then gently shook his arm.

"Huuuhh" he sleepily mumbled. "Oh, are we landing?"

"We're nearly there. I think dinner is coming soon." Kerensa replied. The time on the screen flashed up as 8.05pm locally.

Two airhostesses shuffled slowly down the narrow aisle pushing an overflowing metal trolley between them, and with heavily frozen smiles slammed trays down on each table. The plates were covered neatly with smoothened tinfoil. Kerensa slowly peeled away them away, underneath lay a variety of enticing Indian dishes - a fresh salad made with greens and olives, spicy chicken curry with potato and spinach, yellow saffron rice, roasted vegetables and a selection of tiny desserts, including a mini cheesecake and a bowl of *payasam*, a creamy eastern version of rice pudding, made with vermicelli, juicy currants and crunchy cashew nuts. The aroma rose up enticingly. A sensuous, earthy scent. Kerensa tasted all the dishes, she didn't normally like plane cuisine, but everything was delicious.

Outside, far away, a scattered sprinkling of twinkling lights came through the blackness, presumably from houses and cars. They looked so pretty, she thought to herself. The lights of the runway were aligned in straight lines, like perfectly trained soldiers.

Not long.

Kerensa recalled what she knew about her father. His full name (Kaian Achari), date of birth - 21st of April 1971, and last known address in the town of Nagercoil. That was all she knew about the most important man of her life. A few impersonal, cold facts.

Kaian, or Kai as her mum called him, had been in her and Matt's life for such a short time, she could barely remember him being there. A hazy photo of him holding Matt as a baby, as she wrapped her arms around his neck protectively, had pride of place on her dresser. She had brought it with her too in case it helped, wrapped carefully in a clear plastic frame.

Somewhere in the recesses of her mind she had a memory of Kaian holding her close, whispering "Kerensa, remember that I will always love you. I am right here with you," placing his hand protectively on her heart. She wasn't even sure if it was real or an illusion she had conjured up, her childhood mind playing mean tricks on her.

The absence of her father hurt so very much. A scalpel slicing in and twisting, deeper and deeper into the recesses of her soul, creating endless insecurities which manifested themselves in different ways over the years. The pain never left. It lingered, festering tumour-like in the pit of her stomach. A cancer of longing and abandonment.

The plane descended slowly, landing with all engines screaming onto the Indian runway. The tropical night heat imbued a sultry ambience within the cabin.

"Don't forget Kerensa, if you need anything just give us a shout okay?" It was a parting farewell from a short friendship with a stranger as they disembarked. It hit home that she was on her own from now on. Alone in a country of billions.

Disembarkation was quite straightforward, but the queue was long, and snaked around the Immigration barriers. The humidity within the area was overbearing - even though it was late in the evening, the air felt heavy and the heat, stifling. The monitor on the wall described the outside temperature as 28 degrees Celsius.

As she waited to pick her suitcase up from the baggage ramp in the crowded arrivals lounge, she saw David waiting for his on the other side. He waved, and she waved back.

After visiting the local currency exchange, she headed straight toward the exit.

CHAPTER

9

Walking into arrivals, it was evident to Kerensa that she had landed in India.

Chaos reigned.

Although the middle of the night, the hall was packed with people coming to meet loved ones who had travelled from abroad. The endless noise and bustle were deafening - the invasion of senses overwhelming. Kerensa felt as though she couldn't breathe and almost wished she were back on the plane.

Groups of short, dark-skinned men stood together, staring unashamedly at everyone who went past. She was one of the few foreigners on the flight and could feel many eyes on her, curiously assessing. Women were scattered about in the arrival hall, some with husbands, others with friends, many with small children in their arms, screaming for attention. A few young girls huddled together, Kerensa could feel them looking in her direction - dark hair neatly oiled and tied back in tight pigtails, curious eyes examining her up and down, giggling, turning to each other as they muttered secretively in their own language. A small group of children were chasing each other around the packed hall, laughing happily - there did not seem to be anyone supervising them.

A small brown mongrel with forlorn eyes, ribs pushing painfully through its undernourished frame, hungrily devoured the contents of a torn paper bag left on the ground by the barriers. Scraps of an unwanted lunch tossed aside.

As she continued walking, her senses were overwhelmed by the colourful saris of the women, striking and bold, vivid dancing amalgams of reds, blues, yellows and greens. A world away from the minimalistic greys and blacks that dominated corporate London.

A young man with one leg sat on a small trolley at the front of the crowd and called out to her pleadingly: "*Amma, amma.*" He held out his hands expectantly. Kerensa reached in her purse and pulled out a one hundred rupee note. The equivalent of about a pound, she handed it to him, he stared at it with sheer wonder, as though he had won the lottery and never seen so much money at one time. His smile was dazzling. "Thank you amma!" It made her feel happy to see such utter gratitude from another human being. He scooted off quickly on the trolley, propelling it with his hands, weaving his way back through the dense crowd.

Kerensa had arranged to be picked up and sure enough, a big banner was held up by a tall young man on the side of the crowd which read: WELCOME KIRENSA OLDDFILD.

She laughed to herself at the misspelling of her name and went over. The tall man put down the makeshift placard, offered his hand and smiled.

"Hello Kerensa, I am Samuel de Mello, from Amma's guesthouse. Welcome to India!"

Kerensa reached forward and shook his hand. "Thank you, Samuel." He had coffee-coloured skin, slight stubble sprouting on his face and thick black hair which had been gelled back in smooth streaks. His thin t-shirt, embossed with a Superdry logo, clung tightly against his athletic frame. Handsome, his chiselled features would not have looked out of place in a fashion magazine. His smile, all white teeth, radiated warmth like a sunny day.

Samuel looked at her up and down, appreciatively. His eyes lingered on her face for more than a few seconds, and Kerensa surprisingly found herself going uncontrollably red.

"How was your flight?" he asked as he insisted on taking her heavy suitcase and pulling it along much to her relief.

"It was really long." She tried to keep up with his wide strides out of the arrival's hall. "Samuel, is the guesthouse far from here please?"

"Nagercoil is a two-hour drive, but the cab is comfortable, and you can easily have a nap on the way. Just mind the door on the left side!" he smiled with reassurance as he led her to an Ambassador car, an elderly Indian relative of the British Morris. It had peeling cream paintwork and a broken rear door on one side, which the driver had propped up incongruously with thick rope and strong tape. Kerensa could not believe that this car could possibly be roadworthy, but it was after all India. The rules were different.

Samuel took her bags and handed them to the driver who arranged them in the boot. She suddenly remembered that her handbag was in the back and quickly got out to retrieve it before the boot was closed. She should have kept it by her side for safety, but fatigue had exhausted her. She made a mental note to sit as far away from the broken door as possible.

The journey was a long stretch, the driver playing cheerful Tamil songs, upbeat and happy along the way. Samuel kept reminding him to lower the volume, that their guest could be trying to sleep in the back. A string of colourful beads hung from the rear-view mirror; at the end, a golden crucifix danced with the motion of the car, which at times increased pace to breakneck speed, especially on the wide highways. The driver gave her an occasional toothy grin through the rear mirror at times, almost an apology for the speed. They passed small shanty shops and darkened paddy fields, often through narrow, winding roads. Kerensa was relieved that her seatbelt fitted securely as they sped hastily along the bumpy, uneven roads.

Outside, it was night, but the scenery silhouette was still beautiful. She couldn't wait to see it in the daytime when it's full beauty would come to life. The air conditioning whirred noisily on full blast, for which Kerensa was thankful - even though it was late, the humidity was stifling.

"Samuel, what does the word '*amma*' mean?" She leaned forward, keen to hear what he had to say. She had learnt a little Tamil but wasn't sure about this particular word. "It's the guesthouse name, and the crippled man at the airport called me 'amma' too."

"It simply means mother but can also be used to address any woman respectfully." he explained, flashing her a quick smile. "Our guesthouse is named after my mother, who is the driving force behind it!"

They finally reached their destination. The guesthouse was situated in a quiet area of the town, away from the main highway. The imposing wooden and stone building lay hidden behind a stunning tropical front entrance, where banana trees, coconut palms and colourful bougainvillaea nestled peacefully, bedfellows amongst the vivid green grass. Even though it was night, Kerensa could see that the garden was landscaped and well maintained, long hose pipes snaked through the vegetation to ensure they remained lush in the extreme summer heat. The garden was obviously a focal point, illuminated by solar lights of various hues so that its natural beauty could be admired well into the night.

Kerensa had researched the Indian guesthouse from home, considering its location, facilities and also customer reviews before reserving her room online. There seemed to be an eclectic mix of guests passing through, both Indians and foreigners and it was owned by a lady called Vivien de Mello, and her son Samuel. They had moved from Goa, on the west coast fifteen years before and had spent years working hard together to build up the business. A smiling photo of the mother and son adorned the front page of their website, alongside the blurb and glowing customer comments, stating how Amma's Guesthouse was the best in Nagercoil.

On entry, the reception was imposing. The teakwood front desk had carved ornate scenes of majestic animals in various poses of hunting and reclining - tigers, elephants and buffalo mainly. Stunning, hand-painted artwork featuring beautiful sari-clad women adorned the walls, dark hair plaited down their backs and dreamy eyes lined daringly with black kohl, staring seductively in the distance. Kerensa could not help but be drawn to the gorgeous paintings. A stone fountain spurting cool water took pride of place as the centre piece in the room. Small coins of different denominations could be seen languishing at the bottom of the fountain pool, thrown in by guests hoping for good luck.

Samuel and a porter brought over her luggage and she made her way to the front desk. An elegant older lady who appeared to be in her early fifties, wearing a dark purple saree and hair tied neatly up in a tight bun, came over smiling. Samuel joined her behind the desk.

"Hello, I'm Vivien…you must be Kerensa?" she said in perfect English, with a slight Indian lilt. "So lovely to meet you! Welcome, you must be tired. Samuel will see you upstairs." She glanced briefly at her son.

"Please, may I see your form of payment, and also your passport?"

"Sure" Kerensa said, pulling out her bank card, and pushing her hand deep inside the pocket of her handbag, delving for her passport.

It was empty.

CHAPTER

10

At just fifteen and a half, Vivien had once been described as having the looks of a goddess by a passing stranger.

Vivien always had strong ambitions way beyond her years, but a hasty marriage to Thomas de Mello at the tender age of twenty-one destroyed any dreams for her future.

A handsome, rugged fisherman, she caught his eye at the tail end of a sweltering hot summer. It had been 1976.

She had gone to Calangute beach, one of the largest in Northern Goa, with her friends from college. Dressed in a white mini sundress with her hair swept back, Vivien looked windswept and effortlessly gorgeous. She didn't need any makeup; her creamy golden skin was naturally flawless and delicate.

As she laughed heartily with her friends at the water's edge, she caught sight of Thomas staring at her unashamedly.

His pursuit of the unworldly Vivien was relentless, persistent - 'accidentally' bumping into her at odd times until she finally agreed to go for a movie date in the village. She found Thomas fascinating. He had many interesting stories to tell about his life at sea, and wise opinions to say about most things, she felt.

Her parents, however, hated Thomas, saying he was uneducated and unambitious, a mere fisherman going nowhere with his life. How would he support a family on his meagre income? They tried to discourage their infatuated daughter, but to no avail.

Vivien was determined to marry him, no matter what. Her stubbornness was renowned in the family, as she steadfastly ignored the many warnings of her worried parents.

The pair eloped, and Thomas purchased a humble beach shack by the edge of the sea. However, any blissful happiness was soon overtaken by heated arguments, caused mainly by his continual drinking habits.

The initial bouts of generosity from her husband changed to spending their hard-earned money on tall glasses of toddy from the local shanty bar in town where fishermen gathered to exchange entertaining stories and where Thomas seemed to be spending more and more time.

As cowards often do, Thomas had soon turned his attentions on their young son Samuel, looking for a scapegoat on whom he could take out his frustration. Drunken rages often resulted in unwarranted beatings on the young boy, whom he would pull into a room and hit mercilessly for no apparent reason. Their younger child, a daughter, was spared. Thomas treated her differently.

Vivien had tried to shield their son, but the beatings only got worse, and more frequent.

So, Vivien de Mello made the bold decision to leave him.

CHAPTER

11

The blood drained from her face as Kerensa thought she would be physically sick. Her very first day, thousands of miles from home…and this.

The most crucial travel document, her passport, was missing. Panic was rising steadily, and she could feel her legs wobble, she thought they would give way.

'I... I can't find it!' she stuttered, tears welling up in her eyes. She rummaged desperately again in her handbag, emptying the contents onto the top of the reception desk. She was so sure she put it back after clearing immigration and had not taken it out since. Her mind was racing through a sea of images, and she felt faint.

"Don't worry dear." Vivien reassured her gently, kindness in her eyes. Samuel joined them. "What's the matter?" he asked his mother. She quickly explained.

"Look, don't worry, this has happened before. I will get hold of the taxi driver, will go and check the cab myself in case it has fallen there. I have contacts at the airport who can find out if it dropped there and will get back to me. Don't worry, Ms Kerensa, my mother will take you to the room and when we find it, I will contact you okay?"

Kerensa nodded briefly, unable to speak for fear the tears would overwhelm her. "Thank you" She managed a quick smile of appreciation.

"No worries, don't be concerned. I am sure it will turn up, leave it with me. Please check your bags thoroughly in case it has fallen inside somewhere."

Vivien came around the desk with a set of keys and placed her hand gently on Kerensa's arm. "Come with me," she beckoned gently. "I will show you to your room."

Her manner was soothing and motherly. Kerensa followed her to a large ornately decorated lift, rather like a gold cage. Keys jangling around her waist, Vivien pressed the button for the second floor. Her sari was deep purple chiffon with black and silver thread embroidery, flattering and feminine for her slim frame.

As the lift went slowly upwards, Vivien looked at her for a few seconds, appearing deep in thought. "Goodness, you look so much like my daughter," she said contemplatively, "you could be almost twins!"

Kerensa smiled, as the lift bell chimed to indicate they had reached the floor. Vivien pulled back the internal metal door before opening the outer wooden one, intrinsically carved with clusters of peacocks and doves. It was a quaint lift, Kerensa thought to herself.

"We have twenty-four rooms and yours is particularly nice with a view of the garden. I hope you like it," Vivien said as they came out onto the second-floor hallway, greeted by another huge painting showing several proud maharajahs, atop majestic groomed horses, hunting in a forest with packs of dogs by their side. It was so realistic and intricate in design, Kerensa made a mental note to come back and have an in-depth look. The hallway was long and carpeted in dark green, with carved teak lanterns in strategically placed areas on the walls, illuminated by flickering tea lights within. Alongside the paintings, huge sculpted wooden elephants stood proudly near the window alcoves, as though guarding them fiercely. The whole place had a tasteful, colonial feel to it.

Kerensa's room was at the very end of the hall, number nineteen, and as they approached the large wooden door, Vivien gave her the set of keys and smiled.

"These are for you, my dear. Keep them safe. You should find everything you need inside, but if you need anything, do not hesitate to give us a call, you can just press zero on your phone. And I'm sure we will find your passport, Samuel is very good. If not, I will direct you to the British High Commission in Chennai where they can help you get a replacement quickly, so don't worry. Sleep well Kerensa."

"Thank you so much for all your help. Goodnight!" Kerensa returned the smile, more cheerful now.

She opened the door and was greeted by a stylish stone bathroom, the rock-carved shower was modern, and a large shower head hung majestically from the ceiling. It was surrounded by a double glass door, and the washbasin was carved out of the same matching stone. A great deal of thought had gone into designing it, she thought.

The bedroom was modern and contemporary - a dark red shaggy rug beckoned from the wooden floor near the bed, enticingly warm and comforting. A large steel fan hung low from the ceiling above the bed, whirring incessantly on full blast. The highlight inside the room was an imposing king-size, four poster bed with inviting pristine white sheets. The soft cosiness beckoned to her.

Another quick search of the bags proved fruitless, and Kerensa resigned herself to the fact that the passport had disappeared mysteriously without a trace. Her stomach was churning, and she felt ill simply thinking about being in a strange country without a passport.

She couldn't understand how it could have happened either - she had been careful with all her documents and had not removed the passport from her bag after Immigration. The only time the bag had been out of her sight was for a few moments when it was being placed in the boot, so possibly it could have fallen out then?

The thought that she could be stranded alone with no travel document, and in a place where she didn't know a soul, or the language, was terrifying. Without her passport, Kerensa knew that there was no way she would be able to return home to the UK.

She should have felt stressed, but at that point was too tired to care, it was late. It would be the first thing she would do in the morning, once she had cleared her mind.

The seemingly endless journey from London had been exhausting, and a few moments after collapsing onto the soft pillows, sleep had buried Kerensa protectively within its dark mantle.

CHAPTER

12

I can hear the machine.

A steady 'bleep, bleep,' monotonous and low key from somewhere in the distance.

Where is this place?

Is this another dream?

As the memories consume me, day and night…I no longer know what is real and what is not.

The light coming through is bright. Too bright.

I am leaving the land of the sleeping and returning to the living.

As the light filters through the horizontal peripheries of my eyes, slowly opening, hazy visions enter my world.

A woman, kind eyes, dark hair swept back under a small white hat, is leaning over me. Her face - compassionate. I look at her, unseeing.

"Can you hear me?" She calls out a name, presumably mine.

Eyes opening slowly, glancing down, I see she covers my hand with hers. The bleeps intensify in magnitude.

"Yes," I hear a voice say in reply, it is coming from within.

"You are safe, this is the general hospital in Nagercoil."

I remember being transported to many places. A different land across the sea, a family. My family.

A woman, golden haired and beautiful, I love her. Two small children whom I adore. This is another life.

I remember family pressures, endless furtive phone calls home to India. A father shouting mercilessly down the line, a mother crying ceaselessly about how her daughters would not get married now, because of the shame, the shame I alone brought them.

The terrible, terrible choice is the one I made.

The choice to cut short, to leave this life of total love and return to a life of family duty and obligation. A life of sacrifice and guilt and constant regret.

Only to obliterate shame in the family.

Every day I push these thoughts of what I had done deeper and deeper away, but every day they return, swords sharpened, ready to confront me boldly. In fearsome, unending pursuit.

A relentless battle, of which I was never the winner.

"Preeti!"

I shout out her name.

I remember my beloved angel, my sweet little Preeti, helplessly watching her being snatched by strangers from outside her school, running after her, desperately chasing them. I remember. The dark van, somewhere in my mind's eye, is racing towards me. It is too late.

Panic sets in, I sit bolt upright in shock. The bleeps on the machine intensify violently in pace, getting closer together, screaming for attention.

The woman by my bed calls urgently for assistance. An elderly doctor arrives quickly and removes a board from the bottom of my bed, whispering quietly to the woman for a few minutes, which seem like almost a lifetime. He breaks away and turns to me, his tone matter of fact.

"Mr Kaian Achari, you have been in a comatose state for nearly six weeks."

The woman comes closer, and rests her hand on my arm, reassuringly, about to say something. The doctor hurriedly pulls her away, muttering something about it not being the right time. Too soon to tell me.

Too soon to tell me what?

I can feel myself sinking again...I leave that place and return back to the land of dreams.

The one of peace.

CHAPTER

13

To outsiders, Sheikh Yusuf al-Mahani was a tough man's man, ready to fight tooth and nail in his corner and hold his own in a challenging world. He secured lucrative deals for his Dubai based stonemasonry business from around the world with ease in areas where others failed.

Over five hundred employees remained consistently loyal to him mainly because of his kindness and extreme generosity. Once, Yusuf personally funded an awayday in the heart of the Dubai desert opulent Bedouin tents set up in the remote location, filled by row after row of plump, colourful cushions arranged around the low tables. Seemingly endless platters with roasted meats, their scintillating aroma circulating in the air, alongside mouth-watering, decadent desserts excited his employees. It was still talked about to this very day.

But at home, Yusuf was just a pussycat. He didn't want to admit it, but his wife intimidated him.

Behind her dark burka, Basma hid her many frustrations. And her deep desire for control.

She was intelligent and had wanted a career, but Yusuf had put his foot down from the beginning. He had clever women working in his company, but they were different, westernised. They were forthright, strong and had learnt to fight their way in a man's world, he tried to explain to her. Those rules did not apply to any wife of his. He was liberal with Basma, but there were limits.

They had been married for twenty-five years, and he realised that Basma was bored of the endless mall shopping trips, and lunch dates with meaningless women, who had nothing to say. Rich, empty headed Arab wives with more money than sense. Too much time, but nothing to fill the gap.

"Yusuf, you promised me a boy to take care of the twins!" she had scolded.

After many years of trying for children, they'd had a surprise pregnancy resulting in four-year-old Hasan and Aisha. Basma had been forty-three years old at the time, an age considered positively ancient in the middle eastern world.

"I am meeting the woman soon who will arrange it, be patient dear. The boy will come from India, he has been hand-picked and his journey will be organised. They have found someone and are just preparing him."

"I hope it won't be long," she pouted. The children were a handful, and she had no patience or desire to deal with their liveliness. Their housekeeper helped, but it was not enough. They demanded a lot of attention and energy and needed someone to watch them full time.

Yusuf recalled the last child they'd had. A poor woman's son from the nearby town. Basma had insisted that he sleep in a tiny space under their stairwell, and fed him scraps of leftovers just twice daily, saying that any more would 'spoil him.'

At times, the boy did not listen to Basma, and once, she had beat him so hard in a fit of rage to within an inch of his life. Yusuf had to smooth things over by footing the hospital bill and paid a tidy sum to the parents of one million Dirhams, as compensation for his life-changing injuries. And for their silence.

Her temper was renowned in the household - the servants kept a mindful distance.

"Basma, I need you to promise me that you will treat this boy properly." Yusuf requested, solemnly.

Her reply was silence.

CHAPTER

14

'Can you help me remember how to smile.
Make it somehow all seem worthwhile.'
Runaway train, Soul Asylum.

Maya had not seen the sun for over a year.

She had memories though. As she crouched on her broken mattress, she reminisced about those dazzling rays falling heavily on her arms. The overwhelming feeling of pervasive warmth that encompassed her as she played outside in the garden. An old life now.

However, she knew she would soon catch the sunbeams ricocheting through the dirty glass of the tiny skylight, through the metal bars on the window as they shimmered playfully on her hands. She loved to watch the moving specks of dust somersaulting as they danced within the narrow projectiles of intense light.

It was a game that she enjoyed playing alone. An escape from the ravaging thoughts within her head. Constant and immutable, relentlessly hounding her each and every day.

The muffled sobs of the new girl coming from the next room were unmistakeable.

One day after her morning ablutions, Maya pressed her ear to the door so she could overhear their talk. The girl was the daughter of a journalist, they said, and a big reward had been offered for her safe return.

Maya had managed to survive on mere morsels over the past months. The meals the guards brought for her were inedible, often repulsive. The nauseating, rancid smell of stale food reached her long before the dishes were brought into the room. She just ate a quick nibble here and there, only to satiate the pangs that gnawed at her insides like lions seeking fresh prey expecting nourishment, scraping her internally with their sharpened talons as they demanded satisfaction.

Oh, how she missed her mummy's cooking. The exquisite, wafting aroma of freshly prepared chapattis, alongside pungent golden dals, crispy paneer surrounded by a bed of warmly wilted spinach and mama's special fried chicken were etched indelibly within Mayas senses. She could feel her body slowly getting weaker day by day, crumbling and decaying, like that of an ancient, neglected ruin.

A strange lady walked into her room unexpectedly one afternoon.

"How would you like to spend a while outside?" she asked Maya, smiling. "We thought it would be good for you, and also you can make a new friend. She is in the next room and will be joining you."

Maya's heart leapt with excitement.

A friend. At last.

She remembered her best friend Rebecca, who had joined her class after emigrating from the UK. They had so much fun together, giggling hysterically as they drew funny caricatures, and playing tag in the playground. In her old life in Northern Delhi. Distant memories stirred her mind like faded photos from another century.

Her heart ached when she thought of her parents, who loved her so much. Each day they smothered her with kisses and cuddles, their little princess. Her daddy would pull her cheeks affectionately and her mummy plaited her hair in the morning, before planting a kiss on her forehead at the school gates, telling Maya she was her special angel.

She remembered her little brother, Nitin, gurgling in his highchair, his large dark eyes lighting up with delight when he saw his sister. Would he be crying for his big sister now, she wondered?

She remembered her last family outing, to the shopping mall in New Delhi four years before, where she lagged slowly behind her mother. The strangers who came up stealthily behind, putting a hand over her mouth to muffle the sounds of her desperate screams. Maya hadn't seen them.

She was only five years old.

They smuggled her heavily drugged by truck from the north to the south of India. It was a very long and treacherous journey, full of screams, tears, pain and discomfort. She was told to forget her mummy and daddy, as they never loved her.

Life had finished for Maya on the day she was snatched.

CHAPTER

15

The dark crow sharply tapped its beak against the windowpane three times. The noise was startling in the quiet tropical hum of the early morning sunshine.

Kerensa pushed the sheets aside and pressed her face against the glass. She could see the large bird had flown onto the thin black railings that bordered her balcony. It turned to look at her, beady dark eyes fixed boldly, unblinking, almost in defiance.

Crushing a few biscuits from a packet that had been placed in the room, alongside the welcome basket of fruit and chocolate, she slowly opened the window and held them in her palm, in full view of the bird. Turning its head, the crow watched silently immobile, expectantly waiting.

Kerensa threw the crumbs onto the balcony stone floor, and it flew down and landed near them, pecking quickly. She slowly closed the window. A loud cawing came from outside, an acknowledgment of gratitude.

Heading downstairs, the corridor was deserted. Dazzling rays of sunshine filtered through the wooden frames, dancing in the heat as she walked, with the mild chirp of crickets offering soothing, rhythmic sounds in the background.

It was 7.10am, most people in the guesthouse were sleeping, a normal, peaceful Sunday morning. However, Kerensa had been wide awake for the past few hours, jet lag was always hard, but she had not encountered anything quite as tiring as this journey.

Anxious to find out about her passport, she headed to the front desk. It was manned solely by a young man, no more than eighteen, who looked like it was his first week on the job. He muttered to himself nervously, eyes fixated on the screen in front of him.

"Can I help you madam?" he asked politely as he looked up.

"Hi, yes, please. I arrived yesterday and my passport has gone missing. I'm really worried, but Samuel said yesterday that he would try to locate it for me, do you know if he found it?"

"One moment please." he checked the shelves and drawers behind and below the front desk, shaking his head from side to side as he stood in front of her.

"I'm sorry, ma'am, I can't see it here. Samuel and Vivien are unavailable right now, but I will leave a message for them to contact you. What is your room number?"

The passport was still missing. Oh God. She felt her anxiety return, as she could almost hear her heart pounding heavily against her ribs.

"I'm in room nineteen, on the second floor. Kerensa Oldfield. Please tell them it's urgent."

"I will ma'am. Please don't worry, they will contact you soon I am sure." His smile attempted to be reassuring, however the expression in his eyes conveyed a somewhat different message.

On entering the spacious ground floor restaurant, the breakfast spread on display was impressive.

The first station had fruits of every description - thin slices of honeydew and watermelon, oversized, shiny red apples and bunches of dark, gleaming grapes were arranged side by side on large black platters. Nearby, were local speciality fruits; slivers of ripe golden mangoes, blood oranges (which looked as they sounded) and miniature yellow bananas, which the waiter Arul explained were plentiful in the town.

Other tables had the usual continental items, such as cereal, bread and jams of different varieties, but the last table in the row contained different south Indian breakfast items, including *idlis* (small, and almost spherical in shape) and flat savoury pancakes called *dosais*, both of which were made from rice flour. Accompaniments included a coconut chutney, and several types of dal, or lentil, curry. The nearby corner had a grill area, where a chef was cooking eggs in various forms, made to order by request.

Kerensa was keen to try the local dishes, and after taking what she wanted, armed with a mug of steaming Indian coffee, made her way to a quiet table in the corner.

No sooner had she sat down, than an agitated older waiter came over to the side of the table.

'Ma'am, I'm sorry but this table is reserved.'

'Oh, but there was no sign on the table.' Kerensa pointed out. She didn't want to move as the table was in a private corner and she had already made herself comfortable, spreading out her breakfast items.

The waiter looked uncomfortable. 'I'm sorry, but you will need to move ma'am.' He was smiling, but it was forced, and his tone was brittle, insistent. 'I will help you carry your things.'

Kerensa didn't want to make a fuss, it was early in the morning and she was still tired after the long journey. She moved to a nearby table, but was curious to see who would occupy the cosy, corner position.

The food was spicy, and flavourful. Back home, mum on occasion, made a few Indian dishes which Kaian had taught her when they first moved in together; meat and vegetable curries, dal and also rasam, a peppery based soup, commonly known in Anglo-Indian circles as mulligatawny soup. Kerensa and Matt were quite used to hot flavours, so she found the breakfast palatable and very enjoyable.

She was sipping her coffee, when a sudden commotion made her look up.

A few waiters, including the older one who had asked her to move, were fawning around the table from which she had just moved. Adding cutlery, wiping down and placing extra glasses near the bamboo placemats, they seemed nervous. Their intricate preparations seemed to imply that someone important was coming.

A woman walked in; she was ordinary looking but held herself with a certain charisma that would attract attention. An air of over confidence, almost bordering on arrogance. The clothes she wore looked immaculate and expensive. A white, tailored top and trousers, teamed with a crimson and black scarf knotted elegantly around her neck. Rather incongruous for the extreme Nagercoil heat, Kerensa thought to herself.

The woman headed straight for the table. and sat down.

The fawning began again, with the waiters bending over backwards to attend to her every need. They raced back and forth nervously from the food stations, bringing her various plates of steaming food to try; eagerly watching her reactions, keen to please.

A young waitress brought a large pot of coffee over, and filled her large cup, almost to the brim. Steam rose from the top, little puffs of white mist that evaporated quickly into the air. The woman waved her away, impatiently.

Kerensa chuckled to herself. It was like a scene from Fawlty Towers, almost comical.

Who was this woman? The waiters seemed to know her, so she had obviously stayed at the guesthouse before.

The woman suddenly stopped what she was doing, and glared fiercely, directly at Kerensa.

Their eyes met, fixed and locked in an icy gaze.

CHAPTER

16

Gulab Jamuns were her favourite. Round, moist and delicious, soaked in a sugary syrup, they melted slowly on the tongue, leaving a distinct, delectable aftertaste in her mouth.

Varsha, commonly known to everyone as Jingles, loved sweets. Of any kind. Indian sweets of course, but also the imported American chocolates with the soft centres that one could pick up easily nowadays at the larger convenience stores in Nagercoil. Jingles knew exactly where to look.

However, for the past six weeks, ever since her young daughter vanished one day after school, she had been unable to eat even one.

Her friends came by, when her mother was not by her side, bringing familiar brightly coloured boxes containing cakes of various forms; round golden *laddus* and *burfi* sweets, made with nuts, milk and lots of sugar, hoping to tempt her and change her mind, to alleviate her sadness. But Jingles could not eat even one.

She kept thinking morbid thoughts about her precious girl. She regretted shouting at her over breakfast that dreadful morning, just for eating slowly. The terrible day when the sun disappeared, the day her angel was taken from her.

She was not the best mother, she knew it. But she tried.

Preeti would come home from school, and mention that her friend's mother made exciting packed lunches, with sandwiches shaped liked teddy bears and tigers, each and every day. Followed by homemade chocolate cookies. Now why couldn't her *amma* make ones like that for her?

But she loved the way her *amma* made the funniest faces and impersonated her favourite cartoon characters, little Preeti would laugh endlessly and the two of them would giggle together until their sides ached. None of the other *ammas* were as funny as hers.

Jingles would give anything to have her girl sitting at the kitchen table in front of her right now. Anything.

She did not want to think about her baby being scared, frightened, alone. Preeti had never stayed apart from them, not even for one night, and the thought of her little one sobbing, calling for her was almost too much to bear.

What sort of monsters would snatch a small innocent child from outside their school?

The Chief of Police had visited her on a number of occasions, once with an older English man, who, he explained was a lead in the field and was working with him closely on the case. Over from the UK.

There had been a number of recent disappearances of young children, in the area- mainly girls and all under ten years, the police officer said.

They had talked a lot about the facts of her daughter's disappearance, their plans and next steps. Reassurances that they would get her daughter back safe and sound. It was too much to take in.

After they left, Jingles felt dazed, lost and alone.

Her husband was in a coma, but it didn't make any difference to her. He never noticed her anyway, it was as though she had been dead to him for years.

His thoughts always seemed to be elsewhere, even when he was with her, it was as though he was looking right through her. He cared more about his newspaper role, spending long hours at work, than he did about his wife, or her feelings.

There was affection though, especially when he teased her playfully and referred to her as his 'round ball.' He indulged her love of sweets, little realising that they were a poor substitute for the normal married love she should have expected from him.

And so, she ate. And ate. To compensate for the loneliness.

It had been six long weeks, but on her way to the hospital that day, Jingles Achari reached for an unopened box in her fridge for the first time, and pulled out a huge swirly orange *jelabi*. As she bit into the crisp exterior, the heavenly sugary syrup within the sweet oozed into her mouth. She reached for another one.

Jingles suddenly felt good once again.

CHAPTER

17

The taxi driver would come to the front desk and ask for her, she was told.

He had come highly recommended by Arul, the waiter at breakfast, for having a good understanding of English, which would make it easier for Kerensa to talk to him. Thankfully it was not the same man who had picked her up from the airport, she couldn't face going in that taxi with the broken door again.

She had been waiting for him for a few minutes on the sofa near the entrance, ready for the day ahead. The ceiling fan at reception was on full blast, the cold air giving some soothing relief amidst the tension.

Khaki trousers, with a loose white cotton top were comfortable attire, her hair tied neatly in a high ponytail, to keep cool, and dark sunglasses perched at the top of her head. A hat would have been too much as none of the women wore hats in Nagercoil according to her research, and she didn't want to stand out any more than she already did, as a foreigner in the small Indian town.

The young guy at reception glanced over occasionally. Kerensa made a mental note to catch either Vivien or Samuel on her return; she was desperate to find out what had happened to her passport. She had messaged her mother and Matt in the morning, but didn't want to worry them about her missing passport just yet. Mum would only panic, and didn't need any further stress in her life.

The receptionist briefly left the front desk area disappearing into a back room, there was no one else around.

Kerensa made an impulsive decision to pop round behind the desk to check for herself for her passport, in case it had been placed on a shelf by mistake. Leaving her handbag by the sofa, in eyesight, she quickly went behind the desk and bent down to check a few shelves, but couldn't see anything resembling her passport. She scanned the area briskly, heart pounding as she knew the receptionist could return at any time.

Suddenly something caught her eye. High on a ledge close to the back room stood a large red box file, clearly marked 'biodata (confidential).' She didn't know why but sudden curiosity caused her to reach for the file.

Inside were profiles of dozens of young children, their painful eyes clearly masked behind forced smiles.

Tiny photos were stapled to the front of sets of papers, detailing information about each individual child; their first name, age, height, weight etc. Plus, further down, addresses abroad, outside India, in far-away destinations such as the Netherlands, Dubai, Russia and even Gibraltar. In bold, were highlighted in yellow, large monetary amounts on each page, running into tens of thousands of American dollars. The word 'TRANSACTION COMPLETED' in handwritten capital letters was scribbled next to some of the children's profiles.

What was this? Her heart started pounding, she felt sick at the thought of what was implied by the pages she had seen.

A fleeting thought came to mind of a BBC news report she had watched in England about children who had gone missing in the local Indian town.

Could this be connected? She strained her mind trying to forge the new information into some sort of meaningful link.

She hurriedly put the pages back into the file and closed the lid. By the time the receptionist came back, Kerensa had returned to the sofa. The driver still hadn't arrived.

Her thoughts went over what she had just seen, she mulled it over in her mind, disturbed. She needed to think more about what to do about it, Kerensa knew she needed to contact the police however she didn't know how to go about it with the language barrier. And who could she trust in the Guesthouse? Not knowing who could be involved in this terrible crime was the hardest thing.

She needed time to mull over things a bit more. This latest information, coupled with the thought of her missing passport, felt overwhelming.

Breakfast that morning had been strange, to say the least.

The older woman on the next table had literally summoned her over. The request (more like an order) came via the waiter who had originally asked her to move. Very ironic that he was now calling her back to sit there.

He came over to her side, rather sheepishly.

'Ma'am, the lady at the next table would like you to join her.' The request had rather a firm tone, subtly suggesting that refusal would be at her own peril.

Kerensa looked over, the lady caught her eye and smiled suddenly. The taunting smile of a hungry tiger waiting to devour its prey.

Kerensa made an instant decision to go over; she was new to the place and wanted to make as many contacts as possible. Furthermore, she was curious about this woman.

What did they say about curiosity?

It was the first time the woman had smiled since she arrived for breakfast, Kerensa thought. Until then, she had only glared at everyone.

The waiter helped her moved her things to the place opposite the lady, which had already been neatly set, as though she had been expecting someone.

'Good morning! Thank you so much for joining me. I thought you were on your own, so might like the company.'

She beckoned Kerensa to sit down. The woman had an American

drawl, however there were detectable undertones of an Indian accent underneath, one that had possibly lain hidden for many years.

'Thank you.' Kerensa said, offering her hand 'I'm Kerensa, and you are?' She was curious to know the identity of this mysterious lady.

There was a slight pause, before the woman offered her perfectly manicured hand, and replied.

'My name is Aruna. Aruna Pillai.'

CHAPTER

18

My next dream took me back.

I remember my childhood. It was a happy time.

Playing with my two younger sisters on the large banyan tree that grew outside our house, was a regular activity after school. The tree was our friend, and we let our imaginations run riot. I know I carved my name, 'Kaian,' on one of the thick branches.

We built secret worlds, with invisible doors to lands that only we could see. Hours were spent in complete bliss, until mama called us down for dinner and homework. Childhood memories tease me playfully now, like daisies blowing in a summer breeze.

The girl next door used to look over the fence, watching us enviously. She was always alone. I think she must have been my age or a little younger.

My mother used to tell me to invite her over; I tried to call her from the tree and be friendly. She never replied but would just stare.

There was something about this girl that seemed strange. Her empty eyes screamed of neglect.

I think her parents worked, they never seemed to be at home. Even on weekends she would be wandering in the garden; alone, forlorn. The maid, with whom she was left, used to ignore her.

My mama felt sorry for her and would send over little packets of banana chips and sweet laddus, wrapped in newspaper and tied up with string.

I would call her, and hand the treats over the low fence at the bottom of the garden.

One night, there was a terrible fire in the house.

None of us knew how it started. All we heard is that the girl was the only one who survived.

The last I heard she was put in an orphanage in Nagercoil. Then adopted into an American family in the US.

So, Mrs Kumar across the road told my mama. Mrs Kumar saw everything and missed nothing. She had eyes everywhere. Her gossip was always to be trusted.

I always wondered what happened to her. Mrs Kumar said she heard from another neighbour that she studied law after she went to the US.

I struggle to remember the girl's name, but I would never, ever forget those dark, haunted, vacant eyes.

CHAPTER

19

The taxi drove past rows of tiny shanty shops situated along narrow dirt roads selling everything ranging from cheap beach balls to colourful star-shaped lanterns. The owners sat on stools in the front; some reading papers, others chewing on freshly rolled *betel* leaves, the contents leaving a blood-red rim around their mouths. All looked bored, waiting for customers that never appeared. Their wares hung from string displayed outside, moving side to side in the breeze. All the colours seemed to be represented in those synthetic swaying branches; shades of reds, blues, greens and yellows, bright and bold - a visual delight.

Kerensa finally arrived at Old Pound Street in a part of town called Kottar. The driver Chandu stopped close to number seventeen and switched off the engine, as he'd promised to wait for her as long as she needed. A day-old, crumpled copy of the 'Deccan Herald' newspaper lay rolled up by the dashboard, which he spread out against the steering wheel, humming cheerfully to himself.

Chandu had told her his entire life history, or so it seemed, during the short twenty-minute journey - five children, all aged under ten, whom he needed to support through school, so even though he had a master's degree in English literature, it was the work as a driver that ultimately helped him pay the bills and bring up his family.

She felt nervous when she alighted. This was the last known address of her father. It wouldn't be long until she met him for the first time in years.

He had written a last letter to Catherine soon after he left them, twenty years before citing the reasons why he had been forced to leave. Emotional family blackmail, the marriage prospects of his sisters. He'd told her it would be best for them to part, she deserved better and that he would always love her, Kerensa and Matthew until the end of time. Catherine had written letters to Kaian at the address, begging him to return. However, she'd never received a reply.

No reason was good enough to leave your two small children, Kerensa thought to herself bitterly.

Yes, he'd been young when his children were born, and his family had been from a different world to their lives in London, but surely, he could have stood up to them rather than choose to leave the way he had?

Yet here she was, standing in front of his house.

Kaian had left when Kerensa was only five years old and Matty two, but the pain of abandonment was still raw and fresh, an open wound, as though it had happened yesterday.

He had left them in a cowardly manner, in the middle of the night, without any proper explanations or saying goodbye. How could any father do this to his children?

Taking a deep breath, she went up to the front gate and lifted the latch. The garden was relatively small in front, the vegetation heavily overgrown with weeds. It looked unattended. A large Banyan tree stood tall and proud in the middle, its many arms extended protectively over the front garden, like a complex woven umbrella.

She noticed the shutters were closed, rather unusual she thought; all the other houses had their shutters wide open, so that people could observe the world passing by. She rang the doorbell three times, there was no reply. She then went up to a few windows and tried opening the shutters. They were bolted shut. An elderly woman across the road was watching her intently from her living room window.

The narrow road was bustling in the scorching mid-morning heat, two children were playing a game with stones outside the house next door. A stray dog strolled jauntily across the road, tail wagging as he got near the children who promptly shooed him away. One of the children threw a small stone at him. The dog yelped and disappeared down the road.

An elderly man slowly pushed his rusty bicycle past the gate. On the back, he had bunches of small green tender coconuts, strung together by thick rope. He stopped and gestured to Kerensa. She went over, and the man stuttered in broken English, "Delicious coconut water. Please buy ma'am, very tasty, only forty rupees each!"

She nodded and reached for her purse, giving extra money so the man could take one for Chandu, parked across the road, who was probably sweltering in the car. It was extremely hot, over thirty degrees centigrade already and she could feel sweat trickling slowly down her neck.

The man took a sharp, curved scythe from the back of his bicycle, and sliced the top of the coconuts, swiftly inserting a straw in each, handing one to Kerensa. The juice inside was fresh and delicious.

She didn't know what to do now. The house looked deserted.

Her one chance.

She had come all this way for nothing.

The old woman from across the road came out, leaning against the gate curiously and gestured for her to come over. Kerensa went up to her.

"Are you looking for someone?" the woman asked curiously. Possibly in her eighties, she seemed as sharp as a tack, with her facilities clearly intact. Her spoken English was perfect.

She peered at Kerensa up and down, curiously wondering what this pretty foreign young woman could possibly want with the family across the road.

Kerensa shrugged her shoulders despondently.

"Come inside for a nice cup of tea," the woman beckoned. "I made fresh banana cake this morning which must be eaten! Tell your driver to wait an hour, I am happy to answer any questions you may have."

"Thank you, I will tell him." Kerensa went over to Chandu, who was happy to wait, a chance for him to have a siesta, he said. She walked through the gate, held open by the lady. Her garden was neat with a square tended patch of lawn surrounded on all sides by well-tended beds of colourful greenery and delicate flowers. It was clear she had an interest in gardening.

Kerensa followed the lady inside. A narrow hallway in front led to a compact living area, with pots and vases of flowers displayed around the room, bright flashes of vivid colour that transformed the place.

"Sit down, my dear." The lady pointed to the cane sofa with plump yellow cushions by the window. "My name is Mrs Kumar; you can call me Asha. Let me take your coconut shell, I will throw it away for you." She spoke with a slight lilt which was almost undetectable.

Kerensa thanked her as she perched at the edge of the sofa. The metal ceiling fan directly above was on full blast, a relief from the extreme humidity.

"I'm Kerensa, its lovely to meet you. I have come from London and this is my first trip to India."

"How nice! Let me go and bring you a glass of cold lime juice first before we talk, one moment please." With that, the woman turned around and headed for the kitchen behind. She disappeared through a beaded curtain, and Kerensa was left alone with a tense feeling.

Her thought went back to what she had found that morning at the hotel. She needed more time to think about what she had seen and to explore her options going forward. Her passport was missing. Plus, now there was the possibility that the house on Pound Street may not have belonged to her father after all. Could she have made a mistake? The house looked derelict. A dead end.

A lot to think about, some choices had to be made.

CHAPTER

20

The tall glass filled with icy water, in which swirled pithy strands of lime and broken chunks of ice, was delicious.

Even though Kerensa had just had a whole tender coconut and was sitting directly under the fan, the humidity was incredibly intense with the midday sun perched at its peak over the town. The extra refreshment was welcoming.

Mrs Kumar pulled up a chair opposite Kerensa and sat down.

"So, who are you looking for?" she began slowly, curiously, her eyes not moving from Kerensa.

Kerensa was not ready to spill out her life story, so she took a different approach.

"I am looking for someone called Kaian Achari. We have not been in touch for some time, but I believe he lives across the road?" It was more a question, thrown out to the older lady casually with hope in her voice, clutching at fragile straws that would easily break in the wind.

Mrs Kumar took a sip from the glass in her hand very slowly, she looked like she was contemplating her reply.

"May I ask what you want with this Kaian?" she asked bluntly. Mrs Kumar's expression was inscrutable.

"I have a few things I need to clear up." Kerensa could feel the older lady's eyes probing her, wanting answers that she was not yet ready to give.

"I see. And he is your…?" The lady just would not let go. Kerensa had to admire her unrelenting determination.

She put her empty glass down on a wooden coaster next to the sofa. Her mind thinking of how she would reply.

"It is a bit of a private matter Asha, I'm so sorry, would love to discuss it with you, but I cannot at the moment." Kerensa was pleased with herself for her diplomatic answer. It wasn't easy with the older lady's eyes penetrating her thoughts. It was obvious that Asha was determined to find out what exactly she wanted with Kaian, and her neighbourly curiosity was understandable in the circumstances.

For a fleeting moment, Mrs Kumar's face showed pain, however this was soon masked by a cheerful smile.

"That's fine dear. I totally understand and won't probe anymore." Asha Kumar rather liked the young girl and was enjoying the conversation. She didn't have many visitors, especially since her husband passed on many years before and many of her former neighbours had moved on. The new ones were not so friendly, they were busy with their own lives - jobs, children, family. She had no-one. No-one to share gossip with. Life as a widow was not great, like climbing a dusty staircase, each step becoming more tiring.

"I can tell you however that the Achari family moved out from number seventeen many years ago. I don't remember anyone called Kaian; their only son moved away with them when they left. I believe his name was Adesh."

She looked intently at Kerensa before she continued. "No-one lives there at the moment; the house has been vacant for about fifteen years."

CHAPTER

21

Sophie had paddled out to sea far away from Calangute beach, she couldn't remember for how long, but it was long enough. She just wanted to escape.

Her fingertips had been lightly touching the water as she lazed on her back in the small wooden boat reading a magazine in the intense summer sun. The place was peaceful, solitary, away from everything. The only sound came from small waves lapping gently against the sides of the boat. She could stop thinking of her family here.

Lying on her back in the middle of nowhere, with the stillness of the sea around, Sophie's hand was grazing the watery surface, when she suddenly felt something firm brush against it. Not just once, but twice.

That was when she spotted the shadowy grey striped sea snake circling her tiny wooden boat, its tail flicking side to side as it glided smoothly through the calm water. They were deadly creatures, shy, but aggressive if provoked and were notorious inhabitants along the Goan shoreline. There was no known antidote for their poisonous bite. Her father had warned her to be careful.

Sophie De Mello adored her father. She was very much a daddy's girl.

Her deep-rooted anger was aimed at her mother who had taken her brother away after the divorce, leaving their dad floundering. She could never forgive her. Especially when she'd moved to the South fifteen years before, that was the last straw. Vivian had begged her to come with her and Samuel, but Sophie refused. Who would be there to look after daddy?

Abandonment was the death of the relationship, as far as she was concerned. Sophie steadfastly ignored emails or texts sent from her mother but always had time for her older brother Samuel, whom she adored.

Thankfully, that day out on the water, the sea snake was more interested in the colourful marine life that swam in the water, than it was in biting Sophie's fingers.

It had been two years since she'd had the chance encounter with the woman, at Seashells gourmet seafood restaurant. The fascinating lady had spent hours talking to her one evening when her shift had finished, saying she was very impressed with Sophie - the girl's drive, ambition, and tenacity would get her far and she would like to offer her a business role that could be very lucrative and change her life. It would involve travelling around India as well as abroad.

She had personally trained the eager girl, who was quick to learn and keen to progress, casting aside any inner thoughts that challenged the morality of the work she was undertaking.

Sophie had focus now. Purpose. No thinking of the past. At thirty-two years old, she could finally leave the anger she felt against her mother behind and move on.

She would be always indebted to the American woman who had helped her change her life.

CHAPTER

22

It was a real bombshell.

Mrs Kumar did not remember any 'Kaian' in the Achari family. Kerensa felt as though her world had just collapsed around her.

"One moment dear, I will just get you the tea I promised and some of my homemade cake."

Before Kerensa could reply, Asha had disappeared again through the curtain into the kitchen. She tried to digest her thoughts. What should she do now? She didn't have any other leads about her father's whereabouts.

On her return, Asha handed her a china cup filled to the brim with milky, steaming tea as she leaned close to Kerensa, and said in a low voice, rather conspiratorially,

"I am sure they gave me their new address. If you give me a few minutes, I will find it for you."

Kerensa could not believe it. She briefly held onto the tiny cross around her neck that Mum had given her for protection and said a silent prayer of thanks.

Asha took a bunch of keys hanging on a nail on the wall and went to a narrow, steel almirah in the corner of the room. She inserted a key in the tiny lock and turned the handle slowly. It was stiff, making a loud, creaking noise when opened. There were many shelves inside stuffed untidily with papers and files of all sorts almost spilling out.

She reached up to the top shelf, groping around with her hand, and found a small green diary which she quickly brought back to her seat. It was stuffed with assorted scraps of paper that had been inserted strategically into different pages.

She looked through, and with an "Ahh," smiled to herself, and turned a page to show Kerensa.

"I found it dear. This is their new address. It is in a city called Chennai, quite far from here. Let me write it down for you."

She copied the address and handed the small scrap of paper to Kerensa, who gratefully took it.

At last, a lead. Something positive. A flutter of excitement welled up inside her.

"Asha, thank you so much for this and also for your lovely hospitality, I must go. Your cake was delicious! I hope we can meet again." Kerensa meant it. She rather liked this blunt older lady, something about her was warming.

"It was my pleasure dear." Asha stood up, followed by Kerensa. "I hope you find them. I received Christmas cards every year until about five years ago, when they suddenly stopped coming."

"Good luck on your search, and please do come and visit me again."

"I will." Kerensa promised as she closed the gate behind her and turned to Asha. "Thank you again."

As the car eased away slowly, Kerensa turned back and could see Asha still standing by her gate. She gave her a last wave before they turned the corner, driving away from the narrow residential road, weaving back through the busy traffic through town.

CHAPTER

23

It had taken Samuel a long time to adjust to life in a crowded town, far away from the fishing village he had grown up in Goa.

He missed his younger sister and, despite everything, his father. The awful beatings and his father's harsh words remained with him constantly. They greeted him sorrowfully in his mind each morning, as he woke to face the day ahead.

Moving from a fishing village in Goa to the southernmost tip of India where everything was different to what he was used to, had been a real challenge at first. Mum had a real go-get-'em attitude, which helped, but he didn't enjoy too much change. And the language in Southern India was a real barrier for Samuel.

Back in Goa, on the west coast where he grew up, aside from English, the most widely spoken language was Konkani. This was followed closely by Portuguese, which had been introduced when Goa was a colony of Portugal. Samuel found learning Tamil difficult after coming to Nagercoil at the age of twenty-one. One of the oldest languages in the world, it had a complex alphabet and words which Samuel found hard to pronounce. But he persisted.

His knock on the door was answered quickly.

"Hello Kerensa," he said cheerfully. She was covered with a dressing gown, hair up with a towel after a shower he guessed. Despite being makeup-free, she was just so pretty. He had found himself thinking of her quite a bit since the morning.

"Really sorry to disturb you, I heard you were asking about your passport at the front desk. I wanted to update you."

"Thanks Samuel." Something inside him felt silently pleased to see her look away quickly, cheeks flushing bright-red, nervously pulling the towel tighter around her. He wondered what she thought about him, and if it was anything like the flame of desire, he felt fuelling up inside of him when he saw her.

Leaning on the door frame, arms crossed, he tried to look relaxed.

"Well, the thing is Kerensa, unfortunately it has not been located as yet."

He shuffled his feet uncomfortably, looking down after seeing the upset expression on her face, "But, I can promise you I am giving the search everything, and will not rest until it is found. My mum said she will bring you the paperwork for filing the police report, this should have really been done earlier. Don't worry, I will do my best to find it for you."

"I just feel so worried Samuel." Kerensa sighed. "What if I don't find it? I can't leave the country or return home to the UK."

He could see her eyes swell up suddenly with tears and felt sorry as it was obvious exhaustion had overwhelmed her. She looked alone. In a world far different to the one she had been used to.

For Kerensa the jetlag, combined with the extreme heat, felt suddenly overwhelming. The fruitless search for her father that morning had mentally exhausted her. A solitary tear streamed down her cheek.

'Ahh Kerensa, don't cry!' Samuel stepped towards her, his face showing genuine concern. He looked broken for her and put his arm on hers, giving a squeeze to try and console her.

But for Kerensa it was all too much.

She couldn't control the pent-up sobs anymore, they emerged suddenly - loud, bawling tears of pain and anger running hotly down her cheeks. Mournful sounds welled up within her, causing her to gasp for breath.

She lost her balance and fell against Samuel, who put his arms around her to steady her. As he circled her protectively with his arms, he nestled his face against the top of her head, pressing the damp towel.

Her shoulders continued to shake against him with violent sobs.

He held her for a few minutes, quietly, as her crying subsided, and then tilted her head, as he slowly brought his lips towards hers.

No sooner as he had done so, he quickly pushed her away, mumbling "I'm so sorry, I should not have overstepped my place, forgive me."

He raced out of the room, closing the door behind him.

CHAPTER

24

The phone had been ringing incessantly off the hook for most of the morning.

Constable Gopal Kumar was feeling overwhelmed, and rather under-appreciated.

His shift at Nagercoil Police station had been a long stretch, starting at seven am, it was now past twelve noon. He had hardly had a break the whole morning, apart from a mug of very dark, bitter coffee, made by the maid at around nine am. She had gone overboard with the coffee beans, the colour of the steaming liquid was bordering on a deep black, even though he had asked for extra milk and extra sugar. He took a gulp, it was foul. He made a mental note to admonish her when she came for her next shift. He had enough on his plate without dealing with forgetful maids who couldn't even make a proper cup of coffee.

Nearby, his colleague Krish had been on the phone for about fifteen minutes, trying to placate a woman on the other end. From what Gopal had overheard, it appeared that her new Boxer puppy had gone missing. As Krish talked to the near hysterical woman, he turned to Gopal, rolled his eyes and covered the phone with his hand, mouthing, "Oh God, help me!"

Gopal burst into laughter and turned back to his computer.

A well-built, bearded man entered the room. From his uniform and his smart demeanour, it was evident that he was high in the ranks.

"Right, everyone, we are gathering for a catchup meeting about the missing children in thirty minutes, please bring your latest case updates." It was the Inspector.

In his fifties, Raj Patel had come from Delhi two years before. An experienced officer, he had climbed the ranks quickly in his ten years of service and was well respected. He brought new and innovative ideas to the rather stagnant Police force, as its head in the southern town.

"Don't be late," he added as he glanced around the crowded room, his eyes landing on Gopal.

"Constable, I want to see your latest progress regarding the journalist case okay? We need to be moving forward on this. Quickly."

"Yes sir," Gopal replied humbly, hastily gathering together the loose papers spread across his desk and putting them in a neat pile in front of him. He pushed them into a plastic jacket and headed for the conference room.

He pushed open the meeting room door and took a seat near the middle of the long table. It would be a while before the meeting started, and he needed this time to plan his strategy for tacking the current issues. He knew he would be questioned on it.

The main news at the moment, was the disappearance of little Preeti, the only child of senior journalist, Kaian Achari. His newspaper, the Daily Chronicle, had gone to town with its sensationalised theories of what had happened to the little girl. If she had been kidnapped, then how come no kidnappers had come forward with a ransom? And no body had been found.

Preeti's father had been in a coma for over a month. An eyewitness stated that as he was chasing his daughter's abductors, a van coming at high speed, knocked into him and he'd landed on his head on the nearby pavement. He's lucky to be alive, Gopal thought to himself, as he glanced at his file. The whole case confounded him.

The room started filling up with officers, with all the seats soon occupied.

Krish sat opposite Gopal and gave him a wink, undoubtedly relieved to be finished with the woman he had been speaking to. Head constable Madesh, who was Gopal's boss, came and sat next to his right.

Inspector Raj entered last a heavy wad of files pushed under his right arm, which he slammed down on the table in front of him, as he took his usual space at the end. He stood up and looked around. Silence fell across the room. His presence was forbearing and formidable. Everyone felt it.

"Right" he began, his commanding voice booming. "I need to find out where you all are with the cases. Let's start with you, Gopal."

The constable reached for his file and pulled out some pages. "Sure sir." he began as he quickly glanced through his notes.

"I have been receiving some phone calls about the abduction over the past few days. Some hoaxes, I believe but I now had another eyewitness come forward just yesterday. A woman who was picking up her children from school. She was too scared to contact us before. I spoke to her she has given me a brief description of both suspects. One man and one woman. The man looked Indian, she said but the woman looked like a foreigner."

"Very good." interjected Raj as he nodded for Gopal to continue.

"We are looking into the possibility that they could be part of a network of traffickers. No contact has been made to us or the mother regarding a ransom or similar, so there must be another motive. This is probably connected to the other disappearances over the past few weeks."

Next to him, Madesh leaned forward clasping his hands on the table, and added, "There has also been a report of a boy going missing, aged under ten, from near the railway bridge. He was a vagrant. One of my team went to look around the area and spoke to the local hotel owner. He remembers seeing a young woman come in with the boy one evening a few weeks ago. He thought at the time they looked odd together. We are investigating this lead further."

"Great work team." Raj smiled at both men. "Keep going, we are closing in and we need to get those children back quickly. The Chronicle are already going to town with us for not locating their journalist's daughter. It's been six weeks since she went missing."

The room was suddenly noisy as officers started talking amongst themselves about what they had just heard, their eyes heavy with the burden of too much terrible knowledge about the lost children.

"Can I have quiet please." Raj continued, banging his hand on the table to get everyone's attention just as there was a knock on the door and a silver haired gentleman, dressed in white shirt and trousers entered the room.

He gestured to the gentleman to take his seat, as he moved aside near the window.

"Everyone, we have an experienced Interpol officer over from the UK. Please give a warm welcome to David Holdsworth."

CHAPTER

25

The neatly handwritten note pushed under her door was brief and to the point.

Dear Kerensa,

Please join me for dinner in my room, tonight at 8.30pm. It would be great to have your company.

Aruna.

Kerensa re-read it a few times as she wondered what she should do.

The clock on the wall read 7:25pm. She couldn't believe it had been just two days since she'd arrived in the country.

In that short time, it seemed a whole spectrum of emotions had crossed her path. Coming to terms with the possibility of never finding her father, the devastating loss of her passport, not to mention the shocking information held in the file at reception. She still couldn't decide what to do about the last one; her mind was going around in circles. The place was new, she could hardly converse in the language and it seemed to be one barrier after another.

She suddenly remembered the man she'd met on the plane, David. She had kept his number. Would it be worth giving him a call possibly? He had seemed approachable and kind. She decided she would definitely give him a call.

A part of Kerensa wanted to hibernate, she'd had a short nap in the afternoon, something that she realised was essential in India and a much-needed mechanism to cope with the intense heat. She felt fresh after sleeping, and it seemed to balance her volatile emotions.

Everything in the east seemed to close down in the afternoon. On her way back to the guesthouse after meeting Asha the day before, most of the shops had been pulling down their shutters preparing for an afternoon siesta soon after lunch.

In fact, everything in India seemed to work slowly, whether it was getting things done, or asking people for their help. It drove her mad, she was a woman of action and order, and the culture, with their unique customs and traditions, was beginning to agitate her.

She was rather fascinated by Aruna. The older woman was worldly, interesting and surprisingly rather funny. The invitation to dinner was something not to be missed.

But first, she needed to check something.

As she approached the front desk, the same young man who had been there on the first day, was using the phone. There was no sign of Samuel.

Kerensa wasn't sure what to make of the situation with Samuel. Since the time they'd met, she couldn't stop thinking of him. There were underlying feelings, but he seemed to blow hot and cold, and she really didn't need any complicated entanglements right now. She had enough on her plate.

"Hello, ma'am," the receptionist said, flashing her a smile as he looked up. He put the phone down. "Can I help you?"

"Sorry to bother you again. Just wondered if there is any news of my passport?"

Kerensa asked hopefully.

"There was something." he began, as his voice tailed off. He rummaged through the shelves. Kerensa remembered how she had rummaged through the same shelves too.

She glanced at the shelf on the back wall there was no sign of the file that had been there. What had happened to it?

"Ahh here we are." he said as he stood up to face her. In his hand was a sealed, brown envelope with her name typed neatly on the front.

"I found this here when I came in ma'am." He handed it to Kerensa.

She quickly tore it open - inside was another unsealed, smaller envelope. She emptied the contents onto the bar it was her passport. Finally.

"Oh, thank God!" Kerensa exclaimed with extreme relief. It was like a huge burden had been lifted from her chest. She took a deep breath of gratitude.

"But who put it there please? Do you know?" she asked, turning back to the receptionist.

"I am so sorry ma'am, but I do not know. The envelope was there when I started my shift at five pm this evening." He shrugged his shoulders, as he turned back to read something on the computer.

Who could have put it there? Samuel promised he would let her know as soon as it was found, so it would not have been him. She flicked quickly through the pages - it almost seemed in better condition than she remembered. The whole thing was strange, but Kerensa felt relieved to have it back.

The Executive suite was situated on the top floor and there were three sets of stairs to climb to reach it. It was set apart from the other rooms and had its own private entrance.

To each side of the carved teakwood door were stunning glass panels the left one depicting a young woman holding a clay urn on her shoulders filled with water, looking into the distance. Her kohl lined eyes were limpid and dreamy. She was wearing a tightly fitting short blouse and petticoat, which amply demonstrated her shapely figure. Her bare feet had large, silver anklets around them. The other panel showed two lovers intertwined in a passionate embrace, tiny pieces of cloth, strategically placed to cover their modesty. The scene looked like it had been taken straight from the pages of the Kamasutra.

Kerensa took a deep breath, as she knocked hesitantly on the door.

CHAPTER

26

"You strike me as a red wine sort of girl."

Aruna reached down into the mini bar, pulled out a chilled bottle of Sauvignon and poured a generous helping into a large glass on the table.

Kerensa laughed. It was an astute observation. "Thank you!" she gratefully took the glass from her host. She had been in the room for only thirty minutes so far, but she found herself engaged by Aruna's conversation.

Aruna turned out to be both knowledgeable and rather funny at the same time, telling entertaining anecdotes about her time as a lawyer in New York - in particular about a time when her clerk brought the wrong case file to court, getting it mixed up with another case, causing many red faces.

They had discussed politics - Trump, in particular - global warming and Sudoku. Kerensa was addicted to the game and as it turned out, so was Aruna. She brought out a small book of Sudoku puzzles from the bedroom and turned to a partially finished one as she sat next to Kerensa.

"So, what do you think should go here?" she asked, pointing to incomplete squares.

They sat, debating various options for finishing the puzzle, when there was a knock on the door.

It was Vivien.

She looked back and forth from Kerensa to Aruna. For a few seconds, she looked surprised, then composed herself.

"Hello, it's nice to see you both. I'm sorry to intrude, but dinner will be brought up in ten minutes, just wanted to let you know. Today's special is Kerala style fish curry with white rice and grilled aubergine to accompany it, followed by banana cheesecake, and mango ice-cream. The mangoes come from our tree!"

"Vivien, thank you, that sounds delicious." Aruna smiled, looking at Kerensa. "Does that sound okay for you Kerensa?"

"Wonderful!" Kerensa replied enthusiastically. "Thank you both so much."

Vivien smiled at her. "Kerensa, I heard from Calvin at the front desk, that your passport was found. That's great news!"

That Vivian didn't seem to know about it surprised Kerensa. She leaned forward.

"Vivien, do you know who put it there? I would like to thank them. It is such a relief to have found it."

"I don't know dear but will look into it." Vivien looked away out the window as she gave a forced, reassuring smile. "The main thing is it has been found."

Aruna had been watching Kerensa intently. Her eyes darted away when Kerensa returned her gaze. Something was off.

"Absolutely and am just so relieved that it has been located!" Kerensa looked at both women and smiled. "Vivien, I need to go to Chennai urgently in two days. For about a week or so - something unexpected has come up. Is this something you could arrange, please? I will definitely be coming back to the guesthouse afterwards."

Vivien took a step forward.

"Yes, I could do that for you. And we can keep your room for you, we will talk more about it. On a separate note, Kerensa, I know you have been distressed, so we have decided to do a surprise for you. A visit to the temple has been arranged for tomorrow, a complimentary guided tour.

Samuel mentioned that you wanted to visit the large temple. I think you will enjoy it."

"That sounds wonderful! And so exciting, thank you so much." She had mentioned to Samuel during the taxi journey that she wanted to do this, he must have arranged it with his mother.

Aruna continued to watch Kerensa silently, contemplatively, sipping slowly from her glass.

"You must be relieved to have your passport back." She turned to Kerensa suddenly after Vivien left the room. "Maybe it had been dropped and someone found it, handed it in?"

"Yes Aruna, it's still a puzzle though, but am not going to dwell on it, as I'm just so happy to have found it!" Kerensa replied, taking a large sip of her drink.

A short while later, dinner was brought in by Samuel, who smiled politely at both women but steadily avoided eye contact with Kerensa, as he laid the marble table for dinner. The food looked delicious, and they tucked in heartily.

"Gosh, that ice cream was probably the best I have ever tasted." Kerensa commented enthusiastically, wiping her mouth with her napkin afterward.

"So glad you liked it." Aruna began. "The food here is excellent they really go all out to make sure guests are fully happy."

Aruna gestured for Kerensa to join her on the sofa. "So, tell me more about you."

"What can I say. I'm twenty-seven and work as an accountant for a firm in South London. I love my job; it keeps me grounded. I live with my mother and younger brother Matthew." She didn't know what else to say and didn't feel quite ready to mention yet that she was in India looking for the dad she had not seen for a long time. It felt too personal, and she was not ready to share.

"Tell me more about you Aruna."

She turned the question around to the older woman.

"Well, I live in an apartment, in a great location opposite Central

Park, Manhattan and my work keeps me busy, takes me to many areas of the globe. I specialise in the trading of goods primarily." She smiled at Kerensa and added, "When I come to Southern India, I always stay here with Vivien. The guesthouse is one of a kind, Kerensa, you will not find another like it in the whole of India I am sure!"

"What sort of trade do you do? It sounds interesting."

"Well, it depends." Her expression inscrutable, Aruna got up suddenly and made her way to the window, peering out into the lit garden. "Various goods are matched to the need of the consumer, so we operate in many areas. I work with an excellent and loyal team. But let's leave it at that, I don't want to bore you. I can see your glass is empty Kerensa!"

She quickly brought over the bottle of wine, generously topping up Kerensa's glass before her own.

"Here's cheers to us!" She raised her glass and clinked it with Kerensa's. "And our newfound friendship."

CHAPTER

27

I remember my Kerensa.

Thoughts of her are always at the front of my mind's eye. They never leave.

I still have the beautiful painting of the playground that we used to go to, that Kerensa drew for me at school. She was four years old. I am so scared the colours on the page will eventually fade away and disappear.

Or, even worse, that my memory of her will.

They say there is something special about your first child.

You are absolutely in love with this tiny miracle that blasts into your life and completely dominates the strings to your heart, that, until that very moment, had been locked away deep within layers of human wrapping, submerged in the selfish mundaneness of everyday living. The love for your child has a way of melting away the layers, and you start feeling a type of exquisite love that you never knew even existed.

She had looked like a doll. The porcelain kind, with huge brown eyes and curly black locks, that Catherine used to tie into bunches with shiny ribbons.

I used to come home early from work on a Friday and she would be waiting for me, jumping up and down with excitement. Matthew used to crawl around and follow her everywhere - he adored his big sister.

I remember when I took them to the playground and pushed her on the swings, she would scream with excitement and demand that I push more, so she could touch the clouds.

"Daddy, daddy, higher, higher!" she would shout as her brother watched excitedly from his pram, clapping his hands.

I cannot bear to think that I made the choice to leave them. Two beautiful children. How could I?

This memory is one that is just too painful to bear. I close my eyes, so that I can shut it out, but it never wants to leave.

CHAPTER

28

She had never seen anything like it.

The architecture that greeted Kerensa as she ascended the crumbling stone steps, was breath-taking. Ornate and detailed with intricate stunning stone carvings of Hindu gods carved in various poses on the outer walls, the temple had survived hundreds of years of intense sun and human footfall and remained majestic and tall. It stood proudly erect against the Kanyakumari coastline.

A huge wooden door marked the entrance to the temple. It must have been nearly twenty feet high.

"Come now, follow me everyone." The thin older man, with the salt and pepper hair raced past her to the top and clapped his hands loudly. "I am going to show you some magical sights that you have never seen before. Stay close to me and be prepared to be dazzled by what you are about to see and hear!"

The group laughed excitedly. There were eight in total, including Kerensa; a German couple, Kurt and Frederika, who had been spending the last four months of their retirement travelling around India. They were friendly and raved enthusiastically about their amazing experiences at the Taj Mahal and also on a houseboat trip down a beautiful river in Kerala, where they had eaten freshly caught fish and crabs cooked on a small stove by the captain of the boat. A young Indian couple who kept themselves to themselves and spoke little English trailed behind. Their eyes look empty and bored, as they stayed glued to their phones.

Two American friends, Carl and Mungo, possibly in their thirties were backpacking their way around India and had ended up in Nagercoil by accident. They had decided to be daring and hopped on a train from Chennai, seeing where it would take them. They'd managed to find a cheap hostel, a basic B&B where they had been staying for a week.

Pretty bold, thought Kerensa. It would not be somethings she would do. At heart, she was a true conservative who needed to know exactly what she was doing in advance, However, her trip to India was an adventure, taking her very much out of her comfort zone.

Lagging behind everyone was a slim Indian girl. Youngish, possibly early thirties. She wore thick, black rimmed spectacles which somehow suited her pretty, delicate features. She was smiley and kept trying to get Kerensa's attention, probably feeling a relatable bond – both of similar ages and had come alone for the tour. She had a professional Canon camera, complete with lenses of various shapes and sizes, which she kept changing to take photos of everything around. Her name was Latha.

"Sorry, but everyone will need to remove their shirts before entering the temple. It is the rule." Hari, the tour guide insisted, however on seeing their shocked faces added hastily: "Of course, I only meant the men!"

As they finally went through the gates and into the main temple area. Kerensa gasped - she had not seen anything like this in her life.

On either side of the entrance were row after row of carvings; the gods riding on chariots, and on horses, and endless frescos of many animals, including cows, horses and dogs. There were large shrines dedicated to the god Ganesh and also the goddess Balasundari who, legend said, was a virgin and Hari revealed, possessed a dazzling nose ring which apparently led many doomed sailors to their death as they confused the sparkle emitted to that from a lighthouse, dashing their ships against the rocks.

Everything was fascinating.

"Gather round everyone." began Hari who cast a sweeping glance, making sure everyone was listening. "Can you believe that this very temple where you are standing was built over 3000 years ago? It is a highly spiritual place, one of the most revered temples in the whole of India. It is said that the goddess had her mission at this spot to go into combat with a demon, whom she was born to kill as a virgin."

"Wow, this place is beyond words! I need to make sure I take some excellent photos here, otherwise my boss won't let me forget it." Latha smiled at Kerensa and swiftly raised her long lens to the ceiling as she broke the silence with a series of loud clicks that came one after the other.

"Are you a professional photographer?" Kerensa was curious.

"Sort of, I work for the local newspaper part time, but am more a lady of leisure. I do love photography especially of ancient architecture. That's my true passion."

Before Kerensa could reply, Carl stepped forward and began asking Latha questions about her camera, saying how he planned to buy a similar one in the range.

Mungo turned to Kerensa and winked. "Who would have ever thought that talking about a camera would be a brilliant chat up line!"

Kerensa laughed, it was nice to have some lighthearted banter.

They were left to wander around the temple grounds for thirty minutes, as Hari had given them strict instructions to reconvene at 11am.

"Aren't the carvings just amazing? "It was Latha. She had come and silently stood behind Kerensa who was peering closely at an intricate mosaic carving.

"Oh, you startled me!" Kerensa turned to her, smiling. "Yes, the detail in the work is breath-taking."

"Where are you staying in Nagercoil, Kerensa?" Latha began with a hint of curiosity.

She was surprised that the young woman remembered her name, she had only mentioned it briefly at the beginning of the tour.

"I'm in Amma's guesthouse, it's just off the highway. The owner Vivien is lovely and arranged for me to go on this tour."

"That's nice!" Latha smiled." I've heard they are very good at the guesthouse. Just a quick question, we finish at 11.30, did you want to grab some lunch after? I know a nice place in the town centre we could go to, not too far from here."

Kerensa had been driven to the temple by Chandu, who had been waiting in his car on a side road nearby.

"That sounds wonderful! I am sure my driver won't mind taking us, I will ask him and pay him extra. It would be good." She smiled. It was always nice to connect to other similar young women, and maybe this could be the start of a nice friendship, she thought to herself.

"I'm really excited to get to know you, Kerensa." Latha smiled as she suddenly turned to photograph something that had caught her eye, camera clicking furiously as she headed away into the distance.

CHAPTER

29

Once upon a time, Mano had a home.

A real home, with four walls and two parents who loved him dearly. And there was laughter there, he could never forget the beautiful sound it made as it resonated throughout the house.

His mother adored him - the only child of Krishna and Reena Verma, he was very much wanted. Krishna worked night shifts at the local paper mill, so each day it was him and mama against the world.

She took him to kindergarten, holding his hand tightly when they crossed the roads. She would laugh as she smothered him with kisses dropping him at the gate. Mano would brush her off, embarrassed. Her little man, she would call him affectionately.

"Promise you will never leave me mama," he would plead as he clung to her tightly. He never wanted the blissful moments to end.

"I love you to the very ends of the world, my beautiful son. Even if I am not with you, remember that I am watching over you always."

His five-year-old mind never understood the meaning of her words, but they remained imprinted in his mind. Years later, they would give him great comfort, in his darkest of times. His mama would always be with him. Like a guardian angel, never leaving his side.

As he left kindergarten one afternoon, he was surprised to see papa waiting outside. Papa usually slept in the daytime, after his long shift overnight at the mill and never usually picked him up.

He looked tired, drained of colour. There was something amiss in his eyes that even a young child could detect - something was wrong.

"Mano, come here my child." He knelt down and gently pulled the boy into his arms. "I have some sad news. Your mama has left this world and gone to heaven my son. You must be strong."

The howls that emerged from the child were heart-rendering, and people walking nearby stopped to gape at the sorrowful scene in front of them. Mano sobbed and sobbed as his father held him close. He felt as though his heart had been torn in pieces, thrown to the wind.

Apparently, she had been walking home, after dropping Mano to kindergarten that morning when a speeding car turned a corner and hit her. Death was instantaneous, a small consolation the policeman said as he stood on the steps of the family home having broken the news to her distraught husband.

A year passed, and Mano and his papa got into a comfortable routine. He desperately missed his mother and her loving kisses. But he knew that papa was trying his best.

One day after kindergarten, he brought a lady to the school gates. She was young and quite pretty but looked at Mano with coldness.

"This is Radha aunty. She is going to live with us, and I want you to love her like your mama."

What was papa saying? Had he gone mad? There would never be anyone to replace his darling mama.

The new aunty moved in with them and began cooking and taking over the things that had always been mama's domain. She was always nice in front of papa, but when he was away or sleeping, she would push Mano out of the kitchen roughly, and she once pinched him very hard just for taking a samosa from a batch she had fried for dinner.

He missed his mama so much, why did she have to leave him alone like this with this woman?

Radha even started wearing his mother's clothes and jewelry, which upset him even more. She had been quietly plotting many plans of a new life with her new husband, none of which involved her new stepson. He was simply a burden, an encumbrance.

One evening, when papa was away at work, Radha took him by the hand to the train station. She had packed his school rucksack with some water, and snacks and sat with him on the deserted train bench until the engine started. He felt very sleepy, it was late and past his bedtime.

He was wondering why she would take him to the station. When he asked her the reason why they were travelling so late at night, she told him to be quiet, or he would get a pinch.

His last memory was a sleepy one. He saw Radha looking at him intently, urging him to slumber as he his eyes slowly closed.

When he awoke the next morning, the train was pulling up into an unfamiliar station. Unbeknown to Mano, the train had been travelling the whole night. The sun was burning hot, rays dancing on his forehead. The station was full of people, chatting, going about their business. Vendors were walking around with bamboo baskets on their heads, calling out for their wares. "Superrr corn." shouted one. "Vegetable cutlets," yelled another.

There was no sign of Radha aunty. Where was she? He looked around - the carriage was deserted.

The whole place was unfamiliar, and the language was different to what he was used to. He felt scared. He didn't know his address or how to get back home.

Mano at five years old, had just been abandoned.

CHAPTER

30

Leaning against the soft, white pillow Aruna brought the cigarette stub up to her lips. Her tired eyes watched the puffs of smoke disappear into the ether, filling the air with a musky smokiness.

She was pleased with her stylish room in the guesthouse, it was just how she liked it. The separate living area had a dark-grey Italian L-shaped sofa. A deep piled black rug with small, abstract squares of various colours lay directly in front. In the corner, the marble topped desk was perfect for her to get to work. The executive suite was simply luxurious, a den perfect for a strong woman. Vivien always understood her tastes exactly.

The bedside table clock read 7:18pm.

She'd had a short nap, which thoroughly energised her. It had been a week since reaching India, and the jetlag was still there, but Aruna was determined to keep active. There was too much work to do.

The thick gold bangle on the bedside cabinet sparkled gently as it caught the light from the lamp above. A gift from the sheikh during her recent stopover in Dubai. That particular meeting had been highly productive. Sheikh Yusuf was an intelligent man and easy to do business with. The agreed amount had been swiftly transferred to Aruna's account during their chat. The child was being prepped and prepared to be dispatched to his residence in Dubai, as per the terms of their deal.

The firm knock at the door was expected. She straightened her posture and held her head high. A woman of grace.

"Come in Navin. It's open."

A small, bald headed man put his head around the door, eyes squinting through his thick spectacles, struggling to see around the room.

"Ah there you are," he said, as Aruna approached him through the lounge area. He leaned back against the door, as it closed. "Aruna, we have a problem." He took a deep breath. "One of the girls is refusing to eat. She has been force-fed, but everything is coming back up. She has lost a lot of weight. She is about nine years old, one of those who have been with us for a long time. We have been unable to move her anywhere."

Aruna sat down at the far end of the sofa and gestured for Navin to take a place opposite her.

"I can't afford for this to happen. Tell one of the ladies to talk to her sweetly, give her something tasty to entice her, maybe take her discreetly outside for some sunshine for a while. Keep trying."

"I will Aruna." Navin shook his head side to side in agreement, the Indian gesture of nodding and showing support. "But what do we do if she refuses?" He knew what the answer would be, but still had to ask the question. Aruna was the boss, and even though he had oversight of all the day to day operations, it was ultimately the top lady who made all the major decisions. He admired her greatly for making some very tough decisions of late. She never showed any fear; Navin sometimes wondered if she had a spine made from steel. Everyone around her was astounded by how she held herself. A regal lady.

"You know what to do Navin. Remember, product is always expendable." She brought the small cigarette stub to her lips, drawing a breath and exhaling a light puff. She watched as it vanished into thin air. "We can't afford to waste time. If we are not getting the outcome we need, she will be eliminated." She continued. "Just do it discreetly, make sure her body is disposed of appropriately. Get one of the men to do it. But give her a little longer."

"Yes Aruna." Navin replied meekly, blinking hard. He was in charge of the operational side of the project but leaned on Aruna for the major decisions.

He reached for an empty glass on the table, which he filled with water from a glass jug nearby. Sweat poured off his brow. He had lived in Nagercoil his whole life, but simply could not tolerate the extreme heat. It was unbearable on most days. The guesthouse was air conditioned, but the heat still came through. The stress was testing his faculties immensely.

Removing a white hanky from his pocket, he wiped his forehead vigorously.

'Give me an update on the warehouse situation. What's happening there?' Aruna looked at him rather impatiently. She didn't want to keep prompting him, but it seemed to be always the case with Navin. He got things done eventually, but always needed a nudge. It seemed that in India, everything always seemed to take so long to function. Including the people.

'Okay, things are going fine. We have about five to six vacant rooms ready to be filled. There is always someone there, and of course we have the henchmen on rota duty. We were lucky to get this place. There is a huge expanse of paddy field separating it from the main highway, about nearly three miles, so it is impossible to see it from the road. Only a small dirt road, with a few dim lamps, connects it to the main highway.'

'And there's no way to leave.' Aruna took another puff of the cigarette, as she threw back her head, giving a maniacal laugh.

Navin looked at her intently. He had worked with the American for almost three years, yet she never ceased to surprise him. Truth be told, he felt quite intimidated by her. It was unusual to meet a woman as cold hearted as Aruna. But she paid him an excellent wage, and that was what mattered.

He lived alone. Somehow, despite desperate attempts from family members to matchmake when he was younger, he never found anyone he wanted to settle down with. Or maybe it was because they found him unbecoming. He had comments from girls he had dated when he was younger who taunted him about his height and lack of hair. But never mind. His life was very much trying to prove his manliness, but women always seemed to emasculate him.

He found the Indian women too feeble anyway - he was attracted to Eastern European women, in particular busty Russian females. There was something about them. An assertive beauty.

His latest conquest was a beautiful, dark-haired woman called Natalya. She lived in St Petersburg, with her young son Kazimir. Her first marriage had broken down. They had chatted on skype many times; light flirtatious talk that hinted keenly with anticipation of the raunchy sex that would come. He planned to visit her in a few weeks for the first time in Russia and couldn't wait.

Natalya was in her late thirties, so much younger than him and very feminine, but that was the great thing about Eastern European women. They knew how to make an older man feel like a king.

CHAPTER

31

"Come quickly, I haven't got all day!"

The sound of the bolt moving to the side was deafening as the heavy steel door slowly swung open to reveal a dark, narrow corridor. The smell of cigarettes lay heavy in the air. The man stood there, looking at the child with disdain.

"If you don't come quickly, I will come over there and drag you out myself." he said with contempt.

Maya eased herself slowly out from under the thin cover, that was riddled with holes and placed her feet, one by one, onto the floor. She turned to her side and holding onto the nearby wall for support, managed to pull herself up. At nine, she was so thin that her bones protruded like little knobs, pushing earnestly against her flimsy clothes.

One foot in front of the other, she moved painfully forward, shuffling a little bit at a time. She looked skeletal, like a grotesque caricature of what was once a healthy child. Her gait belonged to someone who was in their last lap of life, not a young child.

The guard watched her, a scowl crowning his face. His shift was nearly ending, and he didn't have time for any nonsense.

"This is what happens if you don't eat. Now go that way, I will be right behind you. And no tricks, mind you."

He pointed to a small corridor to the right, indicating the way she needed to walk.

At the end was a wooden door. It was large, but not solid steel like the door to her room. It had a large padlock, and the man pushed past her, impatiently taking a set of assorted keys jangling around his waist, as he sorted through them. He pulled out the largest one, inserting it into the padlock. It made a loud 'click' as it turned and unlocked.

"Okay, out you go!" He pulled open the door and as he did so, the intense rays almost blinded her with their ferocity. After being in the dark for months at a time, the brightness was too much for her to take. She yelled in pain, scrunching up her eyes and involuntarily shielding them with her bony hands.

In front of her, was a small courtyard area, packed with overflowing rubbish bins, which emitted a rancid smell. They had not been emptied for weeks. A thin puddle of sewage water lay festering by the bins; a multitude of flies danced around it, as they took turns landing on the putrid waste. She tried to suppress heaving in repulsion, with the blinding lights and grotesque smells.

A makeshift cage, acting as a boundary had been erected in the middle of the courtyard, with filthy blankets covering the ground inside it.

A girl sat inside cross-legged; Maya knew immediately she was from the next room. She looked terrified, and looked down, her tiny frame shivering despite the heat. She was terrified.

"*Cheakro*, quickly now." The man urged her, a little more gently. "You have exactly one hour, I will come back. And no funny business," he said, as he closed the door firmly behind her.

Leaving her and her newfound friend, all alone.

CHAPTER

32

David Holdsworth was a man of precise habits.

Waking up every day at 6am, the highlight of his morning was always his sweet milky coffee with two and a half sugars, freshly made in his favourite china mug by the live-in help, Maria. She would leave it ready in his study for him, covered, piping hot, just how he liked it.

As David eased himself out of bed, he turned and looked lovingly at his wife Pat. She was sleeping peacefully, a gentle smile on her lips. He didn't want to disturb her, so quietly made his way downstairs.

There was no escaping the thickness of the file that lay on his desk in wait for him, a systematic approach was the best way to tackle it. The pages inside were harrowing. Details of all the children who had gone missing over the past five years lay within the covers. Interviews with the parents, reported sightings by concerned members of the public. The pictures of the smiling children were the worst part; innocent and trusting, they were happily posing with friends and family, unaware of the tragic fate that lay ahead for them. David had read their stories over and over, hoping to make some sense of what could have happened.

Absorbed, he lost track of time and as the sun was reaching its peak, the rays filtered through the blinds behind him, soothingly caressing the teak wood desk.

The sudden ring of the phone was startling. He looked at the clock. It was 9.30am already.

"Is that David? Hello, this is Kerensa here, we met last week?" The voice was uncertain, nervous.

For a moment, he wasn't sure then remembered the plane journey back from England.

"Hello Kerensa, of course I remember you. How have you been doing?"

"David, I need to talk to you about something very urgent. It's been on my mind for a few days, and I don't know who I can talk to about this. Please help."

"Kerensa, of course." David wondered what could be so stressful, when he'd met her last on the plane, she'd seemed carefree and excited.

"I think I have stumbled across something sinister at the guesthouse where I am staying. I went behind the counter to look for my passport, don't ask, it's a long story. Anyway, I saw a file marked 'confidential.' When I looked, I found details of many children with addresses where they were being taken to and details of large amounts of money changing hands. I just don't know what to do about the situation David."

There was a deafening silence at the other end.

"Hello, are you still there?"

David simply couldn't believe what he had heard. He had spent months researching and following up leads on the missing children in the area, only for a major lead like this to fall into his lap from a stranger whom he had sat next to on a plane.

"So sorry, I think I am just flabbergasted," he stuttered. This was all too much for him. "This file you are talking about, is it still there in the same place?" he continued. He didn't want to get excited. After all, this was highly unlikely.

Kerensa's response was breathless and filled with panic. "Please don't think I am foolish, this happened a few days ago, I know I should have reported it sooner, I just didn't know what to do. I know the police would have been an obvious answer, but the language barrier was worrying me, so I wanted to talk to you first. I checked yesterday, it has disappeared and is not there now." he could hear her voice getting high pitched and anxious as she talked.

"Kerensa, you need to listen to me. Is this a secure line, where are you calling from?"

"I am using the phone in my room David. It appears to be private."

"Okay. Listen carefully to what I am about to tell you. I couldn't tell you earlier of course, but I am the Interpol lead specializing in Crime Investigations in Southern India. I have been looking into the missing children for months, but we have had very few avenues to venture down. It has been like drawing blood from a stone." He took a gulp of his now-cold coffee as he continued. "We suspect a gang of experienced traffickers are operating in this area, preying on small and vulnerable children, especially from poor and working-class homes. They have been very cleverly covering their tracks. If what you say is true Kerensa, you have just given me a major lead!"

Kerensa could not believe it. Her heart seemed to sink into her chest with relief. The one person that she had opened up to be the only person who could really help her.

"Right, first of all, you need to keep this information to yourself, just like you have done the past few days. Don't let on to anyone that you saw that file. Your life could be at risk otherwise. These are bad people Kerensa, who operate with no moral qualms whatsoever."

"Yes David, I won't tell anyone. Just so relieved that I told you, the right person who can actually help!"

David leaned forward in his seat, as he whispered. "Kerensa, this is ground-breaking, vital information for our investigation. Do not breathe a word to anyone there in the guesthouse and carry on with things as normal. I will come quietly there to have a look around, but will not contact you directly, as I don't want to draw attention."

"David, I need to go away to Chennai shortly for some personal business, it is something urgent that cannot wait, but I will be back in three days."

"Very well then, I will contact you after your return Kerensa, this is my mobile number, please keep it safe, and call me anytime you need me okay? You take care, bye for now. And thank you. You did the right thing." After quickly passing his contact details, David hung up.

Leaving a bewildered, and rather relieved Kerensa at the other end of the line, pondering about what she had got herself into. Fear and suspense whirled around her mind - it was going to be an interesting journey ahead.

CHAPTER

33

"Let's grab an auto into town. Have you travelled in one before?"

Latha didn't wait for an answer, as she suddenly yelled and raised her arm, waving it frantically in the air. The passing driver hooted in acknowledgment, as he deftly swerved his compact vehicle out of the way of an oncoming lorry and pulled up in front of Kerensa and Latha on the narrow road in front of the temple, pulling on his brakes sharply.

The easiest way to go into town was in one of the local autorickshaws. Chandu had agreed he would wait in the car for her.

Latha pointed to the entrance of the vehicle urging with a nod that Kerensa should go in first. She stepped up and crouched as she went inside as it was clear the autorickshaws were not designed for taller passengers. The interior was cramped, perfect for just two people. Anymore, and they would have been spilling out.

The decorations inside were gaudy and eccentric, in various hues of red and green. Latha explained that the drivers liked to put their own unique stamps on their rickshaws. The vehicle they were travelling in certainly had done that.

The bright red seat was covered with tiny green and yellow scatter cushions, rather a mismatch. Hanging from the back near the tiny rear window, were strings of small gold and silver shining baubles, which looked like they had been freshly snatched from someone's Christmas tree, and they swung gaily from side to side as the auto swerved round corners and sped down tiny lanes. Similar baubles were fixed near the driver's seat, on the sides and front, and as the vehicle sped along, the shiny beads would move with it, tangling a few times with the driver's hands and the wheel, which he would impatiently push away.

"*Narro po.*" Latha pointed straight as she guided him ahead, shouting over the loud noise of the engine in order to be heard.

Despite the crazy speed the driver was travelling at, Kerensa found herself enjoying the ride. There were no seats-belts fitted in the vehicle the safety of his passengers did not appear to be a major concern.

"What do you fancy eating Kerensa? Where we are going, there is a Chinese, Mexican as well as the usual South Indian stalls. You choose."

They suddenly stopped at the entrance to a small lane. The meter showed thirty-five rupees, however as they got out, the driver demanded fifty rupees. Latha started shouting at him loudly in Tamil; the irate driver shouted back, and soon a heated tirade of insults were going back and forth between the two. The commotion was the last thing Kerensa needed for her nerves.

"Listen, I will pay it." Kerensa hurriedly took a fifty rupee note from her bag and shoved it in the driver's hand, placating him to leave. He looked furious and gave Latha a dirty look as he got back into his vehicle and sped away.

"Idiot!" shouted Latha, loudly shaking her fists angrily to the back of the auto, as it disappeared from sight. "Sorry, Kerensa, but it makes me mad that when these drivers see a white woman, they decide to suddenly skyrocket their prices."

"Don't worry, let's forget about it and have something nice to eat. I'm starving and I'm sure you will be too Latha."

The girl nodded in reply, as they walked to a row of restaurants on the narrow lane.

"Do you like Chinese?" Latha pointed to a tiny place filled with customers which seemed to be very popular with the locals. "This is an Indo-Chinese restaurant and does amazing food."

"Let go here!" Kerensa suddenly felt extremely hungry, and the photos of the various dishes placed strategically near the entrance were deliberately enticing for passers-by to lure them into the restaurant.

"That was delicious." Kerensa sighed, leaning back in her chair after having eaten too much.

The two had chatted for over thirty minutes as they ate a wide variety of mouthwatering vegetable and seafood dishes, brought sizzling to their table. Food really was a wonderful tonic.

Latha talked about her family, work and even her pet chihuahua, Lucky, who she had picked up at a local rescue centre, three years before. He was her pride and joy. She was an only child, her parents lived up in Mumbai in the north of India. She didn't seem to want to talk too much about them. Kerensa chatted about her life in the UK about her mum, Matt and work.

"Anyone special in your life at the moment?" Latha asked curiously, taking a large spoonful of rice. Kerensa found herself blushing as she thought about Samuel, but the other girl did not seem to notice as she continued speaking without waiting for an answer. "So, when will you going to Chennai Kerensa?"

Kerensa looked shocked, she didn't remember telling the other girl that she was leaving town.

On seeing the expression on her face, Latha stammered. "You told me at the temple you were leaving, remember?"

"I don't." Kerensa replied, bewildered. Maybe she had forgotten. A lot had been on her plate recently. "Yes, I am leaving tomorrow Latha, looking forward to it. How is Chennai?"

"It's a big and buzzing city, I think you will like it. Let's stay in touch, this is my number." She handed Kerensa a simple white business card, with her name and number imprinted clearly in the middle.

"I would love to! When I am back, lets meet again for lunch."

"I've had such a lovely time with you Kerensa, it's a deal!" replied Latha, as they headed back towards the temple.

CHAPTER

34

Maya took a tentative step out into the bright courtyard. She could hardly see in front of her - the sunlight was dazzling, and she had to scrunch up her eyes to focus on what lay ahead.

The little girl on the blanket looked straight at Maya. Her eyes spoke of harrowing pain, however a tiny glimmer of a smile appeared on her face when she saw the other girl.

Maya went and sat down in front of her, crossing her legs slowly. "Hello, I'm Maya. What's your name?"

The girl leaned forward and whispered. "My name is Preeti. I am six."

Maya felt shocked, Preeti was about the same age as she was when she'd been snatched. A mere baby. She reached towards Preeti's hands, covering them with her own and gave them a reassuring squeeze. The first human contact Maya had had for over a year was so comforting.

"Thank you *akka (older sister)*!" The younger girl shuffled closer and put her head unexpectedly against Maya's left shoulder. She nestled closer as Maya quietly circled her with her arms, pulling her close as she squeezed her tight.

Words were not required. Both girls desperately needed the human touch of each other to remind them they were no longer alone. "I miss my mummy. I want to see her so much." A racking sob came from the small girl, her shoulders shaking as she leaned against Maya, who reached up her hand to gently stroke the small girl's face. She continued the gentle touch for a few moments.

"I know you do, and you will see her again okay?" Her voice was soothing. "Just keep believing that. Your mummy hasn't forgotten, she just doesn't know you are here. Someone will find us and take us back home. I know it."

'Yes *akka,* thank you.'

Even though Maya was still a child herself at nine she had to grow up very quickly. For her, the happiness of childhood never lingered.

The sound of the bolt moving broke the unspoken silence between the two girls, who quickly moved apart. The look of terror reappeared on Preeti's face.

The surly guard with the moustache from earlier had been replaced by a woman whom Maya realised was the one who had come to see her.

She took a step out into the courtyard, wrinkling her nose in disgust as her eyes fell on the puddles of sewage that festered in the corners. She wore a pristine red and green sari, which she lifted slightly as she carefully made her way across the uneven stones. When she saw the two girls, a forced smile appeared on her face.

"Maya, Preeti?" she asked tentatively.

Both girls looked at her curiously. In her hands were two brightly coloured boxes.

"These are for you. A gift." She stepped forward and handed them a box each.

Preeti remembered her mother having the same boxes in her pantry, filled with sweets. The thought of amma made her feel incredibly sad. She wanted to be at home, and the thoughts of her mummy brought tears again to her eyes. "Please ma'am, I want to go home." She started sobbing, tears cascading down her cheeks. Maya reached forward and put her arm around the younger girl, muttering soothingly under her breath.

The lady bent down, crouching directly in front of Preeti. Her expression was inscrutable. "Look, dear, you must not cry. What I am about to tell you is going to hurt you, but your mama does not want you. We tried to send you back, but she does not want you anymore, so we are going to find a new home for you, okay?"

The words were shocking. Preeti began to sob hysterically, leaning against Maya, who glared at the woman angrily. "It's not true! It's not true!"

The woman looked at Maya, distaste registering on her face. She stood up abruptly.

"I think it's time for you to go back to your rooms. Enough is enough."

She turned and called for the sour-faced guard, who appeared and stood by the door glaring. It seemed to be his favourite expression.

Without turning back, the woman stepped through the door and out of sight.

"Come quickly, it is time for you to be back in your rooms." It was the guard.

Maya got up slowly to her feet helped up by Preeti, who supported her new friend as she slowly stood up. She had the gait of an old lady.

As they walked to the door, Maya glanced at her wrist. She still had the stone bracelet her mother had given her for her fifth birthday, it was a wonder that the people had not taken it away. A little token of her heart still remained.

She quickly pulled it off, and reached for Preeti's arm, sliding it on.

"This is for you Preeti, to remind you that one day, you and I will escape this place and go back home. It's going to happen, never lose faith."

And with those words, the girls mouthed quietly a final goodbye as the door closed behind them.

CHAPTER

35

The phone buzzed loudly, the WhatsApp message breaking the silence of the peaceful tropical afternoon.

It was Emily.

"Hey K! Thinking of you, what is India like? It's raining here, as usual. Nothing interesting at work, it's not the same without you. How's your search going? I need the gossip!!"

Kerensa smiled as she glanced at her phone and placed it carefully next to her on the small table, making a mental note to reply later. Mum and Matt had both sent messages the day before which she also needed to reply to.

Stretched out on a balcony sun lounger, the soothing warbles of a nearby mynah bird were gently lulling. The intense heat made Kerensa feel lethargic - it was nearly 3pm, and the outside temperature had already hit 35 degrees. Overshadowing branches from a nearby tree offered some well-needed shade on the balcony.

It was the raised voices from below that suddenly caught her attention.

"No, I will not do that. You are asking me to do something that is totally out of my comfort zone, I'm sorry but I can't." It was Samuel. Kerensa went quietly to the balcony wall and looked over but couldn't see who he was talking to.

His voice lowered considerably, and then he disappeared inside. *What could be making him so angry* she wondered?

Since the time he'd wrapped his arms around her, Kerensa found she couldn't stop thinking about him. She tried to tell herself her main purpose for being in India was to find her father, and that anything else was a distraction, but that didn't make it better the thoughts of Samuel simply wouldn't go away. His form, his voice, his face had been circling inside her head.

So much had happened over the past few days. The thought of the poor children with the harrowing expressions she had seen inside the file remained on her mind constantly. She couldn't stop thinking about them. Wondering who they were, and the pain they would be feeling at being separated from their distraught parents made Kerensa feel ill at the thought.

Thank goodness she was able to confide in David, it was a relief. She didn't really want to stay at the Guesthouse anymore with everything happening, but David reassured her that she would be fine, she just needed to keep a low profile. And anyway, she would be heading off to Chennai shortly.

The small town of Nagercoil was rarely in the UK news, until a month before when two young girls under ten went missing from near their homes. Children from poor working-class homes, unremarkable in the eyes of the Indian news channels who had more important things to report on with the current elections taking prime time viewing. But the main British TV stations found the story newsworthy, it made a gripping additional report after the BBC headline news. The parents of both girls had been filmed hollow-eyed, traumatised, lost in their grief. Kerensa had found it hard to watch and had to turn the channel.

She needed to take a break from her thoughts, deciding to get dressed and go down to the bar for a drink.

Apart from an older couple sitting chatting in a corner, the area was quite empty. Catchy sounds of 'Dancing Queen' played low in the background.

Looking around Kerensa was fascinated by the bar. It had a unique theme of the London Underground, with what looked like original tube signs behind each of the individual table booths. Near the entrance was a big neon sign which flashed 'Mind the gap' in bright orange lights. Framed black and white photos of tube trains adorned the walls. The whole place was stylish and radical, and seemed to be slightly incongruous within the sleepy backwater town.

"What can I get you ma'am?" the bar woman asked, wiping down a drinks machine vigorously. She looked about the same age as Kerensa, her dark hair had been tied up neatly in a high bun and a large golden ring adorned her nose.

Kerensa positioned herself comfortably on a tall black stool.

"Do you have Baileys, please?"

The woman smiled. "Certainly, let me prepare it for you. Can I take your room number ma'am?"

"Sure, its number nineteen." Kerensa replied. She was looking forward to the drink. After all the stress of the past few days, she really needed something to calm her, however sordid. Baileys always did the trick.

The glass was tall and wide, with a generous amount of the creamy beverage mixed with large melting chunks of ice. She brought it to her lips; it tasted rich and refreshing.

"Would you mind if I join you Kerensa?" The voice from behind startled her. It was Samuel.

She turned to him and felt her eyes drawn to the top opening of his white shirt, where dark hairs were poking through. She felt herself go red.

"Yes, please do, that would be nice."

Samuel pulled up a nearby stool which he brought close to hers looking at the large glass in her hand.

"What is that?" he smiled "don't tell me; Baileys!"

"Yes, spot on." Kerensa laughed. There was something about Samuel that made her feel comfortable. He was easy to talk to.

"Bina get me the same please," he called over the bar girl, pointing to the Baileys.

He suddenly turned to face Kerensa and leaned forward so his face was closer to hers. She felt herself take a breath. "I have wanted to talk to you since the other day," his voice trailed off taking a large gulp of his drink as though it would give him strength to say what he needed to. "The fact of the matter is Kerensa, I simply cannot stop thinking of you." He looked down, a hint of bashfulness and trepidation at her possible reaction.

He squeezed her hands, taking them in his own. Before she could say anything, he leaned forward, and his mouth was on hers. She responded passionately and could almost feel her knees buckling with the weight of their passionate embrace.

"Come with me." He got to his feet quickly and pulled her up gently, indicating that she should follow him.

Ignoring the bemused barmaid, he held Kerensa's hand and led her through a side door. She suddenly realized they had come out into the garden. Samuel led her to a secluded alcove.

He pushed her against the wall and kissed her with a passion, that blew her away. Kerensa wrapped her arms around his neck, as he pressed closely against her. The scent of his body was musky, manly.

He broke his mouth away from her suddenly, and started kissing her neck passionately, down to her breastbone. His breath was ragged, uneven, as he started unbuttoning her shirt slowly, to reveal her black lingerie. Her breasts rose full over the top. It felt utterly bewildering and wonderful to be felt, to be touch by the man for whom she had such powerful, intense feelings.

"Oh my god, Kerensa you are so damn beautiful." His breathing was jagged and hoarse, as he looked unsteadily at her, with glazed eyes. Kerensa thought she would collapse with weakness she had never felt so overwhelmed with passion.

She pulled Samuel towards her as they resumed their kiss his tongue reaching into the back of her mouth. His right hand cupped her breast as he massaged it slowly and firmly.

Kerensa heard herself moaning loudly, she wanted him, but sudden reason slapped her firmly in the face. Her face screwed up as she tried to resist the clutches of passion. She pushed him away slowly, registering the bewildered look on his face.

"Samuel…please…we need to take this slow," she began, her voice hoarse as she struggled to regain herself.

"Kerensa, come to my room tonight. I want you so much." Samuel looked at her intently, his eyes dark with unspoken passion. His voice was unsteady and his breathing ragged, as he struggled to catch his breath.

She tried to tell herself that this was not why she had come to India that her priority was finding her father and that anything else was a distraction from her purpose. She was rational and sensible. Right? She didn't feel any of these things.

She gently stroked Samuel's cheek and took her hand and kissed her fingertips slowly. His romantic gesture made her smile.

"Samuel, I feel the same way, but please let's take it slow. I'm going to Chennai tomorrow, and have got some things that I need to mentally sort out. Let's wait until my return; I will be back in three days. It's not long."

He looked at her and sighed deeply. "I know you are right Kerensa. I want you to know I like you so much. I have never felt this about anyone, not like this."

He reached down and slowly buttoned up her shirt.

"Thanks Samuel, I couldn't have your mum see me like this, she would be wondering what I was up to!" Kerensa joked. Samuel gave a loud laugh and stroked her hair.

"Go safely to Chennai, and I will be waiting for you right here. I just discovered something disturbing, I need to sort it out, will tell you when you get back Kerensa."

She wondered if it had to do with the conversation she had overheard earlier under her balcony. She remembered the file she found. Should she tell Samuel now? She decided she would wait until she returned from Chennai and tell him then.

The feelings that flowed through her as she thought of Samuel's hands on her skin were overwhelming. She had been on occasional dates after work, usually matched by a well-meaning colleague with boring, selfish older men who had plenty of money, but no interest in anyone other than themselves. The disappointment she felt over the years weighed her down. She had a good job and was often told she was beautiful, yet she couldn't meet a half-decent man.

Until now. A virtual stranger in a new country had stirred a passion inside her that she didn't know she even had. Her feelings for Samuel had ignited a fire within Kerensa that she didn't think she could stop.

Three days seemed almost a lifetime to wait to see him again. But finding her father was priority and she knew that Samuel would be eagerly waiting for her on her return.

CHAPTER

36

Geeta and Laxmi Menon, aged forty-five and forty-six respectively, lived alone in a saffron-coloured house at the end of South Street, Nagercoil. Devoted to each other, the two sisters couldn't have appeared more different. Geeta, her silky hair swept up into a smooth bun, was slim, and considerably taller than her older sister, Laxmi, who, with thick black spectacles perched at the end of her nose, preferred to use brightly coloured chiffon scarves and high heeled court shoes to disguise her rotund stature and lack of height.

When they were younger it used to be considered a stigma, to live alone without a husband with only the four walls for company. They learnt to ignore the gossip from neighbours and well-meaning friends who had tried to 'set them up' over the years, with eligible older bachelors; sad, balding, bespectacled men who had plenty of money, but had given up entirely on life. They didn't want that kind of life. To be attached to a man with no ambition or drive. The way they looked at life was at least they had each other, and that was enough.

Only aunt Uma remained in the family. She was their father's sister; austere, stern, but lovable. She was eighty-seven and lived alone in her expensive, one- bedroomed apartment in Central Chennai, fiercely independent, refusing any offers of help from concerned neighbours. Geeta and Laxmi went to spend a week with her each Christmas, without fail.

They earned a meagre living by tailoring saree blouses. Working from home suited them and they were very much in demand with the local women. They earned just enough to get by but without fail put business on hold each December so they could travel up to the coast to visit their aunt. Creatures of habit, they always travelled on the overnight Chennai express train that left Nagercoil in the evening, reaching their aunt's place in Chennai the next morning.

"I wanted you to know that I am leaving you a special gift each," Uma announced unexpectedly one Christmas as they sat in her living room on the wide, biscuit-coloured sofa, sipping hot cups of chai straight after church. Both women protested they didn't expect or want anything from their aunt apart from love.

They returned each year, until one sunny August when the news came that Aunt Uma had passed away. They were summoned to Chennai for her funeral and the reading of her will. And another overnight journey on the Chennai express.

Geetha and Laxmi were on their way to Chennai, and did not realise that, thanks to Aunt Uma, they were soon close to becoming millionaires.

CHAPTER

37

When Manish was just seven years old, and his friends spent most of their time playing endless games of football in the narrow, garbage-filled alleyway that preceded their ramshackle corrugated homes, he learnt to make a good cup of coffee.

He used to watch *amma* as she patiently heated up a small stainless-steel urn of milk on the stove, adding carefully measured spoons of powder from the rusty tin as she stirred in some sugar. She would always taste it and always added a small amount of water later, as it boiled. This was the secret to a great coffee, she told him.

He learnt fast. Money was scarce at home, the middle shack in the row of shanty houses, squashed between a tiny, one room brick house and a derelict hut with a broken tin roof on a narrow lane. His mother worked full time as a maid, and so was hardly there. His father, a chronic alcoholic, left when he was a baby. So, amma was the main breadwinner, and struggled tirelessly to ensure a good future for her only child. Long hours working, meant Manish was often left alone, so he learnt to occupy himself.

He wanted to make *amma* proud of him. So, when he was fifteen years old, Manish started working at the railway station. He had practised making coffee for neighbours and his friends, and they looked forward to the teatime treats as he had become renowned for his coffee making.

Working at Nagercoil station was a step forward and gave him a sense of ambition. Manish wanted to buy his mother a house, with a proper tiled roof, and a garden too. She deserved it and this would make all her struggle and sacrifice worthwhile.

CHAPTER

38

"Matt, have you heard anything yet?"

Catherine had lost track of how many times she had checked her phone over the course of the day.

As he bit into the oversized doughnut, jam the colour of fresh strawberries oozed out from the other side, with large splodges landing on the plate below. Matt looked at his mother, his mouth full of soft pastry as he gave her an endearing smile. "Mum, you worry way too much! You know you are not supposed to, what did the GP say? Remember, you have to take things in your stride and not get stressed. Our Kerensa will be fine. She's as tough as nails!"

He got up and reaching behind his mother put his arms around her to give her a big hug.

"Matty, I can't breathe!" she laughed, pushing him away playfully. She knew her son was right, but she couldn't help worrying. Her only daughter was halfway around the world, alone, on a continent with almost as many traditions and languages as there were people, and unfamiliar with the language. Why had she agreed to let her go alone? She had asked herself that nearly every day since Kerensa left. The house was not the same without her.

The GP had warned Catherine that she should not let herself become upset or react to anything unnecessarily to prevent any more episodes. And for the most part, she tried to follow his advice. But it wasn't easy, especially when the dark thoughts descended on her. The worst time was early in the morning, when the world was silent. The medication woke her up during odd times. Only the sweet sounds of birdsong kept her company in those early hours. She would toss and turn, praying the blackness would shift.

"Mum, I really need to finish my assignment today, but I will ring her tomorrow okay, don't worry. I know you tried to call, but she might not have had a signal on her phone. I was wondering if she had any progress on finding Kaian."

Catherine wondered it too. In fact, it seemed to be all she thought about of late. She tried to push the thoughts from her mind, but they refused to leave. His absence had consumed her utterly, and this search had become a relentless mission from which she could not detach herself.

Kaian. She could still picture the way he threw his head back when he laughed. How he took her into his arms, and into their bed. Pulling Kerensa and Matt playfully onto the sofa, he would tickle them hysterically as they begged him to stop, all falling about laughing. Happy times.

They'd shared a simple, happy life. Every day, he'd told her without fail that he loved her. She trusted him, there was no reason not to.

And he had adored their children. Everyone could see that. It was something that could not be faked. Kaian had always said that Matt was like her-blonde, moody, serious. Kerensa, he'd insisted, had the traits of her father; dark haired, curious and adventurous.

So how could he just get up and leave them one day, without a word, a goodbye, saying nothing. It was beyond comprehension.

As a couple, she and Kaian had passion and an emotional strength of purpose that provoked unconscious envy amongst others. Glancing across the crowded lecture hall one day, Catherine had first noticed him on their English course at Anderson College, based near Clapham Common; shiny black hair gelled back, his chiselled Indian features stood out with long limbs encased in skintight, dark blue denim as he languished lazily against the hard seats. He'd turned to her, smiled, and that was it.

"Hey, let me take you for coffee,' he had insisted as he introduced himself. They'd ventured to the dingy college canteen as he brought over two mugs of steaming coffee alongside plates that had been piled high with delicious cakes, sandwiches and scones with bowls of clotted cream and jam balanced precariously on the tray. He had skin the colour of deep burnished gold, which gleamed under the harsh hall lights. She could not help but contrast his swarthy Indian looks with the usual puny, artistic types who seemed to congregate aimlessly around the dimly lit college hallways. He was handsome, with a depth and sense of purpose that she felt was lacking in the other guys.

Feelings had developed quickly, and they soon moved in together. When Catherine found out she was pregnant, Kaian was ecstatic. He was always attentive and understanding with her. Even after Kerensa and Matty arrived, he was caring and loving with both of them, full of hugs and tender affection. A wonderful dad.

Until the day he suddenly disappeared from their lives. Forever.

Whilst Catherine remained in her thoughts, Matt recalled the trauma of school football practice.

All the other boys had dads who would cheer them from the sidelines, eating hot dogs and drinking beer from tall plastic cups. They would jokingly ruffle the hair of their sons affectionately as they left the field, proud of their achievements.

Matt had no one. No male role model he could call his own.

He often wondered what would happen if Kerensa found their father.

What would he say? Would his father love them unconditionally? Could he ever forgive Kaian for abandoning him?

The fear of not knowing sometimes was the worst.

CHAPTER

39

The overnight train to the city of Chennai had been a unique experience, to say the least.

Vivien had booked a first-class compartment, something that Kerensa had been looking forward to with excitement. She was the first one in - the narrow space had two long cushioned benches on either side, and she made her way to the corner by the window where she placed her small bag under the seat. She had only packed enough for three days a short trip, it was only to serve the purpose of locating Kaian, but she was looking forward to seeing a totally different city.

She had done some research about Chennai and found some interesting facts; formerly known as Madras, it was the capital of the southern state of Tamil Nadu. Rich in history, it was renowned for being the seat of ancient dynasties that ruled India and shaped the culture of many surrounding countries. Kerensa was keen to visit Marina beach, officially rated the second longest beach in the world.

The compartment door opened and the young man who entered looked like an intellectual; dark, round-rimmed glasses and a long-sleeved white shirt, tucked into dark trousers, that clung to his wiry frame. A small goatee beard clung pitifully to the base of his chin. He nodded rather curtly at Kerensa, as he made his way to the seat opposite. He could be no more than twenty-one, she guessed.

'Hello.' He finally smiled, as he reached for a worn duffel bag, taking out a slim laptop and plugging in white earphones, placing them in his ears and closing his eyes as he leaned back in the seat, a clear cue that he did not want to be disturbed.

It was 7:15pm, and the train was due to leave Trivandrum station at 8pm sharp. The platform was buzzing with the mass of people, surging forward to their carriages, towing suitcases and bags of various sizes. Vendors weaved intricately in and out of the crowd, some carrying baskets of wares balanced on their heads, as they shouted across one another in a bid to be heard over the noise.

"Vegetable's cutlets! Hot and delicious!" said one, as he was stopped by an elderly man surrounded by a group of small children. Probably his grandchildren, Kerensa guessed. The vendor brought down his basket from his head and placed it carefully on the ground. The children excitedly pointed out the ones they wanted.

A sudden commotion came from the next platform. A small crowd had gathered, and she could see a stray dog trying to jump up onto the platform from the tracks. In her mouth, was a tiny puppy. It appeared that it was a mother rescuing her pup who had somehow fallen onto the tracks. As she managed to clamber up, the crowd cheered with relief.

She slid open the glass, it was dirty and needed a good wipe. There were three horizontal bars across the window. A young man suddenly appeared outside, trying to get her attention. His badge had the name 'Manish' printed in capitals across it.

"Madam, please try, very good coffee. Only ten rupees. I can give you?" he asked earnestly in broken English.

She could really do with a coffee, but before she could say anything further, the young man had already reached for his large stainless-steel urn, and placing a small paper cup underneath, poured out some frothy coffee, and held it by the window. It smelt heavenly.

"Okay, yes I will have it." Reaching for her purse, she pulled out a ten rupee note and handed it to him through the bars. The coffee was creamy and delicious, dripping down her parched throat, feeding her with energy and warmth.

Manish smiled and headed to another window, where a woman had been desperately trying to get his attention.

The boy opposite Kerensa was still engrossed in his laptop. Suddenly, the whistle blew, a sign that the train was starting. It crawled slowly away from the station. A group of children began running by the side, laughing, trying to race against it.

She sat back in the firm seat, wishing she had brought a soft cushion to make it more comfortable.

The door opened again, and two women entered, talking loudly in Tamil. They looked at Kerensa, the boy opposite and then at each other. It looked like they were debating whether to stay in the half-filled carriage or leave.

After a brief whispered chat, they decided that they would stay, and sat opposite each other, near the door. They seemed to know each other well; both wore colourful sarees, and were probably in their forties, estimated Kerensa. Their names were Geeta and Laxmi. They were very curious about Kerensa asking where she was from and why she was in India. Questions that could have been intrusive anywhere else, but in India they were the norm, it seemed. They were sisters, travelling to Chennai to attend the funeral of an elderly aunt who had been their last living relative.

Outside, the train passed through vast expanses of greenery, that stretched for miles as far as the eye could see; wet, dense paddy fields that ended very close to the rail tracks and were fringed by tall coconut palms, that swayed gently in the distance. It was getting darker outside. Kerensa looked at her watch, it was 9.15pm.

Geeta leaned over as she took a pair of dark rimmed glasses from her purse, putting them on.

"Where would you like to sleep?" she asked Kerensa. "If you feel comfortable, the top bunk can be quite an experience." She pointed to a place above the boy, where a cushioned bed appeared to be folded against the wall.

"That looks great!" It looked fun and would be interesting to try to climb up, Kerensa thought.

Laxmi gently prodded the boy, who had been absorbed in his reading, indicating that it could be time to settle in for the night. The two women made themselves comfortable on the lower two bunks, covering themselves with thick shawls.

Kerensa climbed up slowly to the bunk above, using a wooden makeshift ladder that had been built in at the end of the bunk. It was getting cooler, and she wished she had brought some warmer clothing, maybe a small blanket would have been good. The blanket that had been kept folded on each bunk was wafer thin.

Outside, the train rattled merrily on the tracks. The sound was soothing, and soon lulled her to sleep, thoughts of Samuel and his kiss sweetly caressing her mind, filling her with an aching warmth.

CHAPTER

40

Natalya Kuzmich was a small-town sort of girl.

It was hard growing up in a deeply religious home in the small Russian village of Plyos when you had hopes and dreams of bright lights, stardom and fame.

Growing up, her cold, stern mother had a no-nonsense approach to her aspirations. Natalya felt stifled and bored by small town life and longed to escape from the village. Memories of her lonely childhood still caused her to tremble to this day.

"Mama, I am ready to leave for school now." It was Kazimir, who broke her train of thought. At eight years old he was her only son, her rock. He looked at her with his brown, puppy-dog eyes and she just melted with love. She reached to him, putting her arms around him and drawing him close.

Every morning, his favourite packed lunch was prepared in the Harry Potter lunchbox that he loved; usually ham and cheese sandwiches, with a packet of raisins, an apple or banana, and an orange drink, all purchased from the local supermarket in central Saint Petersburg.

Keys jangling in her pocket, they took the familiar route to school. Kazimir hugged her tight, he loved his mama, she always smelled like scented roses. When she came to watch his school plays, his friends used to nudge him and whisper 'guaracha mama (hot mama).' She was beautiful and always made an effort. Many of the other mothers looked old, fat and aged, but not his mama.

Her lipstick was the colour of fresh strawberries; crimson and radiant. She always wore a light pink blusher, that accentuated her soft cheeks. Looking beautiful was always effortless for her.

After dropping him, Natalya slowly returned home to the empty flat, solitude filling the room. She hated the feeling of being alone. After a painfully lonely childhood, she decided her adult life would be filled with busyness and noise. So, she made lots of friends along the way - friends who used her, betrayed her and then dumped her. They always came running again when they needed something from her.

And then there were the men. Like flies they gathered around, as though she were fresh chopped meat. They plied her with money, jewels, announcing undying love, until they got what they wanted. And then she didn't see them again. Mysteriously, their phone numbers changed, the presents stopped. And their once eager phone calls.

Each time, Natalya vowed it would not happen again. But it did.

One day, she found an international dating website that came up on her computer, linking Russian women to foreign men who were seeking feminine women. She was browsing through the profiles, and one from India particularly caught her attention.

Describing himself as kind, a true gentleman who was solvent and needing a woman who would soothe him, his name was Navin.

They talked, laughed and flirted madly online. He was not conventionally handsome but possessed a certain kindness and charm that was worth more than superficial beauty in Natalya's eyes after her past experiences. He was quite interested in Kazimir; unusually so, especially as most men from her past would glaze over when she mentioned her precious boy. But Navin would ask questions, and admire his photo over skype. A handsome boy, he said.

He was coming to see them in Russia soon, and after a long time Natalya, from the small town of Plyos, felt excited at the prospect of meeting her new lover.

CHAPTER

41

A carnival always brought out the fashionista in Ravi Joseph Malhotra.

Colourful feather boas were the highlight, of course. Especially pink and purple ones.

When he attended his first ever gay Indian Pride march in Delhi, Ravi wore them, with little else. Pride was a time to celebrate - be wild, be hedonistic.

A front to mask the pain.

The only son of two ambitious parents, he had always felt pressure to live up to the dreams and expectations of others. His tightly regimented father, a commander in the Indian Army, was aggressive and disciplined, setting lofty standards for his son that he expected to be followed. Which included marriage to a 'nice' girl, one day.

Scraping through his engineering degree, Ravi had found himself at University. Kissing boys.

On coming out to his parents, their reactions were of intense shock and horror. Their only son, their pride and joy...how could they ever face the neighbours?

Mama was constantly tearful. His father sternly summoned him one Sunday in late June, to tell him that he was no longer considered their son and needed to leave home immediately.

He moved, with all his earthly belongings, to Goa. The party city. Renting a room close to Calangute beach, where on wandering on the beach one humid day, he spotted a cute, blonde haired boy chatting animatedly to a young woman. The boy's name was Mikael, and he was with his girlfriend Freya. From Finland.

"Hi guys, my name is Ravi. If you need someone to show you around the city, I'm your man!" He was always open with people, and now was the time to make new friends.

They strolled to a beachside shack for a coffee and breakfast, entering as three people, however left as just two.

When Freya disappeared to the bathroom, Ravi found Mikael staring intently at him, and he reciprocated by covering the boy's slender hand with his own tanned one.

They knew immediately that they had both just found "the one."

CHAPTER

42

Just a few minutes, and she would be there. At the home of her father. Kaian.

Not long to go.

Kerensa felt her heart fluttering. It was butterflies flapping madly, trying to escape from the steel cage that encircled her soul.

She had caught the autorickshaw from the front of her Chennai hotel. The driver had been leaning against the wall chewing a paan leaf over and over, the familiar red discolouration staining his teeth. He looked up when Kerensa came over and spat a red mass against the wall.

He gestured for her to get inside his vehicle, it was even fancier than the autorickshaw that she had travelled in with Latha. There were twinkling lights adorning the inside that changed colour every minute, it was very pretty. The autorickshaw drivers seemed to take a lot of pride in their vehicles, Kerensa thought to herself.

Racing along the busy road that ran parallel to the famous Marina beach, the driver headed for an area called Adyar, known for its comfortable and exclusive residences. Kerensa glanced again at the piece of paper in her hand, which had been given by Asha Kumar.

"Driver are we close?" she shouted over the noisy engine, leaning forward.

"Just a few more roads madam, nearly there."

He stopped abruptly in front of a block of flats. The address Asha had given was flat seven.

She made her way slowly up the narrow, steep steps.

Flat number seven, on the second floor, was welcoming- the small rectangular hanging basket fixed alongside the door had a mixture of brightly coloured border plants that brought splashes of colour. A large Moroccan style lantern took pride of place near the entrance, rising majestically with a wide, curved dome that was ingrained with cut-out rectangular and diamond shapes that offered windows to the light within. The large polished wooden door had been carved with dancing women in the panels; it was artistic and unusual, Kerensa thought. She paused, nervously outside.

The sound of the door knocker resonated, as she knocked twice. Voices were audible inside.

The door opened suddenly, and a head popped round. It was a young man, possibly early twenties, fair skinned, his light blonde hair flapping loosely around his face.

"Yes?" he looked at Kerensa, questioningly. He looked her up and down, with curious interest.

"Can I help you?" he continued.

"Who is it honey?" another deeper male voice asked from inside.

Kerensa looked down at the paper with the address. Could this be the place? Maybe Asha had made a mistake. This did not sound like her father.

"Hello, I'm so sorry to disturb you. I was given this address. I am looking for Kaian Achari?"

"Who?" he looked at her, puzzled. Another person joined him at the door, presumably the voice she heard earlier. The new man looked older, maybe early thirties, with jet black hair gelled back away from his face and a small scattering of facial hair, that congregated in clusters around his square chin.

"Can we help you?" She could detect hostility in his voice, as though she had intruded upon a private moment.

Kerensa suddenly felt nervous. Could she have made a terrible mistake?

"Apologies for disturbing you, my name is Kerensa, I have travelled from London and need to find Kaian Achari. This is the address I was given. It's the main reason I have come to India, I really need your help please."

Both looked at each other and nodded. The darker hair man opened the door wide.

"Where are our manners, please do come inside." He gestured for Kerensa to enter. She suddenly felt apprehensive, she didn't know these people so how could she go alone into their home? But she desperately needed closure and to find out more. This felt like a pinnacle moment of revelation. She took a step forward. Her mother would disprove greatly of going alone inside the home of total strangers.

She followed them inside. The hallway was brightly lit with golden tea lanterns that flickered as they passed.

The living room at the end of the hallway was an unexpected surprise. Nearly everything inside was red, ranging from the fluffy carpet to the cushions, sofa and drapes. It was vibrant and intense on the senses.

"Come and take a seat, this is our room of hot passion!" The two men looked lovingly at each other and laughed. Kerensa smiled and perched at the end of the cherry red sofa.

"I am Ravi, and this is my partner Mik." The dark-haired man pointed to his blonde boyfriend affectionately.

"Nice to meet you both. Your home is lovely."

"Kerensa it's nice to meet you, we both would love to help," said Mik, "tell us how we can."

Kerensa sighed. She had to open up if she needed their help.

"Well, I am looking desperately for my father, Kaian Achari. I have not seen him since I was five." Both men looked at each other, surprised. "I was staying in the town of Nagercoil, near Trivandrum, and went to the last address that I held for him. The house was boarded up, but the neighbour told me he had moved. She gave me this address."

Kerensa looked at both men hopefully, desperation in her eyes.

They pulled up chairs in front of her.

"Darling, we want to help you. We moved here five years ago, after meeting at a house party in Goa." Ravi reached over, took Mik's hand and squeezed it in his own. "Sorry, I digress. When we moved here, we came across this flat and loved it. There was an Indian family here, I think they were South Indian."

"Sadly, the elderly parents had passed away, they had some children, and it was their daughter who showed us around when we came here."

"But do you remember her brother, who joined us when we viewed the kitchen Rav?" Mik looked quizzically at his partner.

Kerensa felt her heart pound.

"Oh yes!" exclaimed Ravi. "Don't remember his name, but he must have been in his early forties, I think?"

Kerensa felt herself catching her breath.

"What happened to him Ravi?" She had to know.

"Honestly, Kerensa, I feel terrible to say this, but I don't know." He looked at her apologetically. Mik shook his head, in agreement. "We met him only once, very briefly, and unfortunately didn't exchange any addresses or contact details. I have a vague feeling that he moved back to the south but can't say for certain."

It was the biggest blow. All of her hopes and dreams about meeting her father for the first time, had just been shattered.

Suddenly, everything went black.

CHAPTER

43

The seatbelt around his tiny waist felt uncomfortable, especially as Mano was not used to being constrained. The airhostess came to help him adjust it.

Sitting next to him Sophie was deeply absorbed in her chick-lit book with the gaudy pink cover, oblivious to what was happening around her. They had been in the air for over an hour. The take-off had been the best part for Mano, feeling the roaring engine in the underbelly made him scream out with excitement.

Mano had never been on a plane in his life.

Sometimes, on a clear night, he used to make his way to the open grass land near the station where he would lie prostrate and gaze up longingly at the night sky, legs spread-eagled, waiting for the planes to pass. Imagining what it could be like, he dreamed that one day he would be flying in one of those palaces in the sky.

And now, here he was flying on one. Going to his brand-new life. He had done well.

Sophie had visited him a few times at the station, taken him for meals, given him new clothes. Talked to him about mannerisms, interacting with others. He had his own room in the hotel the night before the flight and felt like a king. The best part was his shower. The hot water running over his body was an amazing experience, and he didn't want it to end. He had never felt anything like it. He stood under the cascading waterfall for over an hour, until he could feel his skin gleaming under the soapy bubbles.

Once, as they were finishing eating at a restaurant, two police officers had come in asking questions to the diners, regarding identifying a photofit. Sophie had urged Mano to hide behind her as they quickly exited through a side door. She quickly explained that she had a fear of the police and didn't want any encounters with them. They liked to make trouble for innocent people like her.

"Mano, remember everything I told you." She had closed her book and turned to the young boy, whispering. "If anyone asks at Dubai airport, you are my half-brother David, okay?"

Reaching in her handbag, she'd pulled out the passport. She bore a striking resemblance to the photograph, which, thankfully had not been spotted at immigration. She had been holding her breath as the officer held her passport up to the light, scrutinizing it closely and then peered at her over his thick lensed glasses for seconds, which felt like a lifetime, before letting them through.

She sighed with relief as they walked through the gates. The money would not reach her bank account until the child had been safely delivered to the Sheikh.

"Yes Sophie, thank you." Mano was so grateful for this new opportunity and would listen to everything she had advised him.

He was ready to begin a new life, with a loving family, to help erase the sad memories of the ones he had lost in a previous existence.

CHAPTER

44

"Ma'am, I just wanted to let you know a European man has been hanging around in the bar area for some time. He is not one of our regular guests."

At eighteen years old, young Vik on the front desk, was learning fast. He had been personally trained by Vivien De Mello and had even earned the title 'Customer Relations manager,' which made his mother very proud. As 'Employee of the month' twice in a row, he liked to do everything by the book and make the guesthouse owner, Vivien, feel he was an outstanding employee.

"Vik, thank you for your sharp observation. I shall make my way there shortly and discreetly find out what this man wants. I don't want all and sundry coming to use our facilities for no reason."

Vivien liked to have control over most things. She knew Aruna was very sensitive to strangers hanging around the guesthouse, so she took responsibility for vetting whoever walked through the doors. She had found out however, the hard way, that there were some things she could not control, in particular her son Samuel.

Recently, he had been arguing back with her too much for her liking. He was changing. There seemed to be something weighing on his mind. Something to do with the British girl, Kerensa. She suspected her son had fallen quite hard for her. She didn't like to interfere in his life, but there were some things out of bounds.

Making her way hurriedly to the bar, she stood discreetly at a distance, in the corner, where she could see everyone in a quick glance.

She spotted the man immediately. His silver hair almost glittered under the sparkling neon lights, as he sat with his back to her, slouched casually over the bar whilst looking intently into his drink.

"Don't tell me you are alone, on a nice evening like this?" Vivien appeared by his side, resting her arm gently on his, as she leaned against the bar. Such behaviour in a younger woman would have been construed as overt and flirtatious, however when it came to a woman in her fifties, confidence overtook everything. She was beautiful, but in a simple way that would not draw unnecessary attention to herself. Dressed in a turquoise saree, with a sleeveless blouse, her golden skin shimmered with softness. Her skin, apart from a few lines under her eyes, was flawless, despite her age. Her later years had been very kind.

The man turned and smiled.

'It's wonderful in this place, do you work here?' he ventured curiously.

'Yes, I do.' Vivien replied, quietly.

'Have a seat, do join me.' David beckoned to the seat next to him.

She pulled the bar stool a bit closer. On talking further, the man revealed his reason for coming to the guesthouse; he was exploring South India for the first time as a businessman and tourist. Staying in a rented villa by the sea.

Nothing major untoward, thought Vivien to herself. She would mention it to Aruna though, at some point.

As she got up to leave, a waft of heady jasmine scent covered David with its sweet, narcotic smell. It was intoxicating. The smell of womanly richness and splendour.

He was determined to find out the identity of the mysterious woman, with whom he had just had the brief encounter.

CHAPTER

45

After a while, the darkness shifted into haziness which, in turn, became faces that started to hold a vague familiarity.

"Kerensa, wake up!" As she opened her eyes, Kerensa could see deep concern etched on the faces of the two men standing over her. For a moment, she struggled to place where she was, until she finally remembered.

Ravi and Mik.

Her head ached. "What happened?" she whispered. She was lying in a foetal position on the bright red sofa, and a thin blanket had been placed over her. She tried to raise her head and could feel it starting to throb mercilessly from somewhere behind her left temple.

"Sweetheart, I think you have overstretched yourself. You fainted and have been out for about twenty minutes." It was Ravi who stood over her, holding a large blue mug filled with something hot. Steam erupted hastily in white wisps from the top.

"There is nothing like a cup of hot chai to help make you feel better!" he said, bringing it closer to Kerensa. Mik placed his hand behind her neck and slowly eased her up, supporting her gently.

The tea was delicious- hot and milky, with a generous amount of sugar. It immediately perked her up.

The men helped her sit up carefully, placing fluffy soft pillows behind her.

"Are you okay Kerensa? We were worried about you." Mik knelt down in front of her, his expression kind.

She felt overwhelmed. Not only by their kindness, but by the fact that she would now never get to know her father. The one man she had dreamed of meeting her whole life.

On that day, Kerensa wondered what the point was of going on. She was mentally ready to pack up and leave for home as soon as possible, staying any longer in India would be unnecessary, as she had lost all hope of ever finding her father.

CHAPTER

46

It had been a long day. Gopal Kumar was tired.

Sitting in his favourite spot close to the kitchen window, he could only see darkness outside. Gopal had been tasked with writing up overdue reports, following the recent station meeting. The subject of the missing children was a harrowing one, especially after dealing with it on a daily basis.

The woman's hand on his shoulder squeezed gently as it massaged the back of his neck, with just the right amount of pressure. He groaned. It felt fantastic. He stretched back, closing his eyes.

"Honey come to bed. I will give you an amazing massage that will put you to sleep!"

She took his hand enticingly and closing the laptop cover, pulled him out of the chair, playfully ticking him under the chin with her free hand, as they both went laughing up the stairs.

In the darkness, something stirred. It was 2.31am precisely. The night air was still, the silence only broken by the steady hum of the rickety ceiling fan as it revolved frantically in a vain battle to create a soothing breeze amidst the humid suffocation.

She pulled off the thin quilt, glancing carefully at the sleeping man, before sliding her feet quietly onto the wooden floor.

As she tiptoed down the stairs, she was careful to avoid the ones she knew creaked, which was natural for her as it was her own flat. The half open laptop in sleep mode blinked in the darkness.

She hesitated, as she felt a momentary pang of guilt. It didn't last long. She knew what was at stake.

Reaching over, she typed in a few letters on the keyboard. No luck, it wasn't letting her in.

She sat down slowly, pulling the laptop closer. Thinking hard for a few minutes, she began typing again. Persistently trying different combinations for possible passwords.

It was then that she remembered Gopal's favourite quote: 'Carpe Diem.'

It worked. The confidential police files showing the missing children appeared on the screen. She had the information she needed.

Quietly, she made her way upstairs and back to the bed. Gopal muttered in his sleep and turned, his arm coming to rest protectively over her.

She stroked his hair soothingly, as she smiled to herself.

It had been a productive day.

CHAPTER

47

At the end of Rose Lane in the suburb of Kodambakkam, Chennai, stood the decrepit house that everyone wanted to forget existed.

People often imagined what goings-on took place inside the four walls and whispered to themselves in hushed tones as they attempted to peer over the high boundary walls, past the white and pink Bougainvillea creeping along the surface, struggling to get a glimpse of the hidden secrets that lay on the other side.

It was the brothel belonging to Veena Kumari, known locally as 'madam Veena.' In her early fifties, she sported an unkempt look - wild hennaed hair sprouted out of her bun, her trademark bright red lipstick painted unevenly on her lips like the whore that she was. Life had been hard for Veena, and she made sure that it was even harder for the eight young women who worked for her. She was a tough character who liked to rule the roost by intimidation and bullying.

At sixteen, Anuja, or 'Anu' as everyone called her, was the youngest, and Veena frightened her. The madam had bought her when she only twelve years old, after haggling with her stepfather, a recovering alcoholic, who was eager to sell off the child when his wife, Anu's mother, died of cancer. They had only been married for two years before the diagnosis was confirmed. He promised her on her deathbed that her daughter Anu would be well looked after.

But promises were so easy to break, especially when temptation got in the way. Money was tight at home. After losing his factory job due to missing too many workdays, he took to drink.

Luring his stepdaughter with the promise of a better life, with more fun, travel and new clothes, he handed her over to Veena, for a measly three hundred rupees, and then disappeared. The little girl found herself trapped in the sordid prison.

"Madam Veena, I want to go home, please? she begged the madam on her second night.

She had been forced to sleep on a dirty, stained sheet on the hard floor and endure the strange moans and groans that came from Eva's bed, who at only twenty-seven had already been with Veena for twelve years. Eva had told her to face the wall and not to look under any circumstances, but Anu couldn't block out the guttural noises.

The man in Eva's bed was extremely fat, with round, bulging fish-like eyes. He was one of her regulars, apparently.

Veena looked at the child in front of her, with her smooth skin and baby face. She knew nothing of hardship or challenge. That was all about to change.

"What an ungrateful wretch you are!" she began, staring coldly into the eyes of the frightened girl. "I have troubled myself to give you a home and paid good money; you belong to me now, remember that. You have to pay me back before you can leave." She laughed coldly, her teeth stained red with *paan*, and the old man sitting with her shuffled uncomfortably, as he joined in with mirthless laughter.

Anu felt tears prickling her eyes.

"Oh, the girl is crying!" the woman pointed to Anu's face in mock concern. "Go to your room and get ready. Your debt has now decreased; Mr Biju, who was with Eva last night has paid a hefty price to have you join them today. He will be here in one hour, so you had better get yourself ready."

Eva came and took her away, squeezing her arm for comfort.

"I am going to give you a special pill Anu, you must take this so it will block out what is going to happen later okay?"

Anu didn't understand but she trusted the older girl, and took the pill as requested.

Everything started swimming in her head, and she felt dizzy.

Later, Mr Biju came to the room, full of ugly smiles and leered at her in a way that made her feel uncomfortable. Eva had advised Anu to do what he wanted to get it over with. As she looked at Anu sympathetically she remembered her own start in the brothel. It had been the pills that helped her through those dark times.

Biju told the little girl to dance for him. And then, massage his shoulders.

That night, little Anuja left her childhood behind, forever.

CHAPTER

48

Anu had discovered, by chance, the creaky floorboard that was in the corner under Eva's bed, and during a rare five minutes on her own, was able to prise it open. It served as a great hiding place for the secret stash of money that she had been collecting, little by little, during her time at Rose lane.

She had been at the brothel for four years, three months and seventeen days now, and it was surprising how fast time was moving. She longed to leave, dreaming of a proper, normal life outside the crumbling walls. However, madam Veena threatened her if she tried, and that a bounty would be placed on her head.

"The most popular girl in Chennai and very much in demand." Veena used to boast to all the clients when they dropped by. The price for her could be more than four times that of any of the others. It had taken a long time for Anu to accept her fate though, and she only got through the days by imagining living her life in another far-away place. She often dreamed of being lured away to paradise, a parallel universe. A place where true beauty, and peace existed.

Veena grudgingly agreed to pay Anu a small percentage of her earnings monthly; unaware that it was being tucked discreetly away in the secret hideaway place. Anu had plans and many dreams, plans to leave and go far away. She had barely left the four walls during her years of captivity. Madam Veena always made sure one of the trusted women went with her as an escort to the shops, she couldn't bear to lose her prized possession.

One day, Anu finally had her chance to escape. She had tried once, a few months before, however had unexpectedly heard Veena waking up, and going down to the kitchen in the night, at the time she anticipated to leave, so her plan had been scuppered. But now was another chance. It was four am, and sheets of monsoon rain pelted the roof tiles. The drunken security guard had fallen asleep in his chair, and the house was quiet. Anu had gone to bed fully dressed, covered with a bedsheet, as she waited for the right time.

As she quietly reached for the familiar floorboard under Eva's bed, her friend stirred.

"Anu, what are you doing?" she whispered, slowly sitting up in the dark. Noticing the bag of money in her friend's hand, she begged her not to leave.

"Eva, I cannot take this place anymore. I feel lost and if my mama had been alive, she would have been shocked I am here!" Anu explained quietly.

"Okay, I am coming with you." Her friend quickly got dressed and they both quietly tiptoed down the stone stairwell. The house was quiet, apart from the loud snores coming from the guard.

One of the other women had also tried to leave three months before, however, Madam Veena had suspected her intentions. Her German Shephard, Bullet, had been trained to sleep at the bottom of the stairs as a deterrent and barked noisily at the unsuspecting woman as she'd tiptoed down the stairs. Lying in wait, Veena had screamed; pulling her hair and dragging her back to her room, where she beat her black and blue. "Let this be a lesson for any others who try to leave," she'd threatened, menacingly the next morning, as she glowered at everyone in turn over breakfast.

However, the day that Anu and Eva crept out, it seemed that fate was watching them favourably.

Madam Veena had a rare visit from her cousin, Geetanjali, from Mumbai, who not only brought two boxes of burfi sweets, but a large bottle of Jamaican rum. The giggling women drank many rounds, catching up on family gossip and, after much merriment, proceeded to ceremoniously climb the steep stairs to Veena's room, where they both fell into a drunken sleep.

Loud snores were heard from the room, as the girls made their way down the hall. Bullet raised his head curiously and growled at Anu quietly as she stepped near him, with Eva tip-toing closely behind, cowering fearfully. Anu had always been kind to the dog, feeding him scraps of food and he seemed to remember this, as he soon stopped his growling and wagged his tail hopefully, when Anu gave him a small biscuit she had hidden in her sari petticoat. After this, he stayed quiet.

The final hurdle was at the main door. It appeared that the security guard had participated in the drinking session; he sat prostrate by the door, dribbling from the left side of his mouth as he snored loudly, dead to the world.

Anu gently removed the set of keys that were lodged firmly in his chubby fingers and the two young women glanced happily at each other, as they held hands and tentatively made their way, unescorted, into the chilled morning silence of the dusty Chennai street.

A few hours later, the residents of Rose Lane were wakened by the howls of a desperate Madam Veena who had found the empty room. She vowed to have them hunted down, and the remaining woman incurred her wrath as she stomped through the house, screaming at all and sundry.

Two weeks later, madam Veena realised that they were not coming back.

She had heard through one of her long-standing clients, a former police officer, that a young girl was being offered for sale in the Southern city of Nagercoil. The child was much younger that normally expected, however could be bought and trained.

Veena gathered her passport, and a purse full of cash, as she planned to purchase a new child, who would replace the one that got away. In this world of deep evil, fresh girls were necessary to accommodate the men's ever deepening appetite for debauchery.

CHAPTER

49

With her passport held open, Kerensa tentatively stepped forward to join the long queue at Immigration.

It was nice pm and Kamaraj terminal, the hub at Chennai airport for internal flights, was bustling. People were in a hurry it seemed to be somewhere else.

Kerensa was leaving the city with sadness, her primary reason for coming to India in the first place to find her father Kaian, seemed futile and a waste of time and resources. Every hope, every dream of meeting the man who should have been pivotal to her life, had been wrecked.

Ravi and Mik turned out to be a lifeline. She had spent the day with them in their flat, with Ravi supplying endless cups of chai and slices of homemade lemon cake, which had been made, he alluded, from his mum's secret recipe. She had cried hysterically at the thought of never meeting her father and used up nearly a whole box of tissues. The men took turns in putting their arms around her, to try to comfort, but it was no use. Just three days before, they were complete strangers living in her father's old flat, and now she was pouring out her soul to them. Agonising displays of raw grief and loss.

They had insisted that she come with them to the street vendor, who had rung his bell, calling out for all to come and try the sweetest sugar cane juice imaginable. Kerensa had never tried the beverage before and watched in fascination as the man took long stalks of freshly trimmed cane and pushed it a steel machine that consisted of two large, parallel cylinders, that when set in motion by the turn of a handle, crushed the cane sticks as they were pushed through. Glasses were placed underneath to catch the freshly squeezed juice. It was delicious, with a sharp undertone.

Both Ravi and Mik came to say goodbye.

"We are going to miss you Kerensa! I can speak for Mik too when I say you are like family now. Stay in touch girl okay, you have our numbers; don't forget your new fabulous friends!" Ravi said affectionately.

Kerensa had hugged them both closely and turned to wave goodbye as she disappeared from sight through the baggage checks.

The queues for immigration were long and snaked around the metal barriers. Only a handful of officers were available at all the desks.

The Indian couple in front of her pointed to a lady in the next line and giggled amongst themselves. Following their stares, she could see why. The woman had unkempt dark hair with ginger roots that poked through, her hair was tied loosely up in a messy bun. She wore extremely long, dangly hoop earrings that would have complimented a more youthful face but looked vaguely ridiculous on an older woman. However, it was her face that drew attention, with foundation that must have been at least five shades lighter than her skin colour, and bright red lipstick that was smeared heavily extending far outside her lipline. Huge gold rings adorned her fingers with chains of multicoloured beads gathered around her neck, in a rather gaudy fashion. The woman was a spectacle.

She didn't seem to care that people were staring at her turning to boldly look others in the eye. She stared at Kerensa in a way that made her uncomfortable. It was not the woman's appearance. she couldn't quite put her finger on what made her feel uneasy. The queues surged forward, and the woman disappeared into the distance. Kerensa was nearly at the front and knew it wouldn't be long.

The man at the desk stared at her as she approached. He resembled a man from a bygone era with a long mustache that twirled comically at the ends, like a ribbon. Perched at the end of his nose were thick round goggle-like glasses, which kept slipping off.

He looked stern, peering at her through his thick lenses, as he said, 'Hello madam, can I see your passport please?'

'Sure.' Kerensa laid her passport face up in front of the officer, pushing it towards him through the glass.

He held it up to the light, as he peered closely at the markings on each page, turning them as he examined it in great detail. He looked concerned, summoning another officer who was standing close by. They placed the open document into a large machine on the desk, where a noise buzzed as the machine came to life. Without looking at Kerensa, they muttered quietly amongst themselves for a few minutes as they placed the passport face down on the scanner glass.

She was starting to feel very nervous. What could be wrong, could the passport have expired? That would be impossible as she had no problems at London, and it would have been picked up at the airport when she left. She was sure the dates were sufficient for travel, but her mind was dizzy these days with worry and excitement.

The men both looked at each other and then over at Kerensa, the initial officer glaring at her through the glass.

The people in the queue behind were getting restless; the muttering was becoming more apparent and when Kerensa turned around, she could see a sea of eyes looking at her with mixed reactions of curiosity and annoyance. Everyone was keen to board their flights; corporate businessmen holding their briefcases tight mingled alongside young, trendy couples glued to their i-phones and shouting at their children to behave as they ran excitedly across the barriers. A group of sari-clad, elderly women were animatedly chatting away in their native language as they laughed and joked with each other. However, it felt like all eyes were on her at that point, muttering amongst themselves as they eyed her up and down.

"Hello, can you tell me what is happening?" she leaned forward and spoke urgently through the glass opening, trying to get the officer's attention. Everything seemed to be so slow and take so long in India.

Ignoring her, the officer with the moustache gestured to a uniformed policeman, who hurried over quickly.

Kerensa felt fearful, what was going on? She wished Ravi and Mik were by her side.

The Police Officer stood behind her, placing his hand firmly on her shoulder as he sternly commanded "Miss, you need to come with me. We have some questions we need to ask you."

And, with that, followed by the eyes of many curious onlookers, Kerensa was escorted away.

CHAPTER

50

Despite appearances, Madam Veena Kumari was a sensitive soul, or so she liked to tell herself.

In her own eyes, she had treated the women who worked for her with nothing but kindness and fairness, giving them a free roof over their heads, and a profession they could fall back on. They were earning more than their counterparts who were educated, she liked to remind them.

Yet, to her disappointment, they often chose to disobey her, with two of her best girls recently leaving in the middle of the night. She had been unable to locate them, despite the best efforts of people in the area who were keen to pass on vital information for a small price.

Anyway, she had decided to purchase a replacement. Another young girl to replace Anu who had been her pride and joy. Leaving her trusted older sister, Divya, in charge of the place was a good idea. The two sisters were very much cut from the same cloth.

Veena had spotted the young foreign woman being escorted out of the Chennai airport lounge in full view of crowds of onlookers - she was very pretty and tall. Veena had imagined her in the Rose Lane brothel and the high price a girl like her would fetch from eager customers. She wondered what the girl had done to deserve being taken away publicly in such a humiliating manner. Her head hung down, and she had looked on the verge of tears.

"Madam, would you like tea or coffee?" The question from the air hostess broke her thoughts.

"Coffee." Veena picked up a worn copy of the in-flight magazine, hanging out of the pouch in front and flicked through it absentmindedly.

It was nice to have a rare break from the mundaneness of Chennai life, even if it was just for business.

***

Maya had been fast asleep when she vaguely heard the bolt moving loudly side to side. It was the guard.

"You need to wake up now, there is someone coming to view you."

Maya yawned loudly and stretched out, arms above her head. Who could be coming to see her at this early hour? It could not have been more than seven am, she could hear the happy morning song of the solitary mynah bird that often settled on the slender palm tree, outside her window.

Recently, the food brought to her seemed to be tastier than before, perhaps they had changed the chef she thought. The dishes were varied - chicken curry, dal, fried paneer, samosas. Once, she even had biryani, a rare treat. But everything was covered in *ghee* or clarified butter and Maya could feel her clothes getting progressively tighter. However, her bones still protruded through her clothes. Being locked up in a dark, claustrophobic room for up to twenty hours each day did not help.

***

The woman who joined the guard at the doorway was the same one who had visited Maya the day before for the first time. She was very elegant, probably older than her mother had been, with a pretty lilac saree. She smelt like sweet Jasmine, and on the first day, she had given Maya a long strand of the fragrant flowers, which were traditionally used to adorn women's hair in Southern India, on special occasions.

The woman had brought a small hairbrush and painstakingly began taking out the knots from Maya's hair, running the brush through to the ends. It had been a long time since her hair had been combed, and Maya felt nice. The steady strokes as the stiff brush went rhythmically through her hair were comforting. Human touch was something which she felt unused to, but the soothing strokes were intimately relaxing.

Maya suddenly had a flashback of her darling mother combing her hair each morning before she caught the bus to school. Her hands were always warm, soothing, with her favourite dark pink nail polish and Maya could almost feel the sensation of her hair being stroked, long fingers massaging her scalp reassuringly. Her favourite hairbrush, purple with a pink letter 'M' imprinted boldly on the back, had pride of place on her dressing table. What would her parents have done with it; would they have thrown it away and forgotten all about her, she wondered?

A new dress had been hanging behind the door when she woke. With gingham red and blue checks, it was the prettiest thing she had seen for some time. After being left alone for months on end, it felt strange to have so much attention suddenly. Was it because of the visitor who was coming to see her possibly?

"You have ten minutes to put the dress on and be ready." The guard's angry glare brought Maya back to reality.

He disappeared, closing the door behind him. Removing the dress from the hook, she eased it slowly over her head, slowly pushing painfully thin arms through the two spaces on the sides. It was beautiful and the warm colours made her smile.

"Maya, are you ready?" As the woman opened the door, Maya could smell the intense scent of pure Jasmine wafting in with her. It danced on her nostrils, playing sweet havoc with her senses. The light green sari complemented the woman's golden skin, and her hair was coiffed high in an elegant top knot. She looked like a glamorous Bollywood actress walking onto a film set. Maya couldn't help but stare.

"This is Veena aunty, please come and meet her."

Another woman walked in and looked around the room with a level of disdain that only matched that of the guard. Her hennaed ginger hair was unruly, with strands escaping from all sides, that had a roughness in desperate need of some conditioning. With a face that was powdered heavily, she closely resembled an aged geisha girl past her sell by date, desperately clutching onto some final strands of youth. Maya without realising, unconsciously stepped back, as the woman made her feel uneasy.

She looked Maya up and down, her blood red lips pursed together tightly. She showed no emotion, no smile of encouragement, to make the child feel comfortable.

Something unexpected happened. Veena stepped forward and began prodding Maya from top to bottom; squeezing her arms, checking her fingertips, separating the silky strands of her hair as she looked through the young girl's scalp. She touched the area around Maya's chest, which made the child feel uncomfortable. She wanted this woman to leave.

Veena pulled the other woman aside. "The girl is nothing but skin and bones. I cannot take her, what use is she to me? I have wasted my time coming here." Her hands went up in exasperation, as she turned around and left the room, without a backward glance.

Maya felt herself tremble, and she looked down at the floor, cool tears prickling her eyes.

The pretty lady hesitated before putting her hand on Maya's shoulder, squeezing it.

"Maya, there will be other chances. I know you will have a new life, so believe in yourself."

Her kind words touched the little girl, she had been shown very little affection since she was taken at five years, and the tears finally came.

"Please ma'am, I want to go home." Her moist eyes were pleading.

The woman looked her, a fleeting glance of sadness crossing her face.

"Maya, I am very sorry, but that is not going to happen dear. Your life is here now, you need to accept it and think about the new family you are going to have."

And with that, the little girl was left alone with just her sadness for company, which enveloped her like a black mist.

The woman left, closing the door firmly behind her.

CHAPTER

51

"Miss, I need to ask the reason you are visiting India at this time?"

It was the same officer with the stern expression who was seated opposite her in the bare room, except he had now been joined by a more senior ranked official. The two policeman who had led her away were standing by the door, as though guarding it with their lives.

He leaned forward, her passport in his hand. Flicking through it, he kept it open on the photo page. Without waiting for her answer, he continued.

"How long have you had this passport?" Again, a look of disdain accompanied his words.

"Can I have some water please?" Kerensa felt her throat go dry, and the room was claustrophobic, as though all the air had been removed. She didn't understand why she had been brought to the room, why they were questioning her about her passport. "I don't understand why I am here?" Her voice trailed off.

Ignoring her comment, he reached forward and poured some water into a flimsy plastic cup. Handing it to her, he continued.

"You need to answer my questions. Now, do you have a lawyer?"

Kerensa took a big gulp of water, she felt suddenly very sick. The four men were staring at her.

"I am in India to find my father." There, the truth was out. "I have had my passport for three years now. Can you tell me what the problem is?"

The two seated men exchanged glances.

"I will come to that. So, is your father Indian?"

"Yes, he is."

"So, is he in Chennai?"

Kerensa sighed. "It's a long story."

"Well, we have all day, so you can take your time and tell us" he replied, a thin veil of sarcasm coating his voice.

Just then, a loud knock broke the awkwardness in the room. A short man, with grey hair and a khaki shirt put his head around the door.

"Tea, sir?" he looked straight at the man who was questioning Kerensa and without waiting for an answer pushed in a metal trolley stacked with polystyrene cups, from which thin wisps of smoke wafted gently upwards.

Handing out cups to all the men in the room he paused near Kerensa and looked searchingly at the interrogation officer to see if he should give her one. The officer nodded curtly, and the man placed a cup of the steaming beverage on the table in front of Kerensa. She took a sip. It was sugary and comforting. She needed it desperately.

"Right, let's get back to business." The officer, putting the cup down, turned back to Kerensa.

She needed to be as open and forthcoming as possible, just so she could leave and be on her way back to Nagercoil and then back home to the UK. The whole trip had been fruitless or so it seemed, there was no sign of her father and all the leads she had proved to be dead ends. However, some good had come out of her journey to India; not only had she made good friends in Ravi and Mik, but she also met Samuel. The thought of his passionate kiss gave her strength at this time. But those sweet memories seemed far away as she sat before the officer's cold stares.

"So, tell us more about you Kerensa." It was the first time he had called her by name. It didn't sound friendly.

"Please tell me why I am here. I honestly don't understand." She could feel salty tears prickling her eyelids.

The two men ignored her and spoke animatedly in their local language, which sounded like Tamil. After a few minutes of discussion, the officer who had checked her passport at the desk turned to her and said gruffly,

"Kerensa Oldfield, I am detaining you under the Passports Act of India, 1967, for possession of a false and counterfeit passport."

CHAPTER

52

For the last time, I leave that lonely place with my disconnected memories.

I slowly lift the two windows to my soul, when a sudden intensity of brilliant white light comes flooding in through the peripheries. The brightness is dazzling.

And then the voice.

"Kaian. Kaian," it calls. "Can you hear me?"

I answer, however the only sound that emerges is a low groan.

The voice seems happy with the guttural sound.

"Good, Kaian, I need you now to focus. Your wife, Jingles is here with me. I need you to focus on me, take your time."

Jingles. The image of the golden-haired lady, the one who evokes pure love in my heart, moves aside. There is another woman, of plain appearance, her long dark hair loosely plaited behind. As my windows open, I can see her sitting in front of me, leaning close, concern written in her eyes. Jingles.

Next to her stands the owner of the husky voice, the one who continues to shine the dazzling light straight at me. He sounds pleased. The light stops shining.

"Welcome back Kaian. Jingles has been waiting for you."

Once again, I am back. This time for good.

CHAPTER

53

After looking everywhere, Ravi breathed a sigh of relief as he found his phone squashed down the back of the sofa. A deep frown struck his face as he scrolled quickly through, moving his finger upwards in a quick successive motion.

"Mik hun, it's been two days since Kerensa left and she hasn't been on WhatsApp. No reply to my messages. She promised she would let us know as soon as she landed and she's the sort of girl who keeps her word. I'm worried about her."

The bright red cushions gave a squeaky sigh, as he tumbled onto them with full force, lifting his feet so they balanced on the wide arms. It was mid-afternoon, and the intense heat caused a suffocating temperature in the flat.

Mik stood up and reached for the phone, steadfastly willing himself to turn a blind eye to the trainers that were still tied to his partners feet. The no-shoes policy was a silent rule that Ravi always seemed to blatantly ignore.

As he scrolled down, various messages popped up on the screen from their friends, but there was no reply to the many short messages that Ravi had sent Kerensa. It was strange, she had entered their life just a few days before but already felt like a part of it. Her silence was unnerving.

There was something about her that they had both bonded with strongly, her personality alone shone with kindness and compassion. He desperately wanted to keep in touch.

His heart was beating fast, but he tried to maintain a calm front so as not to upset Ravi further. Out of the two of them, it was Mik with his peaceful Scandinavian demeanor who usually helped to diffuse any arguments at home. Ravi had a hot temper which he proudly claimed was an integral part of his red-blooded Indian heritage. It was hard to bear at times, but Mik liked to keep the peace.

"Rav, there's probably a simple explanation. Maybe her phone died? Or she dropped it somewhere? There is always a reason." Mikael liked to think things through, step by step logically. Calmness was the correct way to find solutions.

Ravi yawned, as he raised his hand above his head in a slow stretch. He turned sideways, head sinking deep into a plump cushion as he gazed at Mik adoringly.

"My love, why are you always right? Yes, it's true, it could be any of those. Let's give her space and trust she will be in touch soon."

He struggled to keep his eyes open in the heat; the intense afternoon sun peeping through the narrow blinds was powerful and it wasn't long before loud snores emerged from the soft red sofa.

Mik quietly removed the slippers from his partners feet and placed them in their rightful place next to the broken coat stand in the hall.

CHAPTER

54

At a certain hour each morning, Preeti knew the sun would shine merrily through the narrow window above her mattress. Pouring rays through the bars, it reminded her of the joy in life. The loud cawing of the black crow on a nearby Banyan tree reminded her that breakfast was coming shortly.

Weeks had passed in the place; days were blurring into one another and it was getting harder to remember a life before this one. A happy life, going to school and spending time with mummy.

The sound of her mama's hearty laughter came to mind, as she would toss her head back, laughing loudly and wink mischievously at her only daughter. Just a glance could cocoon her with a warmth and tenderness that made Preeti feel all was well in the world.

Papa, on the other hand, usually wore his serious face. There would be no smile dancing on his lips, but he would help feed her favourite doll, Anna, at the kitchen table or slice through thick crusts of French toast on her plate that mama had made for Saturday morning breakfast. Quietly, sometimes papa even slipped her a chocolate truffle just before bed, placing his finger over his lips, a gesture reminding her to not tell mama, it would be their secret.

The stone bracelet given by her new friend Maya, was her prize possession. As he took it out, it glinted against the sun. When Preeti felt like crying, just a glance of it would make her smile again.

One day, she would hug her mummy again. Maya had promised her so. She had many, many fears in the terrible place, but the one person who offered her hope, was Maya.

CHAPTER

55

The metal handcuffs were clenched hard around her wrists, as she attempted to rub the surrounding skin. It was the scene she had seen hundreds of times over in the movies, the shamed criminal being escorted away head hung down in shame. It was the stuff of a Netflix drama except this time, she was in the lead role.

The jagged stones scattered on the uneven roads, made the journey uncomfortable as Kerensa found herself mercilessly jolted in the back seat. She tugged on the frayed strap that cradled her chest, thankfully it was secured tightly. The Police jeep bumped up and down as it raced down narrow streets, swerving to avoid open-mouthed bystanders, who stood and gaped at the speeding vehicle, not bothering to move out of the way. Some even attempted to peer inside its darkened windows.

She had been in the vehicle for what seemed an eternity but was, in fact, about ten minutes. The bumpy journey, and cold stares of the policemen in the car mirror, made her fret with a numbing nausea. Her pounding heartbeat was deafening, she wondered if they could hear it above the grumpiness of the stuttering engine.

Leaving the crowded streets, the jeep swerved into a quieter stretch of road that seemed to go on forever. Suddenly row after row of neatly ploughed areas and darkened symmetrical paddy fields appeared on the horizon, laying side by side stretching as far as the eye could see, and even further. Slender green offshoots rose proudly from the murky pools, that had cocooned them from infancy. Tall, graceful palm trees interspersed randomly amongst the foliage. No houses were in sight.

The two officers seated in front looked straight ahead, stiff as surfboards, as they stared tersely ahead. The driver tapped his finger rhythmically on the steering wheel, almost an attempt to break the soundless monotony. The female officer, greasy grey-peppered hair swept harshly up into her cap, glanced at Kerensa momentarily with a solemn expression that eclipsed glimmers of lightly veiled sympathy.

It was the cracked sign on the side of the road, that brought her back to reality. The two stark words that hit home: Pulyam Prison. Simple and clear. She was a traveller on the road to dark desolation.

Was this really happening? Surely it was a nightmare that she would wake up from - any minute now?

The grim, imposing building emerged unexpectedly into sight. After the green luxuriance offered by the rich paddy, the monochromatic dullness of the barren concrete walls that lay before them stood in harsh contrast, their bleakness desecrating the surroundings.

"Please, you need to listen to me." She moved slightly forward, away from the firm black leather seat, her desperate voice pleading. Without a word, the female officer swiftly removed a slim baton from the side of her uniform and hit Kerensa squarely in the chest; a warning to sit back. Wincing in pain at the impact, she was determined to continue speaking, her trembling voice cracking under the icy dread and fear.

"This is a genuine mistake. My passport was lost at the guesthouse, I think it has been tampered with. You can contact Vivien at Amma's guesthouse, she can confirm what I am saying. Please, I shouldn't be here." Her voice trailed off.

The younger officer in the front turned to face her directly, a derisive sneer covering his pock-filled face with a mocking sarcasm, as he taunt-ingly commented. "Tell that to the judge!"

Kerensa peered out into the lonely bleakness, hot tears pricking the back of her eyes, as the jeering laughter of the officers echoed cruelly in her mind.

CHAPTER

56

There were times in his life when Samuel simply wanted to disappear.

He found it hard living under the same roof as his mother Vivien, much as he loved her. It was suffocating with maddening slowness, bit by bit, piece by piece, like living inside a balloon from which the air had been slowly released.

Thoughts of Goa and his friends were always on his mind, drunken evenings spent at the *old Calypso bar* on Baga beach where they would tunelessly sing along at the top of their voices to Bob Marley, as they downed shots to much hand-clapping and resounding cheers. Just a few lines were enough to set the party atmosphere off. *One love, one heart, let's get together and feel alright!*

Grabbing overstuffed plates of freshly fried juicy shrimp and battered calamari, surrounded by oil-soaked chips, they would race down to the powdery sand, lit in unnatural hues by strings of gaudy, flickering Christmas lights, strewn carelessly across the stone beach wall. It was there on the sand that the real fun began.

Parties would go on until the early hours; gyrating to dated 80's music, playing beach volleyball and even skinny dipping if the mood took them.

The memories returned to him randomly, at unpredictable times, rather like they were replaying over and over, on a big television screen in his mind.

"Samuel, I need you to concentrate." Mama's sharp voice broke his thoughts, as she thrust a wooden tray into his hands, bringing him back to reality. The tray contained a square, white china plate filled with slices of toast, neatly cut into triangles, fluffy yellow scrambled eggs, plump fatty sausages that were literally bursting out of their tight skins, alongside clusters of grilled mushrooms, swimming desperately in tiny puddles of oil. A large cup of freshly made coffee was steaming invitingly on the side. The aroma that wafted across was irresistible, Samuel could hear his stomach rumbling.

"Now, take it to Mr. Holdsworth, the British gentleman staying in room four. He stayed over last night. Don't spill anything!" she warned, throwing him a quick smile.

Samuel carefully made his way past the buffet dining area, clutching the tray firmly, as he glanced in. It was just nine in the morning, yet busy. A small queue had formed by the egg station, where the Goan chef, Patrick, was dramatically putting together the final touches to his speciality Spanish omelette. With an Indian twist, the bulky egg pancake contained finely sliced red peppers, mushrooms, diced potato and shreds of green chilli and fresh coriander, that added a touch of spice to the flavour. Word seemed to have gotten around that it was delicious, and each morning a queue would form around the chef in eager anticipation of receiving a slice of the delightful dish.

"Room service," Samuel announced as he gave a firm knock on the door. There was a thud that came from inside followed by hasty footsteps that grew closer. An older man put his head around the door, squinting at the tray held by Samuel.

"Oh, hold on." David began, as he reappeared with a pair of narrow tortoiseshell spectacles perched at the end of his nose. "Ah, that's better!" he said. 'Sorry about the noise, I knocked over my cabin bag and everything went flying. Gosh breakfast looks wonderful!"

He looked with interest at the breakfast items and gave a grateful smile to Samuel.

'Please say a big thank you to Vivien for me.' he said, as he took them from Samuel and when he reappeared, he held a hundred rupee note in his hand.

"This is for you, thank you." He thrust the note into Samuel's hand. "Tell me, does Vivien run the guesthouse alone? How many staff work here?"

His curious questions caught Samuel off guard.

"Well, Vivien is my mother, and we co-own everything here. We have about seventeen staff I believe, ranging from the cleaners to the receptionists who man the front desk."

"It sounds like you are well organised! I am so impressed by the excellent service offered here. Just one more question Samuel." He looked briefly at the name printed on the lanyard around the younger man's neck. "Security is very important to me; who else has access to our personal records behind the front desk besides you and your mum?"

"It is only really us and of course, the receptionists, who are Vik and Calvin. I can assure you they are both trustworthy. We are the only ones who are allowed to be behind reception at any time."

David looked relieved.

"Thank you, Samuel, I am here just for one more day and am really enjoying your hospitality."

Samuel smiled warmly. "Thank you sir, please don't hesitate to contact me if you need anything else."

As the door shut, David made a note of what Samuel had said.

He intended to spend the day doing some more digging and then later in the afternoon, he promised Gopal he would help him retrieve some computer files.

In the isolation of his room, it should have been thoughts of Pat who came to mind, however David found himself thinking about the beautiful, sari-clad guesthouse owner and the intoxicating scent of her heady Jasmine perfume that she left behind.

CHAPTER

57

M anish had never worn a tie before. He simply wanted to make a good impression, even if it meant doing things out of his comfort zone. Mama had painstakingly stood in front of him and weaved the silky ends around and around tugging and pulling at his neck, until she was satisfied with the end result. He knew she was incredibly proud of him.

It was his first proper job interview, and Manish felt fidgety. His coffee was finally going places.

The previous Monday morning, no different to any other, he had walked the length of the stationary Kanyakumari express, carrying the heavy black rucksack that clung to his back, weighing him down. The straps had been chafing his right shoulder, so he'd stopped to adjust it, making it more comfortable. Inside were a stack of small paper cups, and a large flask, containing his creamy milky beverage.

A voice had made him look up. "Boy, come here." It said. He looked over to where the sound was coming from. Out of the window, a rolled-up newspaper was being waved frantically, in a bid to get his attention.

As he had ventured over, he had seen an older man, with a thick black moustache looking out through the metal bars that framed the train window. Dramatically pouring the coffee from one metal cup to another, over and over, it gained a frothy consistency.

The man took a lingering sip and smiled broadly at Manish.

"This is good coffee. Did you make it son?"

"Yes sir." Manish had answered truthfully.

"Well, we need someone like you where I work. It is hard to find a decent cup of coffee anywhere. Tell me, how much are you making each day?"

Manish thought quickly as he calculated the average number of customers against the price of his coffee.

"I think about eight hundred rupees sir." *Maybe that was an overestimation*, he thought to himself.

He was eager to sell, but business was hard and there was often stiff competition from other vendors, especially those that sold soft drinks as well. Fanta, a fizzy orange beverage was the most popular followed by Limca, a sweet lemon and lime drink, that was especially loved by children. The vendors who were selling these were minting money.

"Right Manish," began the man, as he glanced at the boy's name badge. "How old are you?"

"I am seventeen, sir," Manish said casually as he wondered what the purpose of the conversation was. There were other customers trying to get his attention and he didn't have time to dawdle.

"I would like to offer you a job where I work, a steady job where not only will you make the best coffee for all of us, but you will also be doing other roles such as cleaning and security. I will give you a starting salary of forty thousand rupees per month. How does that sound?"

Manish nearly dropped the coffee flask with shock. The amount was incredible, and more than double his current earnings.

The man continued on to say that he was inspector Raj Patel, the head of the local police, and that Manish should come for a quick informal chat on Friday at eleven am, ready to start his new job at the police station the following Monday.

As the train pulled away, it left an excited and bewildered Manish overwhelmed as he imagined the luxurious house with a garden, he would be able to purchase for his hard-working mother one day, sooner than had been expected.

CHAPTER

58

Standing outside the stylish wooden door that led to the Executive suite, Vivien hesitated for a few moments before knocking.

"Come in." Aruna's voice was gruff with tiredness, as she sat stretched out on her sofa, a large cup of tea in hand.

. 'Oh, it's you. How is everything? Are you okay?" Vivien stepped into the suite, nervously looking down at the floor, her hands trembling.

"Good morning Aruna, I am sorry to disturb you, I wanted to discuss something that has come up. It concerns Samuel."

Aruna patted the sofa next to her, a sign for Vivien to sit down.

"Tell me, what's the problem?"

"Samuel…he knows." Vivien brought her fingers up to her mouth as she bit firmly on her thumb nail. She felt her breath catch in her throat.

Aruna put down her cup and glared at the other woman. She eyed her up and down with distaste.

"What do you mean 'he knows'?" The curtness in her voice was evident and cut sharper than any knife.

Vivien could feel her heart beating rapidly. Her hands were visibly trembling, almost as if they had a life of their own, she wondered if the other woman could see. Aruna Pillai was definitely not a woman to cross under any circumstances.

"He…he found the file." She blurted. The words tumbled out rapidly, almost having a life of their own. She could feel her throat constricting tightly.

Aruna suddenly stood up, turning to face Vivien. Her face was thunderous, with hooded eyes that spat daggers at the nervous woman seated on the sofa.

"Vivien, please don't concern yourself. There is nothing to worry about. I know everything will work out. Will you please excuse me?" The words of dismissal dripped like sweet honey, thinly masking a layer of vitriol that lay beneath.

As Vivien closed the door behind her, she leaned against the stained glass to steady herself. She could feel her stomach churning, and a deep sense of dread engrossed her. She remembered her first meeting with Aruna.

Five years before, money had been very tight. The guesthouse desperately needed an injection of cash to revamp the tired looking rooms. Complaints had been received from customers who were disgruntled with the faded carpets, broken shower heads and toilets that did not flush. Worried that they would lose customers, Vivien knew that they needed to do something drastic, but she did not have access to any more funds; all her savings had been used up and a bank loan was out of the question.

Aruna had brought over two large glasses of a vinaceous looking beverage to the small table in the corner of the bar where Vivien was seated, one evening.

"I hope you don't mind, I thought I would stop by to say hello. My name is Aruna."

It transpired that she was a businesswoman with easy access to funds. As the evening went on and the wine flowed, Vivien found herself opening up to the understanding American, telling her about the financial issues affecting the guesthouse, and how she needed a cash injection to renovate the place.

Aruna offered her a lifeline. In return for staying in the Executive suite at the guesthouse whenever she was in India, Aruna would give her a lump sum of £150,000 dollars, a huge sum of money. Vivien did the maths, and it more than added up. She gratefully accepted the businesswoman's offer, however, regret soon seeped in when she realized the reality of what she had inadvertently agreed to.

The first time Vivien had an inkling of the business that Aruna was undertaking, was when she noticed a small girl at breakfast one morning, sobbing her eyes out. Vivien thought it strange that Aruna ignored the distressed child whilst laughing with the mother heartily. Seeing her puzzled expression, Aruna invited her to her room, explaining meticulously how she was helping children from impoverished homes find a new home with a loving family, who could offer love and a good upbringing. She spent a long time trying to convince Vivien of the feasibility of what she was doing.

Vivien was not convinced, however. She had confronted Aruna on many occasions knocking at her door, asking her anxiously about the children who were being held. Aruna was calm in her replies, telling the guesthouse owner that she worried way too much about the children's welfare. She also told Vivien in no uncertain terms, that she was legally bound to the terms of the businesswoman's deal, and should not poke her nose where it was not welcome. So, much against her better judgement, Vivien reluctantly agreed to take a back seat. Over time, she found herself resigning herself to the situation she was trapped in, helping Aruna more, as though she had become immune to the children's plight. And the morality of what was taking place seemed to affect her less and less.

Until Samuel confronted her about the file held behind the front desk, which he stumbled on when Calvin was off sick. She had been talking to Rahul, the chef, in the kitchen when he stormed in, demanding to know what the file was for. His voice raised higher and higher, as his words turned to shouts of anger.

Vivien persuaded him to go to the garden, away from the curious eyes of the kitchen staff, where they continued a heated discussion, until Samuel walked away in a huff.

"That bloody woman, she needs to leave." He had screamed as he walked away, referring to Aruna whom he despised.

Vivien begged him to reconsider his stance and help them her son retorted that it would be something he could never do. The fact his own mother was assisting that vile woman was sickening and he could not believe it. It was too much to deal with and Samuel had stormed off.

Caught between the devil and the deep blue sea, Vivien was worried for her son. Aruna Pillai was not a woman to mess with.

CHAPTER

59

The young man seated behind the glass twitched spasmodically as he stared fixatedly at Kerensa. Possibly in his late thirties, he looked older than his years. Months spent sitting in the cramped airless cubicle, at the main entrance to the women's prison had aged him.

Tony D'Souza was bored stiff. The only sound that kept him company most days was the slow ticking of the corporate clock, high up on the white-washed wall, reminding him endlessly of the mundaneness of his life.

But staring at the pretty new addition as she was escorted in by the female guard Rohina, he felt a pang of something. It was not just her beauty that shone through her desperate tears, dark eyes scrunched up in tears and hair untidily poking out through her messy bun high up on her head. He could sense a vulnerability that stood out amongst the harshness of the prison walls.

Rohina tapped her baton impatiently on the glass whilst holding on to Kerensa's manacled arm tightly.

"Tony, I have one more to log in for today. Caught her at the airport. One of the forging gang members, we think."

Tony lifted up the glass flap and slowly pushed a chewed pen through the gap, pointing towards a thick black signing book. He continued to stare fixatedly at the foreign girl, without blinking. She looked at him, broken, her eyes brimming with unshed tears.

The female guard grabbed the pen, and hurriedly began filling in a row of sections in the book. Kerensa lifted her head so the cool breeze emitted from the overhead ceiling fan puffed against her thirsty skin. She could not believe the predicament she was in. Not even a week since she left the UK and she had been arrested. Was it a dream?

Angry tears prickled against her lids, as she forced them back. She didn't want to make a scene. This was just a temporary measure and surely everyone would see that a mistake had been made. She would be released and be on the plane home in no time.

A black plastic tray was slammed in front of her. "Put your phone watch and any electrical items here. Nothing sharp allowed." The guard Tony yawned widely. Kerensa wondered how many times he had said these words before in his flat, monotone voice.

None of the officers had allowed her to use her phone. Or even any official phone at the airport. The immigration officer who questioned her told Kerensa that she would get her chance to speak to family but didn't say venture to say when she would be able to do this.

"Please can I make one quick phone call? I won't be long. No-one knows I am here" Kerenda found herself almost begging, as she pleaded with her eyes. She could imagine mum being sick with worry. Not to mention Mik and Ravi, whom she promised she would contact when the flight landed.

Sudden thoughts of Samuel came to mind. He would be expecting her. Memories of his eager hands on her body gave her strength.

"You can make a phone call tomorrow." Rohina's voice was terse. "Come quickly with me now, you need to change into the prison clothes."

As Kerensa went into an adjoining room, it hit home that she had left the safety of the familiar life behind and entered a new and frightening world.

CHAPTER

60

Prema knew no other life apart from that of a call girl. If people asked what she did for a living, she told them she worked in retail.

From the age of just six, Prema Naidu had been expected to look after her little brother and sister; Rahul and Sima. Her parents worked long hours in low paid jobs- her father was a porter at Chennai railway station and mama worked herself to the bone, nine hours a day for an elderly Bollywood actress who seemed to be stuck in a time warp, caking herself in an unflattering shade of gloopy, thick foundation, refusing to believe that she had passed her sell by date.

The responsibility for her brother and sister fell naturally on young Prema's shoulders. She would wait outside their classrooms after school, to escort them home. Mama left flaky chapattis, and creamy yellow dal, with puddles of golden ghee floating lazily on the surface, in small tiffin carriers, ready for them to have after school.

Life soon changed for Prema.

When she was seventeen, she left school to start her first ever job working at the India Bazaar supermarket, on the corner of Kamarajah road, close to the famous Marina beach. It was a simple role; she stacked up the shelves when stock became low and took turns on the tills with her friend Anita.

One day, a man entered the supermarket; he was very tall, with a dapper grey suit, a thin moustache and dark shades perched on his head. He looked not dissimilar to the top Indian actor, Shah Rukh Khan. Anita nudged Prema excitedly.

"Shah Rukh has come personally to collect you," she teased, as both girls giggled excitedly.

The man spent some time looking at shaving creams in the men's section but kept glancing over at both girls. He beckoned Prema to come over to the aisle he was standing in.

"Hello, how much is this cream?" he asked innocuously, holding up a brown container.

As she turned towards him, he suddenly grabbed her hand.

"You are very pretty, has anyone told you that?" His dark brown, penetrating eyes with thick lashes crinkled as he spoke to her. His clothes smelt of musky sandalwood, his scent was intoxicating. She felt herself get dizzy.

"My name is Dinesh. What is your name?"

"I am Prema," she replied quietly.

"Well, Prema, I would love to talk to you more. This is my card, how about I take you for ice cream tomorrow evening?" He handed the nervous girl a small, rectangular card with blue and gold edging. On it, were the words:

Dinesh Iyer, Entrepeneur

He told her to meet him at the Delectable ice cream parlour the next night at seven pm and to bring her friend along.

Both girls agreed the vanilla chocolate chip ice cream they tasted the next day was the best they had ever tried. Afterwards, Dinesh brought them a brightly coloured drink, which contained something called alcohol. He told them that it was very popular in the west. Called a gin cocktail, it made their heads spin. Unbeknown to them, Dinesh had laced their drinks with Ecstasy. As they stumbled outside the parlour, into a nearby alleyway, three men came from a waiting car bundled them inside and sped off.

Taken to a secret location, far away from town, the desperate girls were sold at an underground auction to the highest bidder. Prema was claimed by a woman referred to as Veena, who ran a brothel at the edge of town.

For Prema, it would be the last time she ever saw Anita.

Her life as a prostitute was just beginning.

CHAPTER

61

The sheets of icy water pelting down against her bare skin was a shock. Kerensa let out a sharp scream as the impact caused her to nearly topple over.

The communal shower in the prison could be described as basic, three large rusty pipes hung precariously from the ceiling emitting powerful gushes of water that made a deafening sound as it bounced off the tiled floor. Tiny streams formed neat criss-cross patterns between tiles, as they raced towards a drainage hole that had been crudely bored in the middle.

"That's enough," Rohina snapped, as she stood by the imposing steel door, arms folded tightly. Her face was expressionless. The flow of water suddenly ceased. Despite the humid temperature, Kerensa found herself shivering uncontrollably.

"Prema, get a towel!" The guard's brusque voice echoed in the confined space.

A younger woman, dressed in dark navy overalls, hair scraped high away from her face opened the door tentatively, as she stared at Kerensa. Her deep brown complexion had a troubled expression, furrowed lines were etched on her forehead. She quickly unfolded the dark towel in her hands, and made her way to where Kerensa was standing, wrapping the towel deftly around.

"Don't let her know you are scared because she's just a bully,' she whispered conspiratorially as she quickly turned and walked away, to stand with head bowed meekly in the far corner of the room.

As Kerensa followed the guard outside the shower room, Prema caught her eye and gave her a brief smile before looking down again towards the floor.

The military style prison uniform, stiff and neatly ironed, had been placed on a low bench outside the shower room. Rohina nodded curtly, indicating that Kerensa should change into them. All her belongings had been confiscated at the entrance by the male guard in the cubicle, including her phone and the precious cross given by her mother. She hadn't been allowed to even make a phone call to her family.

It suddenly hit home for Kerensa that there was no going back.

She had left the comfort of her life in London, for the harsh reality of a new one in a terrifying Indian prison.

CHAPTER

62

Maya liked to spend her time reminiscing.

Spending time on the old, broken mattress there was not much else to do.

She liked remembering the happy times at home, with her mummy and daddy. Nitin would follow her around the house, crawling on all fours, trying to keep pace with his beloved big sister. Her favourite games involved arranging all her dolls around a large tablecloth, she would grab her baby brother and prop him against a fat cushion at the head of the table, so that they could all have a picnic together. It would be an imaginary feast; crispy samosas, followed by slices of cream cake and washed down with cherry lemonade, and she would talk to her dolls as she fed them, encouraging them to eat quickly. Nitin would throw back his head and laugh with delight, as he gazed at his sister in adoration.

It was these vivid memories of love, and of happier times, that kept Maya alive.

***

A few days later she woke up startled and wondered why the Mynah bird on the tree outside had stopped singing.

The familiar grinding of the bolt side to side indicated that breakfast was on its way. She knew the routine ran like clockwork, and yawned lazily, stretching her arms over her head., as she sat up in anticipation propping herself against the dirty stone wall.

The sullen guard stepped into the room rather nervously as he gave her a fleeting smile. Maya startled by the unexpected gesture smiled back. She had never seen him smile before. His hands were empty, and the usual tray of breakfast was missing.

He stepped aside, and a short balding man, with a greasy face entered. Sweat cascaded down his brow, which he mopped away hastily with a hanky. She was certain she had seen him once, many months before. He came and knelt in front of Maya, reaching forward as he attempted to take her hands in his. She instinctively recoiled, and moved closer to the wall, feeling its solid comfort behind her.

"Hi Maya, I'm Navin. Don't be scared, I need you to come with me."

He spoke in hushed tones but had an authoritarian air about him. She quietly followed him outside the room into the corridor. The guard held the door open and threw Maya a strange glance as she passed.

Walking past the room where she knew Preeti was being held, she called out for her friend.

The response was quick. 'Maya, I am here. Please don't leave me akka!' Desperation came out of the pleading words of the little girl.

Navin stopped walking and turned to face Maya, his silence and brief nod offering unspoken consent for her to speak to her friend.

"Preeti, I'm not leaving you, am right here. You stay strong and wear my bracelet to think of me. Remember that you will see your mummy and daddy soon."

"Okay, okay, that's enough." Navin interrupted impatiently, as he threw Maya an annoyed look. "Follow me."

"Sir, where are we going?" Maya was curious. Apart from meeting Preeti for the first time outside, she had not been out anywhere."

Navin ignored her and opened the large door that led to the courtyard. She followed him across, and they opened a gate that led to an open field. The guard had been following them from a distance, his head held down as he kicked into the sand as he walked.

They continued for a few minutes. Maya could not help but gasp at the greenery. It had been years since he had seen any grass or plants, and their scent invaded her senses.

They finally stopped at the edge of a large hole, which had a pile of earth surrounding it. It looked like it had been freshly dug.

What is this, Maya asked herself. *Is it a game?*

Navin turned to her and pointed to the hole.

"Maya, I need you to climb down. It is not for long, and we will bring you up again."

Maya felt her body tremble, and her heart beating fast. Something did not feel right about the situation.

"Sir, I cannot, I feel so scared. Please don't make me do this," she said as fear engulfed her.

Navin looked at her with annoyance. "Get down there right now!" he muttered through gritted teeth.

It was then that Maya took her chance, she knew she had to escape. The swaying palm trees in the distance, at the far edge of the field, would offer a place to hide and could be near the highway. She had to try.

She started running towards the trees. Ignoring the frantic shouts of Navin and the guard coming from behind, she bolted away from them. Her body was weak and fragile, but somehow the strength appeared from within to run as fast as she could.

It was the large boulder sticking out of the ground that unexpectedly caused her to trip suddenly, at the edge of the clearing. Maya screamed in pain when her toes stubbed against the hard surface and she hit the ground with full force.

Everything went black.

When her eyes opened, she could see nothing but soil walls and mounds of loose earth around her. She realized with horror that she was lying at the bottom of the hole.

"Please, get me out!" she screamed, fear strangling her with its tight grip. "Please sir!"

A heavy shower of soil came from above and landed on her. *What's happening, are the sides caving in?*

More soil landed on her face, and she coughed violently as the grainy particles entered through her nostrils.

When she looked up, she was shocked to see the guard with a spade in his hand, shoveling the piles of earth into the hole, on top of her. Navin looked at her intently from above, squinting through his thick lenses.

"Maya I am so sorry we have to do this. There is no choice, God bless you dear." He said, as he moved away from the edge. "Finish the job," he ordered the guard curtly, as he walked away.

Maya released a blood curdling scream.

More earth filled the hole, landing on her legs, her arms and her head. Everywhere. *Thud, thud, thud.*

At that moment, mamma appeared, arms outstretched as she smiled and wrapped her arms around her. "My darling child, don't worry, this will all be over soon. Daddy, Nitin and I will love you until the end of time."

"Mamma don't leave me, please," Maya begged, as her mother faded slowly from sight.

More earth fell on her, larger clay mounds that soaked her hair and skin with its sticky wetness.

Maya could see her baby brother smiling at her from a distance. She smiled and waved back at him.

Thud, thud. The soil covered her entirely, as she tried to make a loose hole to allow her to breathe.

It continued to fall, engulfing her in total darkness.

And then there was nothing but the chill of morning silence.

CHAPTER

63

"How much are the aubergines?" Natalya picked up the fattest, gleaming purple vegetable that caught her eye, perched on top of the overflowing crate, at the market stall, holding it up to the light so that the stall holder could see.

"For you beautiful, only fifty roubles for half a kilo." The man winked knowingly; it was not often that he encountered such beauty at the market. The place was usually filled with elderly *babushkas* who would walk around the stalls many times, either alone or with friends, simply to pass time and ease the mundaneness of their daily routines. They would cling to their wooden canes for support, smiling brightly, excited to be outside and as they hobbled away, the stale smell of death followed them quietly.

She was refreshing, this one, the thick sable coat that was wrapped tightly to keep out the early morning Russian chill complemented the richness of her creamy complexion, and her thickly kohl lined eyes spoke seductively of understated passion. He had seen her once before in the distance at the market, but she had not approached his stall.

Boris wanted to be bold. He was not getting any younger and at thirty-five, his mother was constantly nagging him to find a wife. His soul was old, and he did not care for dating apps, or the like to find his dream woman and bars were not his scene, he found them superficial. Maybe the almighty had brought this beauty to him, as a gift?

"I will give you a special offer today only ten aubergines for thirty roubles *zaika*. You can't miss it!" He blew her a quick kiss.

Natalya was taken aback by his overfamiliarity of calling her *zaika,* a Russian term of endearment. But the price he was offering was good, she didn't want to miss it. She knew that Kazimir loved her spicy beef lasagne, which she layered with roasted aubergine and herbs, and she couldn't wait for her new love to try her signature dish.

Pulling out a thin cloth bag, Natalya nodded and handed it to the stall holder. He was handsome and well built, with light blonde hair, and speckled signs of morning stubble that he had not bothered to remove. As he handed the filled bag back, he brushed his hand over hers and squeezed. Natalya recoiled instinctively. She nervously reached for her purse, quickly pulling out some notes, which she thrust into the man's hand, as she turned and walked away quickly, ignoring his disappointed look.

Her thoughts lay only with her new love, Navin, who would be visiting them in the next few days from India. He had ambition and drive and was the one opportunity to help Kazimir and her escape from a life of poverty. She had dreams that were bigger than her one-bedroom studio flat, situated near the famous square.

He had made it clear that she was his number one and she intended to keep it that way.

CHAPTER

64

Ben Travis felt emotional. His large canvas suitcase was stuffed to the brim, but he had managed to finally close it, a sign that he was finally ready to go.

His last working day at the Olive Tree bar, Croydon, a few days before, had been unexpectedly heart-warming. The manager, Melanie, and her husband Greg had surprised him with a beautiful buttercream cake, which had the words 'Good luck Ben' inscribed in cursive writing and surrounded by small fondant balloons. Greg had stood unsteadily on a wobbly table, as he made the announcement in the bar and, much to Ben's embarrassment, his regular customers gathered around to cheer and pat him on the back as he moved on. He had only been there six months, but it felt like longer. The bar team were like his second family.

"Ben, are you sure you have everything now? Passport, your wallet?" Jenny stood in front of him, turning down his polo shirt collar as she wiped a miniscule fleck of dust away. It was as though she didn't know what to do with herself. Her only child was leaving her shortly for six long weeks in the far East. Staying with her brother, Peter, a senior Embassy official Ben would be shadowing him for a rare traineeship opportunity which they both knew was a highly valuable opportunity, perfect for utilising his degree in International Relations. But it still didn't make it easier.

"Mum, you're fussing too much! Please don't worry, I will be fine. Looking forward to spending time with Uncle Pete."

First stop was Singapore, where his uncle would be waiting, followed by a brief stint in Chennai, India where he would be on the front line helping out.

Ben couldn't believe his luck - after waiting months for his security clearance and filling out endless questionnaires asking about any possible links to terrorism, everything had finally fallen into place.

His thoughts of late had been on the beautiful girl, Kerensa, that he had spoken to a few weeks before in the bar. He couldn't stop thinking about her. Finding himself checking his phone at odd times during the day, in the vain hope that she had called or sent a message, Ben was disappointed to see there was nothing. When he returned to the UK, he made a mental note to himself to try to track her down.

As the taxi hooted loudly outside, breaking the peaceful Sunday silence on the leafy suburban street, Ben turned and planted a kiss on his mother's forehead, trying to ignore the watery tears that had gathered in her eyes. His father had passed away unexpectedly five years before, of bowel cancer, and Ben knew that she lived only for him. It wouldn't be long until his return, as he reassured her gently that six weeks would pass in a jiffy.

As the car sped hastily on the motorway in the direction of Heathrow airport, Ben felt his exciting new life was just beginning.

CHAPTER

65

Somebody wise once said that we do not appreciate what we have until it is gone.

As Kerensa shuffled slowly along the corridor thoughts of home and her family were forefront in her mind. Her feet had been chained together, something she did not understand the need for; it was not as though she would be going anywhere. Yet, the guard Rohina insisted on it after her shower, as a precaution, she said. Along the length of the dimly lit corridor were a series of symmetrical windows, each of which had been barricaded by chunky metal bars. Rohina paused outside a door at the end, waiting for Kerensa to catch up.

The stubby guard standing outside looked at her with bored interest, as he mechanically sifted through a bunch of keys in his hand and handed Rohina one. When the door opened it was like entering a parallel universe.

The sea of faces that greeted her was unexpected. There were possibly about forty or so women, Kerensa estimated, sitting cramped together in the tiny room. Every inch of floor space had been taken up. There were even children who were weaving their way from one end of the room to the other as they played an incongruous game of hide and seek, moving deftly between the women as they ducked and dived, trying to catch one another.

The overwhelming human stench smacked her in the face as the door opened; a crude mixture of unwashed sweat intertwined with undertones of dried urine drenched the air with its suffocating odour. She could hardly breathe and thought she would collapse as the overwhelming putrid smell filled her nostrils.

The shock of the room made her take a step backwards. Rohina prodded her sharply with her baton.

'Miss, you need to go in, this is where you will be staying for the time being. Find yourself a place to sit down, quick!'

She then shouted at the women loudly in Tamil to make way and give Kerensa room to go through.

As Kerensa stepped forward, the sea of women parted in an orderly way, creating a space for her to walk towards the wall in the far corner. She made her way tentatively, stepping carefully over endless legs, arms and feet that were splayed across the room, and settled uncomfortably in a corner.

An elderly woman, who appeared to only have one tooth, seated next to her against the wall, pulled out a thin scarf that she had been sitting on and handed it to Kerensa with a smile, urging her to take it. Kerensa gratefully accepted, she knew the evenings would be much cooler.

Two younger women, dark hair disheveled and heads covered, seated near her stared with friendly curiosity. She was the only foreigner in the room, or so she thought, until she looked round, she caught a glimpse of a blonde-haired girl, head bowed into her lap, sobbing quietly at the other end. She wondered what the girl had been arrested for.

She realized suddenly that this would be where she would sleep that night. And probably the night after that. Thoughts of mum, Matt and her comfortable room at home teased her mind.

As the enormity of her situation hit home, tears of despair trickled down as she fell uncomfortably into a fitful sleep.

CHAPTER

66

It was the loud ring of the bell that woke her with a startled jolt. The early morning rays were making their appearance through the barricaded skylights, as the darkened room was soon illuminated by golden beams of light.

Women were yawning, stretching, some standing up raising their arms high in an attempt to bring their aching limbs to life. One of the children started bawling, his arms around his mother's neck clinging desperately, her voice soothing him to be quiet, as she covered him with her scarf.

Kerensa had a broken, uncomfortable sleep, and had woken up to find her head was resting on the lap of the one-toothed elderly woman, much to her embarrassment. She quickly raised her head and apologised, however the woman gently eased her back onto her lap, as she whispered a tune soothingly and stroked her hair, as though comforting a small child.

The show of affection touched her, and she could feel overdue tears gathering in her eyes. A solitary droplet trickled down Kerensa's nose and fell onto the woman's black cotton saree. As the woman continued to hum a melodic haunting tune under her breath, Kerensa fought hard with herself to keep her eyes open.

She was dozing off, when the bell rang again, this time the sound had more urgency. She could hear the heavy lock moving then the door opened and Rohina entered the room with an annoyed expression on her face. She was beating the baton into her other palm impatiently, as she scoured the room.

Her eyes fell on Kerensa. "Time to get up! Everyone is going for breakfast, so come on," she shouted curtly across the room.

As Kerensa sat up slowly she mouthed a quiet 'thank you' to the one-toothed lady, who said, in stilted English,

"My name is Esther. We need to go now, but I will look after you here. Some people are not nice, you be careful." Her tone lowered, almost as a warning.

The women had formed a line going around the room, and Kerensa and Esther joined at the end as everyone filed out of the room quietly, their manner subdued, intimidated by Rohina.

They walked along the corridor and passed a small doorway. The smell from the room reeked of human waste.

"This is the bathroom we can only go once in the morning, so use this chance," the voice came from behind her, and as she turned, she realised that it was Prema, the girl who had given her the towel in the shower. She spoke English well. Kerensa wondered to herself what she could be in prison for.

It took a long time for her turn, and Kerensa found herself holding herself, as the need to go became more urgent. She saw the blonde-haired woman waiting in front; she seemed more composed than the previous night, but looked down at the floor the whole time, ignoring everyone around.

Prema pushed something into her hand. 'You will need this, keep it quiet.' It was a few loose pieces of toilet tissue.

As Kerensa turned to thank her, Rohina came to stand directly in front of them.

"What are you both doing?" she bellowed, glaring with irritation. Kerensa had discreetly stuffed the tissue up her sleeve, before the guard could see it. Rohina suddenly walked away, distracted by two women who had started arguing further down the line.

"Thank you Prema!" Kerensa whispered, feeling grateful for the kindness she had been shown. The prison conditions were terrible, but both Prema and Esther had made her first night more bearable.

Soon it was her turn. The putrid stench from the toilet hit her as soon as the door was opened, and Kerensa was mortified to see that the latrine was nothing more than a crude hole in the ground with two stone slabs on either side on which to place her feet. A large bucket, that had been filled to the top with water, had been placed next to the hole; it contained a broken plastic cup, which she presumed would be used to flush the toilet.

Carefully removing her overalls, she straddled the toilet, pretending to herself that she was somewhere else, to take her mind away from the disgusting conditions in the prison. One day, she would get to escape from the hellish place, she just knew it.

CHAPTER

67

The stunning view of the garden overlooked by her penthouse suite was priceless. Even though Aruna had stayed countless times at the guesthouse, the scenery from her room never bored her.

Shades of green interspersed with splashes of colour, the well-tended grounds of the guesthouse were a delight on the senses. Exotic birds, honeybees and unusual looking butterflies, flitted from plant to plant. Giant swaying palms guarded the stone walls, as vibrant pink and purple peonies and primroses cradled their feet lovingly.

Stretched alone on the rattan lounger on her balcony, Aruna took small sips of her ginger and chamomile tea that room service had brought. She had expected to see Samuel, and was surprised to see Arul, one of the waiters from breakfast bring up her beverage instead.

It was seven am, and there was a lot of work to get through; contracts to be signed and new deals to be finalised. A family had contacted her from Gibraltar through a mutual acquaintance; desperate for a child, they had spent years trying but to no avail. Could Aruna help? The husband was Indian, and they longed for a darker skinned baby to pass off as their own. The money they were offering was higher than expected and Aruna was putting together a plan to grant them their wish.

Aruna stretched out, propping her laptop sturdily against her knees.

The network she had created were loyal to a tee and could be counted on for their unfailing support.

Navin, her right-hand man, could be relied upon in a crisis to take effective action. He had provnd that recently with the way he dealt with 'the Maya situation.' It was problematic, but the only way forward. Vivien had been terribly upset when she found out.

"How could you?" Vivien had screamed as she burst into Aruna's suite without so much as a knock. "We would have found a home for Maya; you didn't have to kill her." Tears had flowed down her cheeks. Aruna had long suspected that she had a soft spot for the little girl.

"I need not remind you Vivien that it is highly unprofessional to become attached to product, there is no place for emotion in our business," Aruna had replied icily, as she'd glared at the other woman before turning abruptly away.

"She was not 'product,' she was a little girl. A child, who had hopes and dreams, like any other." A desperate sob had choked Vivien, as she gasped to catch her breath. "I don't want to be a part of this anymore. All the lies, schemes. It's too much, I want out."

Aruna had walked slowly towards Vivien and stood facing her, arms crossed, her expression dark, inscrutable.

"There is no exit from this. When you signed up, I made it clear from the start what our work involved. You are very much implicated in this Vivien - if I go to prison, you will too. For a very long time."

She'd let out a mirthless laugh. "You made a foolish mistake by your carelessness in involving Samuel. Good day to you."

She'd immediately turned away, a cold dismissal of the other woman. Vivien had turned and exited the room without a word, letting out a cry of frustration as she closed the door behind her.

This incident made things very clear to Aruna about what needed to be done next. She would devise a plan to be implemented with immediate effect.

As she dozed lightly on the lounger, basking in the warmth of the morning Nagercoil sunshine, a knock came on the door. It was Navin.

"Excuse me Aruna, I need to ask you something." His head was bowed slightly as he entered the room, the bald crown at the peak of his head greasy with perspiration.

"Hello, I was waiting to see you Navin to offer congratulations regarding the Maya situation. I know it wasn't easy, but you handled it effectively." Aruna said, ignoring his comment.

Navin felt himself glow; it was not often that he received praise from his boss.

"Thank you, I need to ask please for some leave, I am planning a short trip to Russia." He blurted hastily, sweat trickling down his cheeks.

"Why are you going to Russia, Navin? Do you have family there?" Her stare was penetrating.

"Sort of. I have actually met a wonderful woman online and am going to meet her." Navin knew Aruna always expected the truth, and nothing less, from her employees.

She smiled at him warmly "Navin, of course you can have the leave, you have earnt it. I need a few more favours from you first though." She informed him about the couple in Gibraltar and their requirements.

Aruna knew she could rely on Navin to complete things to her satisfaction.

CHAPTER

68

Tracey Myers had always been confident that by placing her bets on red it would ensure that she would strike gold at Roulette. Surely it was inevitable that it would happen one day. The anticipation of not knowing when it could have thrilled her the most.

The waiting gave her goose bumps, her heart pounding loudly as adrenaline flowed through her veins. Her superstitious mother always said that she was born lucky, having survived a difficult breech birth unscathed, without a single mark.

Walking past the imposing Dreamlands casino, located against the Brisbane river, each day on her way to work, Tracey always wondered what it would feel like to step inside the place. The tall building, with its rows of twinkling silvery white lights going horizontally from top to bottom, came to life in the darkness. On the ground floor, the windows had huge panes of glass, through which one could see row after row of imposing slot machines and one-armed bandits, with a central area that contained Roulette and Blackjack tables.

The ceiling of the casino was crowded with gigantic glitter balls that spun round constantly, catching the light, creating a myriad of colours that lit up every area of the floor. It was an exciting place to be, and Tracey was determined that one day, she too would be playing inside.

Life was lonely. Yes, she had a job, but working shifts at the Moreland grocery store on the famous Queen street stacking shelves was not stimulating in any way. Days were spent mundanely moving products from one place to another, only to come back, and move them back again a few days later.

Anita, her good friend from work, had suggested one day that they visit the casino. Just the once. So, with fifty dollars each of their hard-earned cash, and dressed up to the nines, with dark, smoky eyes and heavily painted lips, they walked up the steps leading to the gaudily lit entrance, just as Tracey had always imagined she would do.

The smartly dressed manager greeted them at the door, a Hollywood smile frozen on his heavily botoxed face.

"Come through ladies! First time? You are so welcome here." After showing them around, the women were left to their own devices. The roulette table beckoned them first.

Laying bets of ten dollars each, Tracey placed hers on red, her favourite lucky colour. Jumping up and down in elation when she won, she immediately increased her bet to twenty dollars. Finally, she went all in… the ball whizzed around the sides, bouncing onto various sections, before landing finally. On black.

Tracey felt a lurch in her stomach. That was nearly a week's worth of groceries; gone. She had to win it back, no matter what.

As she ventured towards the ATM machine, to withdraw more money, Anita prudently pulled her friend back, reminding of their vow to not spend more than they had entered with.

So, they left, but Tracey returned the next day, lured by the bright lights and the addictive rush of adrenaline. This time alone. And with five hundred dollars, her entire savings amount.

She started with a slot machine, called 'Lucky Vera,' in the corner of the casino, close the main bar. Its flashing amber neon lights seemed to be calling her personally. Lucky Vera lived up to its name - after placing her first ten-dollar bet, Tracey won ten thousand dollars, whooping excitedly as the jackpot sign lit up, to a fanfare.

She was going to win again; it was just the start, she felt it in her bones. And so, at the roulette table, she placed the entire amount of winnings, over ten thousand dollars, on a solitary bet for red. She had faith she would be lucky. It was all or nothing.

An older woman, her silver hair neatly coiffed and wearing expensive diamond earrings, standing next to her gasped. "Are you sure you want to do that honey? You could lose everything," she whispered anxiously.

But Tracey was determined to go ahead. She pushed the tall pile of chips hastily into the red marked section of the roulette board, all eyes on her around the table. The croupier shouted, 'no more bets,' as he leaned forward across the table to spin the wheel. The adrenaline pumped through her veins, as Tracey could feel herself flushing in the heat of excitement, watching the ball as it travelled round the wheel.

Continuing to spin, round and round; the metal ball concentrically circling along the inside of the rotating wheel, as it clattered finally to a halt in the middle.

It landed on black.

The hush was almost deathly around the table.

Tracey felt her stomach lurch, she thought she was going to collapse. She had just lost ten thousand dollars, in one go.

She returned to the casino many times afterwards, determined that she would recoup her losses. Having spent her income, Tracey soon turned to credit cards and loans, desperately scrabbling for any money she could get her hands on, in true addict style.

One day in the casino, she was approached by a mild-mannered, slender Chinese woman, in her forties, who promised that her debts would be taken care of, and wiped clean, if she would just personally deliver a small parcel to a contact in India. She agreed in desperation, having spent her evenings avoiding hounding nuisance calls from those chasing her for money.

Little did Tracey realise that the parcel was a heroin stash and would land her in the biggest trouble she could ever imagine.

CHAPTER

69

Sitting cross-legged on the tiled floor, Kerensa had a chance to look at the women seated near her. There was a mixture of all ages, ranging from young to much older women, including Esther. She wondered to herself what exactly they had done to land themselves in prison.

The spacious dining room was situated on the front wing of the prison; an open plan, it had no windows and resembled a large verandah. Everyone had been directed to sit in neat rows by a middle- aged guard, with a thick mustache. His uniform was neatly pressed, and a khaki cap fitted snugly on his rather large head. One of the women seated nearby whispered that his name was Gautam, he was from the north of India and he was a married letch, actively pursuing any women who took his fancy in the prison. It would be the last thing she needed, and Kerensa made a point to herself to stay clear of him.

Two women with their hair scraped back into netted hats, walked around the lines, carrying large buckets, with ladles sticking out. A small girl went in front of them; in her hand was a metal tray which appeared to have what looked similar to large pancakes, and she placed one carefully on each plate. The women then dropped a ladle of dal, followed by a vegetable curry, on the side of each plate, as they made their way around the waiting lines.

As she took a bite of the pancake, its sourness lined her mouth. She remembered the crispy *dosais* she had tasted at the guesthouse, and how fresh and delicious they had been. A world away from the food in her present environment.

The woman with the blonde hair was seated in the row in front of Kerensa. She stuffed mouthfuls of the *dosai* hurriedly, after dipping into the curries. It was as though she had not eaten for days. She didn't try to interact with anyone around her, she was more interested in cramming the food into her mouth.

Prema sat to the left of Kerensa and was toying with a piece of the *dosai* in her hand, as she moved it around her plate.

"Are you not hungry Prema?" Kerensa asked gently, as she turned to her.

Prema sighed deeply, her brow furrowed anxiously. "I was just thinking about my life. There is nothing much else to do in this awful place."

"If you want to talk, I am here to listen." Kerensa forced herself to eat a piece of the stale, tasteless food, as she didn't know when lunch would come. Listening to Prema, she could hear the sadness in the girl's voice.

"I have been in the prison for four years now. Four years, three months and twenty days to be precise. My parents don't have a clue where I am, or what happened to me."

As she saw Kerensa's shocked face, she continued. "I was with my friend; we were just seventeen. Lured to a bar for the first time, it seemed so exciting, except the man who lured us there plied us with a drink which made us pass out. Next thing I knew, I had been bought for a brothel in Chennai."

Prema continued to recount how she was kept, locked up at the brothel by the owner; a woman called Veena Kumari who refused to give her any food until she agreed to meet one of her clients. When she refused, Veena slapped her with such force that she passed out.

The next thing she knew when she awoke was that she was lying on a bed, her clothes in disarray. A strange man was by the side, tucking his shirt into his trousers. Taking a five hundred rupee note out of his wallet, he pushed it into her curled-up palm as he walked quickly out of the door without looking back, locking it behind him.

Prema stifled a sob, as she continued to talk about how Veena would come to her room with the security guard, who would hold her down while the brothel owner injected her with something that would make her head spin, causing her to hallucinate. Different men were sent to her each night for weeks on end.

One morning, she woke to find that the customer who had been with her would not stir. She poked and prodded him, but his body was stone cold. He had died during the night.

Madam Veena panicked. Before the police came, she took a hunter's knife and made an incision in the neck of the still warm corpse. She then planted the knife underneath the drugged girl's pillow. After bribing one of the senior police officials, Prema was arrested, and thrown into jail, having been found guilty in court of murder in the first degree. DNA results, confirming Veena's fingerprints on the knife, had mysteriously disappeared from the evidence lab.

Kerensa could not believe what she heard.

"What? That's ridiculous Prema. What about evidence?" she asked, bewildered.

"The police official arranged it, so that I would look guilty. They had the upper hand."

Kerensa did not know whether to believe the girl or not, it seemed too shocking to be true. She found herself feeling very sorry for Prema, who had been caught in such a warped and devious situation.

After breakfast, Gautam came around the lines, ordering everyone to get up, and file out in an orderly fashion to the courtyard. It was a spacious area, with a few concrete benches and a grass field. Feeling the breeze blowing gently on her face, felt wonderful after being cooped in the claustrophobic room.

The courtyard area, securely barricaded by a high barbed wire fence and surrounded by armed guards, was a stark reminder to Kerensa of the bleakness and desperation of her situation.

CHAPTER

70

Standing in the prison grounds, Kerensa looked longingly through the gaps in the barbed wire fence to the dried wasteland beyond. Thoughts of home and mum raced through her mind. *How on earth had she got herself into this mess?*

Her passport was the key. The immigration people had said that the passport was false, the only way this could have happened was if it had been swapped when it went missing. Thoughts of her stay at the guesthouse came to mind. The only person who had handled her handbag on arrival, apart from the driver, had been Samuel. Could he have taken it then without her knowledge? She had trusted him implicitly, the thought that she had nearly given herself to a man who had been lying to her was too much to bear.

"Hi there, I thought I would come and say hello." The blonde-haired woman had come to stand next to her, extending her hand as she threw Kerensa a friendly smile. Her hand felt sweaty. She looked in her late thirties, however, there was an air of exhaustion about her, which combined with the fine lines around her eyes and mouth, made her seem older. Her bleached blonde hair was scraped away from her face in a messy bun, and Kerensa could see the first signs of grey roots poking through her hairline. A dark mole stood prominent on the base of her left cheek. She had an accent which sounded Australian, but Kerensa was unsure.

"My name is Tracey," she continued, managing a faint smile. "What you are in here for?"

Kerensa couldn't help but think that her question would be one of the first ones that inmates would probably ask each other the world over.

"I'm Kerensa, it's my second day here. I was arrested at the airport for allegedly having a counterfeit passport, it went missing at the guesthouse I was staying at, and when it re-appeared, I think it might have been swapped." Her voice trailed off as she looked down at the ground, the reality of her predicament hitting her.

"Good lord, that's rough." Tracey began. "All of us have a story to tell here. I was caught with half a kilo of heroin packed in my belt at customs, after landing from Brisbane. I was foolish, I see that now. Stupidly trying to make some fast bucks." Her look was unapologetic, she seemed more bothered about having been caught.

"Well, I will leave you alone Kerensa. Just get as much fresh air as you can, it's the only exercise we get every day. Forty-five minutes straight after breakfast. And watch out for Gautam the guard. He's slimy!" She laughed as she turned and walked to the other side of the open field, joining a small group of women who were deep in animated conversation.

Prema was sitting alone on one of the wooden benches in the compound, her face tilted upwards, and eyes closed, basking in the warmth emitted by the sun. Kerensa didn't want to disturb her, she enjoyed chatting with Prema but felt deep sadness at hearing her unjust story.

"Time to come in everyone." Rohina yelled, as she scoured the women scattered about in the compound. "Form an orderly line in single file."

Kerensa joined the long winding queue that had formed to go back inside as she steeled herself to face her second harsh day behind bars.

CHAPTER

71

As they walked through the bleak prison corridor in single file, Kerensa noticed a wooden door which had a sign 'Prison Warden' in block capitals by the side. Prema, who was walking behind her, whispered that the room belonged to Ashok Reddy, a warden to be feared, she said. Overseeing the prison for more than fifteen years, apparently Ashok ruled with nothing less than an iron fist.

Rohina came from the back of the line and stood next to Kerensa, as she muttered coldly, "The warden has said that you need to meet him tomorrow. I will let you know the time." She stared at Kerensa, trying to discern her reaction to the bombshell she had just dropped.

Kerensa threw Prema a bewildered look. Why on earth would the warden need to see her? Fearful reasons crossed her mind. She realised that this would be one of the few chances she had to talk to Rohina directly, without the other guards nearby.

"Rohina, you did say I could make a phone call today. None of my family know where I am, they will be so worried." Kerensa implored, her voice pleading in desperation.

The guard paused and looked at her watch.

"Okay, straight after lunch, I will come and escort you to the phone room. Five minutes only, mind."

"Can I call England? I live with my mother, and she is ill, she needs to know I am safe." The guard's face softened slightly.

"Okay, that is fine. Now hurry along." Rohina sounded surprisingly kind for the first time. Kerensa knew that to Indians, family came first and mentioning her mother had seemingly touched a nerve.

As the women quietly walked single file back to the room scrabbling for a space to sit down, Kerensa found herself next to Tracey, squashed close to the wall by the high window. The putrid odour that lingered heavily around the air clung to their clothes and hit them as soon as they walked in however Kerensa found that, strangely, she had almost become accustomed to it. Somewhere in the room a child started wailing.

"I can teach you the ropes about this place Kerensa, but the rest is up to you." Tracey said in a matter-of-fact tone, with the air of someone who was used to looking out for trouble. "Rohina is basically okay once you get to know her, but she can be difficult when she wants to be. It is Gautam who you need to look out for." Tracey rolled her eyes, as she continued. "He basically sees all white women as easy game."

"When I first came here, he came up to me in the locker room. Rohina wasn't around and all the others had just left and were standing in the hallway. He pushed me against a locker and began pressing his lips against mine. It was disgusting. I kneed him hard between the legs, and he yelped so loud and ran out, the funniest thing I had seen." Tracey chuckled to herself. "If he does anything to you then you need to fight him back, remember that. Good girl ways don't work in here."

She stared intently at Kerensa for a few minutes deep in thought. The look on her face seemed to convey to Kerensa that she would not have the guts to stand up for herself if the need arose.

For two hours, they sat in the same cramped position. Kerensa could feel her legs becoming increasingly numb with the lack of blood circulation and slowly got to her feet, holding the wall for support.

The bell rang loudly Kerensa guessed for lunch and everyone got up slowly forming a single file, similar to the way they had done in the morning.

Suddenly, there was a commotion.

Two women started fighting, screaming and pulling each other by the hair as they shouted obscenities at the top of their lungs. It was hard to see what had caused the fight. The door flung open and Rohina and the stubby guard who had been outside came in, hitting both women with batons in a desperate attempt to separate them.

Finally pulling the women apart, the guards dragged them out into the corridor and beat them mercilessly. As Kerensa and the others filed out for lunch, they could see the two bloodied women lying in crumpled heaps in a corner of the corridor.

"Let this be a lesson for all of you that we will not tolerate misbehaviour of any kind in our prison," Rohina screamed, her face flushed red, as she frantically scraped away messy strands of loose hair falling in front of her eyes and glared at no-one in particular. The women walked silently past, with their heads bowed.

Lunch was even less appetising than breakfast. A slice of stale bread that had small speckles of mould forming on it, lay beside a watery curry containing miniscule pieces of meat and potatoes. A small mound of what appeared to be mashed vegetables was dumped onto the plate by the small girl who had brought round the pancakes for breakfast.

Kerensa took a few mouthfuls tentatively, trying not to think too hard about what she was eating. The thought of calling home dominated her mind. Rohina had promised that she could make a call, and Kerensa only hoped that she didn't go back on her word.

The dining hall was bustling with animated conversations, lunch seemed to have brought the women to life. Two children were walking slowly amongst the lines weaving in and out of the seated women, trying to alleviate the boredom and pass time. Kerensa could not believe that children could be allowed to be kept in prison and was curious to know the circumstances under which their mothers were detained.

Suddenly a skinny woman at the end of her line screamed loudly, throwing her plate to the floor. The contents spilled everywhere as the woman ran towards the window, shrieking noisily. Two guards came from the other end of the room to see what had caused the commotion, trying to placate her calmly. The woman next to Kerensa explained in broken English that the woman had put her spoon into her food only to find it moving. A small rat had crawled out of the bowl! Kerensa thought she would be sick as she looked away queasily.

Rohina stood in front of Kerensa, thumping her baton rhythmically onto her palm.

"Follow me." She ordered tersely, turning abruptly on her heel, as she marched out of the hall with a bewildered Kerensa trying to keep up behind.

CHAPTER

72

Rohina stopped outside a narrow door and nodded at Kerensa, indicating she should go inside. The room was tiny, only slightly bigger than a box room, with a musty antique desk that dominated the entire space. The clinical, grey coloured paint was peeling from the walls. An old-fashioned black dial phone stood on the centre of the desk, a thin layer of dust coating the surface indicated it had lain unused for a long time.

"You have five minutes," Rohina said gruffly, shutting the door firmly behind her. Kerensa squeezed through the narrow space around the desk and perched on the edge of a wooden stool on the other side.

She had to be quick, Rohina seemed to be a person who always meant what she said, so five minutes would be exactly that. Kerensa desperately tried to remember the code required to dial the United Kingdom from abroad, after thinking for a few moments, it thankfully came to mind. She hurriedly dialled her home number, her heart lurching in anticipation.

"Hello?" a woman's voice answered tentatively. It was mum. Just hearing her voice was soothing, Kerensa had to steady herself so that she wouldn't cry.

"Mummy, it's me." She whispered quietly, her voice breaking with emotion.

"Oh my gosh. Kerensa? I have been so worried darling. Matt and I have been desperately trying your phone, over and over. Are you okay, where are you?" Catherine asked, her anxious voice thick with emotion.

"Mum, I haven't got long. I don't want you to worry, I have been held at a prison in Chennai since yesterday, they accused me of falsifying my passport."

"What?" The eerie silence that followed was palpable.

"Mum, are you there?" Kerensa whispered.

Rohina popped her head round, tapping on her watch. "Two minutes,'" she cautioned sternly as she closed the door.

"Kerensa…darling…I'm here. I…I just can't believe what you said that's all. Matt's here, I am just passing the phone to him." Before she could say anything, her brother came on the line.

"Kerri just heard. Don't worry, I will call the British Embassy immediately, we will get you out of there. Sit tight." Hearing Matt's confident words were comforting. He always would be her little brother, but it seemed that he had suddenly stepped up considerably.

Growing up without a dad in their life there were times when he couldn't cope with the expectations being the only male in the family. Dealing with mum's illness was difficult for both of them. His coping strategy was to retreat into his own world but lately Kerensa noticed he was changing. She almost couldn't recognise the nervous young man that he used to be hiding away in his room, shying away from the world outside. The new Matt was a world away from the nervous brother that she once knew.

"Matt, thank you. I love you both so much." Kerensa felt her throat catch with emotion, hearing their voices brought to mind images of mum's cinnamon French toast. She could almost smell the musky scent that would waft up to her room each Saturday morning. Matt and his constant practical jokes that often caught her unawares, making them both laugh until their sides ached. She longed to put her arms around them. An aching void filled her with hunger for home.

"Okay, that's enough, put the phone down." Rohina had entered the room quietly and stood motionless in the doorway, glaring at Kerensa.

"I have to go now, love you, please fight for me," Kerensa pleaded.

"Darling, we are going to get you out of there, don't." Mum's voice was cut off abruptly as Rohina slammed her baton down hard on the receiver. Her face was thunderous.

"When I say five minutes, I mean five minutes. Do not mock me."

Kerensa gulped and muttered an apology contritely, she didn't want to incur the wrath of Rohina on just her second day.

Following the guard quietly down the corridor, they reached the room where she had spent the night. Again, the sea of faces stared curiously at her when she entered the room. However, as Kerensa settled down for the afternoon in between a crush of female bodies, she had a small consolation that help would be on its way.

CHAPTER

73

The silence that echoed inside Samuel's room was unusual.

On that particular day, Vivien remembered her morning had been demanding but nothing unusual. Waking up at five am as she always did, a steaming cup of strong tea was brought up for her at 5.30am like clockwork by Nalini, one of the house girls.

In the kitchen by six am, Vivien had lost sense of time as she raced around instructing the chefs and maids on arranging the fruit platters neatly, making spicy dosais, grinding freshly picked coconut for a delicious chutney as an accompaniment, amongst many other things, as they prepared for the first onslaught of guests to enter the breakfast area. It was after seven am that she suddenly that Samuel had not come down.

"Arul," she called over one of the breakfast waiters who was busy laying a pristine linen covered table with cutlery and napkins. "Please can you go and give a nudge to Samuel, he's usually down here by now helping out. Think he might have overslept, just knock on his door please."

"Certainly ma'am." Arul nodded obligingly and disappeared up the stairs.

Samuel's room was tucked away in an alcove behind the east wing of the guesthouse. Arul banged on the door twice.

"Samuel sir, your mother wants you downstairs. It's 7.30am." There was no reply. He knocked again.

Still silence.

Vivien was busy welcoming guests for breakfast when Arul approached to let her know that Samuel was not answering his door.

Politely excusing herself from an elderly gentleman with whom she was deep in conversation, Vivien raced up the stairs to her son's room. After no response to calling his name, panic set in as she fumbled hurriedly for the key bunch around her waist.

On opening the door, she was greeted by an empty room. Next to the bed, his pyjamas were neatly folded and placed on a crimson armchair. Vivien felt this was strange, she knew how messy her son was on the best of days.

A white envelope with 'Vivien' handwritten on the front lay propped up on his desk. Vivien tore it open.

It read:

Dear mother,

I know as you read this, you will be anxious.

Please don't be worried about me, I am now in a much better place, and at peace. It all got too much.

I love you,

Samuel

Vivien dropped the letter to the floor as she felt her head pound, throbbing painfully as she thought she would pass out. Waves of nausea pressed against her; she could hardly breathe. Surely, she had misunderstood - her son, her precious Samuel, could not have left her? Gone forever. No way.

It was then that the scream came. Loud and howling, it left her like that of a primal animal as she crumpled into a heap on the floor.

***

Constable Gopal was the one who took the call. The woman at the other end was hysterical, said that she owned Amma's guesthouse, something about her son being missing, suicide note. It was a lot to take in.

"Madam, please slow down, I can't hear you properly. Now, let's start from the beginning."

He took the stubby pencil from the holder on his desk, quickly opening his notebook, whilst holding the receiver pressed against his ear.

"Right, first give me your name."

"Vivien De Mello." Her voice was resonant amidst her sobs.

Gopal paused, and wondered why she sounded familiar.

"Okay, do you mind if I call you Vivien?" Without waiting for an answer, he continued. "Are you sure that your son is missing? When did you see him last?"

"Of course, I am sure, he left a note. His bed is empty, and phone switched off. We have searched everywhere."

A racking sob came from the other end of the phone.

"Does he have any enemies? Anyone who wants him dead?" Gopal cleared his throat, before asking nervously. "Has Samuel suffered from any sort of mental illness before?"

"No, never, nothing like that. He felt down when we first moved here from Goa, but nothing more. Regarding enemies, he has none." It was then, having uttered the words, that the awful thought suddenly struck Vivien.

Aruna. Could the American possibly have had anything to do with his disappearance? She suddenly felt sick.

"Vivien, I will be at the guesthouse this afternoon. Please do not touch anything in his room, we may need forensics. I will take a statement from you too." Gopal put the receiver down and realized that the afternoon ahead would be a difficult one.

***

It was a young boy who found them.

The shoes, battered and worn, washed up on opposite ends of the famous Muttam beach were wedged between jagged rocks. And then, further down, on a bare strip of sand lay a torn, scrunched up t-shirt bearing the slogan: Goa is forever.

Krish took the call from the boy's father, who felt it strange that such good quality clothing should lie scattered on a beach. Gopal felt his stomach lurch when he heard the news.

A huge rock lay off the coastline, famous for its suicides. Old, young, of all religions had decided over the years to exit the world from its craggy, slippery surfaces.

Yes, that afternoon at the guesthouse was not going to be easy.

CHAPTER

74

Opening her eyes, Kerensa realised she didn't know what time it was. The solitary skylight up high on the wall offered little clue. The sky was bruised purple at that awkward time when the dawn was rousing after a deep sleep.

She looked around the room sleepily. Most women were fast asleep, legs and arms flailed in the depth of their slumber. The small children were curled up close to their mothers, seeking some comfort from their bleak environment. Kerensa had been shocked to see children in the jail. She counted five of them in total, under the age of about seven.

Prema had explained that most of their mothers were pregnant when convicted and locked up. Instead of being kept separately and looked after, they were expected to live cramped in the room, in close proximity with the others. They had been denied check-ups and access to health care, a basic need for expectant mothers.

Kerensa knew she had to get out of the place. She had ensured two nights of snatched naps whilst sleeping awkwardly, trying to remain up-right but waking up from fitful short bursts of sleep to find herself lying on someone's foot or, worse, their hips. Her body had never ached so much in her life, restricted within the tightly cramped space.

She longed desperately for the comfort of her warm, clean bed at home. Hearing the voices of mum and Matt brought back buried memories of safety and security.

"Hey dear, how are you doing?" Tracey came up beside her as they walked single file towards the shower room, her blonde hair scraped high into a messy ponytail, with tufts of wild strands loosely escaping from the sides.

"Not too good to be honest. I don't know how much more of being here I can take." Kerensa had felt like her world had collapsed around her over the past days.

"You are a brave girl and will get through this. I know you mentioned about the warden, have you met him yet? I can say he's a real character!"

"Rohina said that I will be meeting him today."

Tracey grimaced, as they entered the crowded shower room.

Later that afternoon when they were back huddled in the room, the door opened and Rohina stepped in.

"Miss Oldfield, where are you?' She quickly scoured the room until her eyes fell on Kerensa. 'I need you to come with me please. Immediately." Her voice was abrupt.

Kerensa got up and stepped over the curled-up legs of some women to reach the door. Following Rohina down the corridor, they came to the door of Mr Ashok Reddy. Rohina knocked once, the sound loudly resounding in the quiet hallway.

"Come in!" The voice was commanding and authoritarian.

Kerensa felt her stomach lurch as Rohina pushed the door open and going inside, she was met with an elaborately decorated room that was in complete contrast to the squalid conditions that she was living in.

Bright, airy and spacious, the heady smell of freshly cut Jasmine lingered in the air. Painted in shades of cream and grey, the walls offered a contemporary feel, which was highlighted by a large black veneer desk that dominated the room. Beautiful vases were scattered strategically on the window sills and table, containing cut stems in vivid shades of purple, red and yellow that brought a simple beauty to the stylish décor.

From behind the desk stood a diminutive man in a tailored suit, with a fading head of hair swept away from his face. A long moustache stood proud below his nose, twirled at the ends. Kerensa discreetly suppressed a laugh.

"Ah, Miss Kerensa, it is nice to finally meet you!" His command of English was perfect, with a slight lilt, hinting at a private school education. He pointed to a solitary chair in front of the desk, gesturing for her to sit down. Rohina hovered by the door.

"It's okay Rohina, you may go." The warden instructed the surprised guard, who nodded obediently as she quietly left the room.

"My name is Ashok Reddy, and I oversee the day to day running of the prison. I understand that you were caught with a counterfeit passport. I am sure you realise that is a very serious offence." He stared intently at Kerensa, as though he was attempting to bore into her psyche.

Without pausing for breath, he continued, "I must admit you don't strike me as the sort of girl to be devious. But these days, you never know!" He gave a hollow laugh and perched uncomfortably against the edge of the table.

Kerensa leaned forward. "Mr Reddy, I can promise you that I don't know how it happened. My passport was lost, but turned up a few days later, so I thought everything was okay. I think it must have been swapped at this stage."

Ashok gave her a sympathetic look, as he replied slowly, "Kerensa, I want to believe you. I do. However, I have a contact who has done some digging and there appears to be no record of a police report being filed. That is something that would have gone in your favour considerably."

She could not believe what she was hearing. Vivien promised her that the report had been filed, Kerensa was sure she did. She felt her world sink around her.

"I do have some good news for you though. I don't believe you have a lawyer and can get one for you. But I have just received an email from the British High Commission in Chennai. They have been contacted by a relative of yours, Matthew Oldfield? They are sending a top official to see you tomorrow as priority."

Kerensa's heart leapt with joy. Good old Matt. She suddenly felt she could breathe again, with a glimmer of hope for the future.

CHAPTER

75

"I am here to see Vivien." Gopal leaned over the reception desk, as the young man picked up the phone and quickly dialled a number. From his badge, Gopal could see his name was Calvin.

Calvin gestured with his free hand to the sofas situated by the guest-house entrance, indicating that Gopal should be seated.

"Vivien, sorry to disturb you, I have a police officer here to see you."

Krish was outstretched on the cream leather sofa closest to the entrance, head buried in a glossy magazine. Gopal tapped the magazine and then sank into the other end of the deep sofa. Krish had insisted on coming along, which Gopal agreed to, he understood the need to get out of the cramped station room even just for a few hours.

An elegant looking lady wearing a crisply starched peach and white saree came through the lift doors towards them. Her face was crumpled, and she had dark circles around her red-rimmed eyes.

Gopal stood up, khaki cap in his hand. "Hello ma'am, I am Gopal, and this is my colleague Krish. I am so sorry for your situation. Is there somewhere private we can talk?"

"Follow me please." Vivien turned on her heels and the two men followed her to a tiny, closed room next to the reception desk as she pulled a red curtain across the glass door for privacy.

"Sorry, this has been a bad day for me." She began tearfully, as the policemen settled into two white wicker chairs. Gopal took out his notebook and looked at her sympathetically.

"Ma'am, I can only imagine what you must be going through. I know it is difficult, but I will need to take a statement from you." Removing a stubby pencil from his shirt pocket, he sat poised, pen to paper, as he waited for her to talk. Krish reached in his trouser pocket pulling out a slim packet of mints, popping a few into his mouth.

Vivien sighed. "He's my only son. I love him dearly. We did have a minor argument the night before, but nothing important."

Gopal looked at her intently. "What were you arguing about? It could be relevant."

Vivien looked down at her hands as her voice dropped. "He doesn't like someone I work closely with, that's all. It's really not a big deal."

"Okay, can you tell me exactly the timeline of your interaction with your son last night?"

Her eyes became watery thinking about her son. "We had dinner and then he excused himself early saying he had a headache and went to his room."

"Do you know roughly what time that was Vivien?"

"I think about nine pm. I only realised he was missing this morning, when he didn't come down for breakfast as he normally did. When I entered his room, I found the note." She suppressed a sob.

Gopal went silent as he scribbled furiously and then took a deep breath before continuing.

"Ms. Vivien, I don't know how to tell you this, but a few items were found on Muttam beach which could possibly belong to your son. At this stage, bearing in mind the contents of the note, we do not suspect foul play."

Krish passed over a black case and Gopal unzipped it, pulling out the clothing encased securely in a clear plastic pouch. Putting on a pair of latex gloves, he opened the pouch and held up a single shoe and the tee shirt.

As soon as Vivien saw what Gopal held in his hand, she immediately started wailing loudly. Both men looked at each other, bewildered and unsure of what to do next. Krish jumped out of his seat and offered Vivien a tissue from his pocket.

Gopal stood up. "Vivien, I am sorry for your loss. The area is a notorious suicide spot, but as yet, a body has not been washed up. Please can you direct us to his room so we can examine his environment. You need not join us."

Vivien dabbed her eyes and stifling sobs, explained how to get to his room.

On opening the door, Gopal noticed immediately how neatly his bed was made and pyjamas were folded. He read the note and seemed puzzled - why would a seemingly happy man, with a loving mother and a thriving business feel the need to end his life?

There were some things in the disappearance of Samuel De Mello, that definitely did not add up.

CHAPTER

76

It had been ten days since Kerensa's life had changed completely. In the prison, each day dragged into the next - endless days of nothingness. Each morning, after waking up from another uncomfortable night of broken sleep, she would have a fleeting moment of excitement at the thought that that would be the day that she would get the visit she needed to release her.

But nothing.

She was sure that Rohina was avoiding her. Each time when Kerensa approached the guard she turned the other way or suddenly seemed to be occupied with something else. However, on the tenth day, she approached Kerensa during lunch when she was seated on the floor of the dining room. Standing in front, arms crossed, she spoke abruptly.

"You have visitors, looks like they are from the Embassy."

Kerensa felt her heart leap. She got up, leaving her half-finished meal and quickly followed Rohina out to the corridor.

Walking through a different wing, they came to a section of the jail that Kerensa had not visited before. It was painted in hues of turquoise and cream and even had large potted plants at regular intervals on the corridor. The sun shone warmly through the large windows, bringing an air of cheeriness to the place in total contrast to the dreary area where the women were dwelling.

Rohina stood outside one of the wooden doors in the corridor and nodded for Kerensa to go in as she opened the door, remaining in the corridor outside.

A man, possibly in his late fifties, was sitting on a large wooden desk facing towards her. His flecked grey hair was swept neatly to the side, and a small sweat bead trickled noticeably down his forehead, which he swept away impatiently with a handkerchief. As he saw Kerensa, he smiled and stood up, politely reaching out his hand.

"You must be Miss Oldfield. I am Peter Travis, a senior official at the British High Commission here in Chennai. It's nice to meet you. I know a few things about your case, but I need you to fill me in."

Kerensa shook his outstretched hand and promptly sat down facing him. The ceiling fan whirred noisily as it rotated tiredly at full blast. The cool breeze that brushed lightly over the top of Kerensa's head was refreshing.

Peter reached for his leather briefcase taking out a thick file overflowing with sheets of paper and muttered to himself as he skimmed through it briefly.

Just then, a knock came on the door.

Peter looked up past Kerensa and smiled as the door opened.

"I hope you don't mind I have my nephew who is shadowing me for a few weeks, he just popped to the car to pick up some papers, are you okay if he joins us?"

Kerensa nodded and turned around. The man who entered looked so familiar, she wondered where she had seen him before. Then, it struck her. She stared at him in shocked disbelief.

It was the man behind the bar in London. It couldn't be, she felt as though she was imagining it.

As Ben raced in, he saw the back of the prisoner's head with her dark hair dishevelled and tied loosely in an untidy ponytail. When she turned around, he could not believe his eyes.

"Kerensa!' he blurted in a shocked voice. 'Oh, my goodness."

They both looked at each other, incredulous. Peter broke the eerie silence.

"Do you two know each other?" His face was surprised as he looked from one to the other, back and forth.

Ben couldn't take his eyes off Kerensa. "We met at the bar I was working in London just a couple of weeks ago!"

Peter shuffled his papers noisily to break the awkward silence. "Now, that's an amazing coincidence. What are the odds of that happening? But we need to crack on now, so let's continue."

Kerensa felt comforted at the thought of Ben being there. A familiar and friendly face.

Peter coughed loudly, as he turned to look directly at Kerensa.

"As I said Miss Oldfield, Ben is shadowing me for a few weeks, as this is a career that he is keen to take up." He looked at his nephew proudly. "My job is to ensure that British citizens who need urgent legal help are given the best support we can offer. I need you to tell me everything that happened before this, in detail. Ben, can you take some notes please?"

Kerensa relayed all the details of what had happened at the guesthouse regarding her passport going missing and how it turned up mysteriously a few days later. She talked about being stopped at the airport and the harsh interrogation by the airport officials. Then about how she was ignored when asking for legal support.

Peter's face fell, as he replied quietly, "I am so sorry that you have been through so much. Let's see how we can help you."

"Kerensa, are you okay?' Ben leaned forward as he whispered in a concerned voice. "It must be difficult in here."

'Ben, it has been a real struggle. I have never experienced anything like this place. Words cannot describe it. I did not falsify my passport, or do anything untoward, as they have been suggesting. Please help me.' She pleaded, a solitary tear sliding down her cheek as she stifled a sob.

'Listen Kerensa, Peter is the best. We will make sure you get out of here okay, don't worry.'

Peter continued, 'Kerensa, I don't personally have the power to get you out of here unfortunately, however I can get you a very good lawyer, and support you through this process. Your brother said that the family can cover the costs and also, they will be sending money for anything you need. I am also going to speak to the warden about letting you have a visitor, is there anyone that comes to mind?'

Kerensa thought immediately about Ravi and Mik; they were the closest in distance and would bring a smile to her face but couldn't remember their address or phone number; everything was on her confiscated phone.

'Right, that's sorted for the moment, I will arrange for the lawyer to contact you urgently and we can work towards getting you out of here, as soon as possible. We need to go now, but will be in touch okay, I am going to speak to Mr Reddy now about suggestions that can help you and will also contact the guesthouse to let them know your situation.'

Both Peter and Ben stood up slowly, shuffling papers hurriedly into the file.

'Thank you both so very much, please help me get out of here and I will wait to hear from the lawyer.'

Ben looked at her, a cheeky smile suddenly appearing on his face.

'Now I bet you really wished you had got in touch for that delicious meal I had promised you!'

They all broke into laughter, and on their way out, Ben turned to Kerensa and muttered:

'Hang in tight there Kerensa, we are going to get you out of here soon!'

CHAPTER

77

I can't stop thinking about my little girl, Preeti.

Where she is. How she must be feeling - all alone, scared, with no-one to comfort her.

For God's sake, she is only six years old. Just a mere baby. I have already lost one beautiful daughter and cannot bear the thought of losing another one.

Jingles visits me every day out of habit and respect, bringing me fresh, tangy coconut water to soothe my parched throat and luscious, overripe custard apples, their pungent scent filling the bleak room with delight. She is covering her duty as a good Indian wife, all kudos to her.

I watch from my hospital bed - her broken, melancholy eyes staring blankly ahead, like a gazelle that faces a hunter in its last moments before death. Her slow shuffle as she crosses the room, dabbing her red-rimmed eyes with her saree pallu, is pitiful. Without our little girl, she is lost.

Preeti was our whole world. Our universe.

And once that world comes crashing down, what is left behind?

Nothing but screams that disappear soundlessly into the night, and a broken, empty heart.

CHAPTER

78

The day had been long and emotionally draining but Kerensa now had something to cling to, something she thought she would never feel again - hope.

Later that evening, huddling together in the crowded room, Esther came to sit near her as she had done the first night. Prema was sitting opposite and manoeuvred around so that they were facing each other. Wrapping her saree pallu around her thin shoulders, Esther closed her eyes and started singing quietly in Tamil. The song was soothing and melodic.

"She is singing a popular lullaby." Prema explained, her voice reducing to a whisper. "Did you know that she is here because she killed her husband?"

Kerensa's jaw dropped. Surely not mild-mannered Esther, she thought to herself.

Prema continued by explaining that her husband was seeing another woman, and was abusive, thinking nothing of hitting Esther in front of their children. Trivial things used to irritate him. Once, he had been drinking heavily and coming home late, he pulled her out of bed and started hitting her on the face for no reason, resulting in a broken jaw and most of her front teeth being knocked out. Kerensa felt sorry for the gentle older woman, and the pain she would have experienced. Prema continued to describe how, one day, it all became too much and after sending her children to her sister's house, she laced his dinner of dal and rice with arsenic, causing him to die in agony while she sat and watched. It was only after a few hours, of sitting next to his body in the dark, that she picked up the phone and called the police, turning herself in.

Esther continued to sing the melancholy song, closing her eyes and swaying slowly from side to side, oblivious to everything around her.

Kerensa's sleep that night was fitful, and in a deep slumber, she dreamt that Kaian came to visit her in the night, his arms were outstretched to her as he smiled and called out her name. However, when she went towards him, he disappeared and she was left alone, crying for him forlornly. She woke up with a start, and yet again, found herself leaning against Esther, who was soothingly stroking her hair.

"Shh, go back to sleep child." She whispered softly under her breath.

The next morning in the grounds, Gautam approached her.

"You have visitors. Come inside." He tapped his baton on her arm sharply. Tracey who was standing nearby shot her a warning look, concern written on her face.

Walking through the same quiet corridor as the day before, Kerensa could uneasily feel Gautam's lecherous eyes on her, assessing her up and down, as he sauntered slowly behind. She was determined to keep contact with him to a minimum.

"Miss Oldfield," he said as he caught up with her. "I wanted to let you know that if you need anything at all, you can rely on me. Just let me know, and I have a quiet place where I can look after you properly."

Kerensa felt herself go queasy as she increased her pace. There was no-one else in the deserted corridor.

Turning back to Gautam she muttered a quick thanks, determined to keep contact with him to the bare minimum. They soon reached the visitor's room.

As she turned the door handle to go in, Gautam covered her hand with his, squeezing tight in a painful grip. His breath reeked of alcohol mixed with a putrid smell that she could only attribute to a severe case of gingivitis. The odour of old, unwashed sweat covered his body.

"Remember my offer doesn't hold forever, and there are limits to my patience." His voice was low but menacing, as he removed his hand abruptly. "I will be waiting outside, you have ten minutes, no more."

Kerensa felt her heart leap with joy when she caught a glimpse of the familiar faces sitting inside. Ravi and Mik.

Ravi immediately stood up and came towards Kerensa, arms outstretched, his face lit up with happiness at seeing her.

"Babe, come here."

She fell into his open arms and Mik joined them as they circled Kerensa protectively, holding her tight and stroking her hair as she sobbed uncontrollably.

After a few minutes, she composed herself and threw them an appreciative smile.

"Guys, you don't know how happy I am to see you both. Thank you so much for coming to see me, it means the world, I cannot begin to tell you."

Mik leaned over and took Kerensa's hand in his, pressing it reassuringly.

"I don't think I can express how worried we were Kerensa," he quickly glanced at Ravi, who nodded in agreement "When you didn't reply to our messages, we kept trying to think of reasons, blaming the phone signal etc. I contacted the guesthouse last week and when they told me that you hadn't reached, we both panicked and spoke the British Consulate. It took days for anyone to get back to us but finally we got permission, thankfully, and here we are."

Ravi reached in a clear plastic bag by the side of his chair and removed a neatly tied, bulky parcel, placing it on the table in front of Kerensa.

"This is for you, my love. They checked it thoroughly at reception. There was a gormless idiot there, I think his name was Tony, who insisted on taking it all out to check every centimetre." Ravi rolled his eyes despairingly which made Kerensa laugh and realise how much she had missed the two of them and their quirky ways.

Mik continued. "There is a toothpaste, toothbrush, soap, magazine and a few chocolate treats. Oh yes, and erm, some sanitary items." He stuttered, his face turning a light shade of red.

Kerensa thanked them and proceeded to tell them about the prison and her experiences. She described her new friends - Prema, Esther and Tracey and also the guards, touching briefly on her encounter with Gautam.

Both men looked shocked.

"Wait until I see that fool, just wait!" Ravi said, his face thunderous as he glanced towards the door.

Just then, the guard put his face. "Two minutes." He insisted curtly glaring at Kerensa.

Ravi rose from the seat and called him over angrily ignoring the pleading glances that Kerensa threw desperately at him.

"I just want to let you know Mr Gautam I work closely with the Senior prison commissioner and if I hear of ANY untoward behaviour or inappropriate actions towards Kerensa, I will report you and you will lose your job. Do I make myself clear?" He had stretched himself to his full height and stared at the startled guard menacingly.

"Yes, yes sir." Gautam answered meekly, his head bowed humbly. "I am very sorry, and sir, I cannot lose my job, I have a family to look after."

"Well, you had better behave then. And remember my words, I mean what I said." Ravi shot him another angry look as the guard looked contritely down at the floor before making a quick exit from the room.

"I don't really know the prison commissioner, if one even exists." Ravi whispered, trying to suppress a laugh.

The three of them looked at each other as they burst into snorts of laughter, covering their mouths to try to stifle the sounds.

"Thank you both so much for coming to see me, it means the world, love you!" Kerensa got up and went around the table, to give them both a heartfelt hug.

"Kerensa, we are always here for you remember that, and will bring more things next week. Stay strong okay? Give me your brother's number,

I would like to call and update him and your mum." Mik looked at her with genuine concern as Ravi took her arm and gave it a squeeze, his voice breaking with emotion.

She quickly gave them Matt's number before the nervous guard suddenly re-entered the room and insisted that it was time to finish up.

She turned to give her friends a final cheery glance, before the door closed, and a rather subdued Gautam led her back to the cell.

CHAPTER

79

There surely had to be some perks to being one of the most sought-after lawyers in Southern India Varun thought to himself as he pulled on the pair of size nine burnished Ralph Lauren boots which had set him back a cool ninety thousand rupees. If his mother could see him now, she would have a fit. Scrimping and saving all her life, mama believed strictly in the old-fashioned approach to only buying the essential necessities of life, nothing more. He tried not to think too much about how the money for his boots could amply feed an entire Indian village for a day.

His specialism was Immigration. After graduating from Yale with a first-class honours degree he headed straight home to Chennai where Varun commenced work experience at a prestigious law firm, Anand and sons Associates on Thambuchetty Street as a lowly paid intern, filing reports and corresponding with clients. It was boring work and not what he expected but Varun had lofty ambitions. The head of the law firm Pravin Anand was impressed with his credentials and positive attitude.

However, two senior lawyers at the firm, Subash and Jay, both in their forties and set in their ways resented the new intern with his 'American swagger', as they termed it, and the fact that his degree was obtained from the number one law school, Yale, secretly irked them no end.

Subash had his office right next to Jay. The former with his heavy head of thick black hair gelled back with 100% coconut oil had the height of a basketball player with a trim frame, and a sour expression, that looked as though he had swallowed a handful of acidic gooseberries all in one sitting. The latter with his stocky, diminutive stature compensated for his lack of height by wearing high heeled cowboy boots shipped from Texas. Sweat made his balding scalp almost luminous.

"Boy, come to my office." Varun heard Subash shouting one afternoon and tried to consciously ignore the derogatory term used when he was summoned. "This report you sent for my Immigration case for court is not up to scratch. I need you to take it back and resubmit it in an hour. All three thousand words of it." He gave a conniving smile as he crossed his arms and reclined back in the black leather armchair.

Varun was determined to show them what he was made of. So, in that hour, he reworked the report cleverly factoring aspects of little used law tenets into the report, and submitted it straight to Pravin, right over the head of Subash.

"This is one of the best caselaw arguments I have seen!" The praise from Pravin was glowing.

The next week, Varun was promoted to a senior post within the firm much to the chagrin of Subash and Jay. And he continued to shine. Within a year, he had successfully won the highest number of Immigration cases in the whole city of Chennai.

Having been approached one day by Peter Travis from the Consulate, he was fascinated by the situation of the seemingly innocent British woman in question held in jail, Kerensa Oldfield, and decided to take on her case personally.

As he approached Pulyam Prison, its bleak exterior brought home memories of a previous case he had won. A British grandmother, Stephanie Black, who was found with a stash of Heroin in a soft toy that had been packed in her bag. Varun managed to successfully prove that a younger friend who travelled with her, an avid drug user, had planted them in Stephanie's suitcase to avoid the chances of being caught herself. Stephanie was released from Pulyam and returned to the UK where she gave numerous interviews thanking Varun prolifically and attributing her newfound freedom to the dynamic lawyer.

Sitting in the familiar visitor room, he flicked through her file as he waited patiently for Kerensa. It wasn't long before she entered. With her hair tied back in a simple ponytail, her makeup free skin was soft, clear and with her slim frame, she looked much younger than her years. Tiredness and vulnerability were etched under her eyes, and she had the expression of one who had endured a lot of hardship.

"Hello, are you my new lawyer?'" she asked tentatively, placing herself in the seat opposite him.

Varun stretched out his hand, smiling. "Good to meet you Kerensa, I am Varun Raman and have been keen to take up your case. I have an excellent success rate and am determined to help you. I always work to win, that's my motto!"

Kerensa felt relieved and silently thanked Ben and Peter in her mind. It appeared they had managed to get her one of the best lawyers available. She proceeded to update Varun with the timeline of events since the day she landed in India.

"Right, I can see there is work to be done. Kerensa, can you first of all tell me the reason why you came to India, motive plays a big part. It's not usual for a foreign girl to come to these parts totally alone and the judge will look at that."

Kerensa sighed heavily. "I came primarily to search for my father, he left us when I was five and I am the only one who was able to come to India to try to locate him."

Varun nodded as he silently wondered to himself what kind of man could just up and leave his children so heartlessly.

"Sorry to hear that, well, let's focus on what we have now to move you forward. You say you lost your passport for a few days did you file a police report?"

"The guesthouse owner, Vivien, confirmed that she would be doing that on my behalf, I trusted her." Kerensa felt a creeping sense of betrayal come over her.

"Right, I will contact her urgently. And I am going to look into the reasons why you were not given a lawyer as soon as you entered the prison. I have links with Immigration officials, and it appears that someone used your real passport a week ago to enter Dubai and then re-enter India, a few days later. There is a local gang whom police are trying to track down, they operate in Nagercoil and apparently have produced many excellent document forgeries. It is believed they are linked with the cases of missing children in the area who have simply disappeared without a trace. We suspect many of them have been smuggled abroad."

Kerensa could not believe what she was hearing. Her passport, used by someone to enter the Middle East? She wanted to desperately tell Varun about the file she found however had promised David profusely that she would not breathe a word until his investigations had finished.

"Varun, I have a friend David Holdsworth who I need to contact urgently, he works in Interpol and I promised I would contact him as soon as I reach Nagercoil. He must be wondering what happened to me. It's urgent. Please could you let him know my situation?"

"I will Kerensa, if he's Interpol the police can put me in touch with him. I will work my magic and let you know okay?" Varun gave her a reassuring glance.

"Right," he continued "Leave things with me. I will work hard on your case and update you when we meet next time, okay Kerensa?"

"Thanks Varun, appreciate it."

On her walk back to the cell Kerensa thought suddenly about her father. She had been so absorbed in her problems, that she had pushed the search for Kaian to the back of her mind, but it was something she needed to really think about. All the avenues she had explored seemed to have come to a dead end.

Was it worth carrying on the search in the future, or was it simply a futile, hopeless dream she had been chasing for much too long?

CHAPTER

80

Things were moving fast. Aruna was getting prepared for the unexpected.

She had been noticing subtle changes in Vivien - a certain abruptness when she spoke to Aruna at breakfast, a coldness and emotional distance that was not there before the Maya incident. Emotion was something that really baffled Aruna, she suppressed any sign of it within her own psyche but found it even harder to fathom in others.

She had to watch Vivien whose faultless loyalty to Aruna and the business had been unquestionable before, but it was wavering now. And after her son had gone missing, who knows what she might do?

Navin had left for a well-deserved five-day break in Russia. Aruna was on her own for the time being but that was fine, she always planned ahead for such eventualities.

Before he left, Navin had supplied her with a checklist of things she needed to be aware of. Making herself comfortable at the desk in her suite, Aruna pulled the silver Macbook Pro towards her and clicked on the spreadsheet.

Update on warehouse:

34 children are being held in total (thirty-five before Maya) with capacity for five more. The vacant rooms are being prepared as we speak with minimum impact on the business. Looking to prepare a nursery for a toddler/baby too.

We now have twelve guards working on rotation, four per shift. Each shift is eight hours long. Main duties include: guarding the children, taking thee meals per days for each, escorting them to the toilet (three times per day max). One guard is always on watch at the front perimeter. All armed. Contracts have been signed by all to ensure security is always maintained.

As you are aware, it is a three-mile stint to the main highway. Little to no chance of escape. I am planning to extend the foliage further to obscure the front of the building. Rebuild the front boundary fence.

Update of member movements:

Our network continues to remain loyal and tight knit, Aruna. All members are reporting to me by close of play each day of their achievements. Current total number of members across India = 29.

Sophie De Mello has now returned safely to India. Mission successful. Boy placed with family in Dubai. I am in constant touch with the Sheikh, advising him on security, to minimise the chances of the child running away.

Sophie had no problems with impersonating the British girl, Kerensa Oldfield, enroute to Dubai due to similar physical characteristics shared by the two.

Other updates:

Planning for abduction of next baby on my return. Discussions currently taking place with a member in Delhi, she has access to a new orphanage, where security is lax. This is our next project.

The daughter of the journalist, Preeti, continues being held in the warehouse and we are in talks for possibly sending her to the Hernandez cartel family, in Cuba, who are offering a good sum for her safe delivery. Their daughter is infertile and is keen to adopt a child from the east.

Vik, who works behind the front desk, could be trusted with the file. He stored it safely at the back however, I can confirm, that it was returned directly to you Aruna, before my trip.

The update from Navin was informative Aruna thought to herself, taking a sip from a china cup of lukewarm coffee brought up by room service earlier.

Aruna had admired the way in which Vivien had stepped up. When Aruna originally made the plan to substitute the British girl's passport, it was Vivien who offered to take it forward, keen to prove her worth. She bribed the taxi driver, who slipped it in his pocket at an unsuspecting moment and subsequently Vivien handed it over to a contact in the forgery team, who produced the duplicate. It had been effortless.

But a lot had happened since then. Maya, and now the disappearance of Samuel. Enough to turn a levelheaded woman.

Her thoughts were interrupted by a firm knock on the door. An unfamiliar officer, wearing a khaki uniform stood outside, with another officer in the background, chewing fervently.

"Ms Aruna, I am sorry to disturb you. We are going around all the guests, taking a statement from everyone. Not sure if you are aware, the guesthouse owner's son, Samuel, has been missing since yesterday. Can you confirm the last time you saw him please?" Gopal leaned across the door frame holding his pencil poised against the small notebook.

Aruna smiled compliantly at the officers. "Of course, officer, happy

to help. I last saw Samuel I believe at breakfast that morning. He escorted me to my table. He seemed a good boy, from what I knew of him."

"Thank you, did you see or hear anything unusual in the past few
days concerning Samuel?"

Aruna paused for a few seconds before replying. "Now that you mention it, I did hear a terrible argument that evening. He and his mother
were screaming at each other. My balcony is above their wing so I can
hear what goes on below very clearly."

"Do you know what that was about ma'am?" Gopal was busy scribbling notes hurriedly while Krish stared open-mouthed at the provoc-
ative glass screen painting outside Aruna's door, amusement written
over his face.

"I don't but they did argue often. Was there a note left behind?" Aruna
queried innocuously.

Gopal was surprised at her accuracy. "There was Ms Aruna, but I am
not at liberty to reveal the contents, not yet." He snapped his notebook
shut. "Thank you, ma'am, you have been helpful. Have a good day." He
bowed slightly in respect and they made their way down the stairs.

Aruna closed the door and leant heavily against it breathing a deep
sigh of relief. She hoped Vivien would not be foolish and spill the beans
- any wrong move, and everything would be out in the open. Aruna's
undercover operation, all the hard work of the past years, would be com-
promised in an instance.

That was something that Aruna Pillai simply could not allow
to happen.

CHAPTER

81

It had been three long days since Varun had visited the jail. Kerensa reassured herself that he would be occupied with her case, but the wait didn't make it easier.

Gautam had kept a safe distance from her and also the other women over the past few days, thankfully. The harsh threats of Ravi had probably hit home, Kerensa chuckled to herself.

Whilst seated for lunch, Prema had pointed to a young woman behind trying to feed a small toddler on her lap, pushing mouthfuls of rice into his mouth with her hand. Her name was Asha, and her story was one of courage and sadness, Prema said.

Apparently, Gautam had taken a shine to her when she was first incarcerated for persistent shoplifting designer clothes at one of the posh shopping malls in the city. The enamoured man showered attention on her and arranged for her to be in solitary confinement for a week where he visited her often in the dead of the night when the prison was quiet. She would scream and flail her arms trying to fight him off, but it was useless. Before long, after returning back to the main cell with the others, Asha found to her horror she was pregnant.

She decided to talk to the warden Ashok who unsympathetically roared with laughter, telling her that she must have seduced the guard for such a thing to happen in his prison. The furious girl threatened to talk directly to the press, which would cause reputational ruin in the prison if it leaked out.

The next day, she was moved to a private cell with her own personal midwife to attend to her needs. Her little boy was born, whom she promptly named Gautam. A sore constant reminder to the guard of the consequences of his lecherous actions.

Little Gautam and the other children had a wide support network in the room. The younger women often took turns in looking after the children to give their mothers some much-needed rest.

One afternoon, Prema was seated against the wall and crossed her legs urging Kerensa to do the same. Esther sat nearby and watch them. The children were brought over by their mothers and placed in between the two women. They looked at Kerensa with particular curiosity, gaping open-mouthed at the pretty foreigner.

Prema started to clap her hands, as she sang in broken English.

Humpty Dumpty, sat on a wall, Humpty Dumpty had a great fall.

The children clapped hands excitedly as they joined in. Kerensa laughed and ruffled the hair of little Gautam resting his head against her arm, happily beaming up at her.

Kerensa then started singing on of her favourite childhood rhymes, and as she did, a sudden flashback came to mind of sitting on her father's lap and singing the same song.

I'm a little teapot, short and stout.
Here's my handle, here's my spout.
When I get all steamed up, hear me shout.
Tip me up and pour me out!

Moving her hands demonstrating the actions brought delighted peals of laughter to the children. Gautam nestled his head onto her lap and whispered, 'I like you,' as he gently tugged at her sleeve affectionately.

Days went by, each one falling into the next and Kerensa found herself accepting her new life, little by little. On the worst days she sobbed herself to sleep, a whole day of stale, tasteless food and a severe lack of proper sanitation affecting her deeply however there were times when the sheer resilience and strength of spirit of the other women motivated her to keep going.

Esther was always smiling, despite having being horribly abused by her husband and poor Prema, being thrown in a desperate situation - separated from her family and inadvertently thrown into prostitution, nothing could match that.

The next day, whilst walking in the grounds after breakfast and enjoying the warmth of the sun on her face, Rohina called her over.

"Ms Kerensa, you have a visitor."

It was Varun. He was seated at the table tapping his pen noisily on the surface absentmindedly as he stared out of the window. This time, he wore a smart navy suit, which was causing him to sweat profusely as perspiration slowly trickled down his forehead.

He stood up as Kerensa entered the room. "Kerensa, it is nice to see you again. Come and have a seat, I will update you. The past few days have been eventful to say the least."

He removed a thick file from his briefcase and dropped it onto the table, hurriedly looking through the papers inside. He appeared to find what he was looking for and looked up at an anxious Kerensa intently.

"Right, I can fill you in with what's been happening. I got in touch with Vivien at the guesthouse, she confirmed that she had made a mistake and did not send the police report after all."

Kerensa felt perturbed - if Vivien did not file the report, why on earth did she say that she did? Something did not make sense.

Varun continued, 'She is willing to back up the fact that your passport went missing for a few days and was eventually handed in. She was able to give a sworn statement, which was exactly the evidence I needed Kerensa. I have been in touch with your family, they send their special love to you, and have been working hard alongside me, to help you out of this situation.'

"Thank you, Varun." Kerensa felt grateful that there were good people in the world. Anxious to hear what the lawyer had to say, she wished he would get to the point quickly. "Just one thing, did Vivien say how Samuel was?" Kerensa felt herself blushing at the mere mention of his name.

"Erm, I don't recall that she did." Varun suddenly looked nervous as he slumped back into his chair, eyes glazed staring blankly out of the window. "I think that is something you could ask when you get back to Nagercoil."

What exactly was he saying?

"All your belongings at the guesthouse are safe, and Vivien reassured me that your room has been kept for you. I have liaised with local police and spoke to your friend David who said that he is working on some findings at the guesthouse, he confirmed he would catch up when you get there. Everything has been taken to the High court judge who fast tracked your case."

Kerensa almost stopped breathing for a moment, in anticipation of what Varun would say next.

"Kerensa," he began, a broad smile appearing on his face. "I am so pleased to be able to tell you that you are now free to go."

CHAPTER

82

As she stretched out her legs from an uncomfortable metal recliner at Chennai airport departure lounge, Kerensa almost had to pinch herself. She could not believe she was finally free.

Even the watery airport coffee tasted luxurious, the pungent woody odour wafting through the tiny hole at the top of the plastic cover filled her nostrils with an intense pleasure that she had never truly appreciated before. It felt so good to be free.

Peter had visited her just before she was released and came alone. He handed her a note from Ben wishing her well and insisting that the offer of dinner was still on whenever she was ready to accept it. Her missing passport was still being investigated by senior immigration officials and the police, Peter said. He organised a temporary emergency document which would get her back to Nagercoil, and then finally home to the UK. Her flight back was just two weeks away and Kerensa could not help but feel overwhelming feelings of sadness.

Her mission to find her father, Kaian, had miserably failed. All the dreams she had built over the years full of hope and anticipation had materialised into nothing like hazy sandcastles in the sky.

She had spent hours planning her trip carefully – researching the local Indian towns, having endless chats with mum and Matt about finding Kaian. He was the missing piece of their broken puzzle which now seemed to be lost forever. There seemed to be more chance of finding a thread of spun gold tossed into the sea than of locating her father, it seemed.

Sipping her steaming coffee, Kerensa thought of the friends she had left behind at Pulyam. Prema, Tracey, Esther, to name a few. She never thought she would feel it, but she even missed Rohina and her stern, bossy ways.

On her last day, Gautam had approached her in the breakfast line and briefly smiled. He wished her well, but she quietly reminded him to stay away from the woman otherwise he would have to deal with the consequences. He walked away slowly with his head held down.

It was hard leaving behind her friends and she felt pangs of guilt knowing how much they too longed for their freedom and to be outside in the real world once again. She promised she would stay in touch and send them food and other items, also toys for the children. An online charity, Friends of Pulyam Prison (FPP) caught her eye whilst browsing on her phone and she joined, vowing to offer any support required and fighting for better conditions. At least some good had come out of her stay she hoped, determined to fight for their cause was a way she could show support for the women still inside.

Prema had hugged and held her close when she found out that Kerensa was due to be released.

"Don't forget me please." She pleaded imploringly.

"How could I forget you Prema?" Kerensa replied, giving her friend a tight squeeze. "You helped me so much in these past few weeks, looked after me like a sister and I will never forget you, ever."

Tracey approached her whilst she was waiting to be seated for dinner that evening.

"Babes, I heard the good news and I'm so happy for you." She smiled at Kerensa enthusiastically. "You have been through a lot and didn't deserve to be here. So glad justice has been done."

"Tracey, I will miss you. How much longer do you have in here?" Kerensa asked.

"Only another eight years, eight long years in hell!" Tracey gave a wry laugh, rolling her eyes and Kerensa found herself laughing.

"I promise I will be sending packages for you all to share out. Just stay strong okay, one day soon you will be out of here and get your life back again." Kerensa hugged the older woman tightly.

Esther sat next to her at dinner. It was rare that they had dessert, but that day had a special treat of moist *Gulab Jamun*. They were given one each and Kerensa wrapped hers carefully in a piece of banana leaf and passed it to Esther, whose eyes lit up at the sight of the sticky, delicious treat.

"Esther, I will miss you so much," Kerensa squeezed the older lady's arm as Esther covered Kerensa's hand with hers, clasping it tight as though she didn't want to let go.

"I know I won't see you again dear, I am old now and will not last much longer. God bless you always child." Her eyes filled with emotional tears as she raised her arm to brush them away.

"God bless you Esther." Kerensa felt pangs of sadness overwhelm her.

She vowed to herself at that moment that she would never forget the friends she had made and work tirelessly to ensure she could help make them as comfortable as possible, in their circumstances.

Indian airlines, flight IA633 is now boarding for Trivandrum. Please can all passengers proceed towards the gate and await further instructions. Thank you.

The loud tannoy message interrupted her thoughts. It was almost time to enter the aircraft. Pulling out her phone, the local time read 2:17pm.

Thankfully, her belongings had been passed back to her as she left by the same guard who signed her in when she had arrived. Her clothes had been kept neatly washed and ironed, in her hand luggage so she could change before leaving.

The guard Tony sat in his booth and stared at her transfixed, just as before, his eyes bulging and mouth open. Kerensa cheekily blew him a kiss knowing full well she wouldn't see him again, and watched in amusement as his round face turned bright red.

Rohina escorted her to the main door and standing stiffly against the wall, a hint of a smile came to her lips as she nodded towards the exit.

"Stay well, ma'am," She whispered, closing the door behind Kerensa.

Turning back in the taxi the imposing concrete building had slowly disappeared from sight.

Kerensa was excited at being free and in anticipation of what lay ahead. A short journey to Trivandrum, followed by a taxi ride to the guesthouse.

And back to the arms of Samuel, who was waiting patiently for her.

CHAPTER

83

Everything looked exactly the same as when she had left a few weeks before.

The gangly coconut palms that reached majestically into the sky, gently sprinkled by snaking hosepipes were the peaceful scene that welcomed visitors who entered the guesthouse gardens.

Kerensa felt she had changed after just three short weeks in Chennai. She couldn't help thinking of the turmoil she had endured such a short space of time, ranging from the inability to find her father to being arrested and thrown into jail in depressing conditions. It felt like she had been through the mill and back again, but she had come through at the other end.

She couldn't wait to see Samuel. Thoughts of him had kept her going at the darkest times.

The taxi drove slowly up the path, crunching the gravel underfoot and pulled up abruptly in front of the entrance. The driver was a different one to the first run from the airport and his cab was smarter. The black dashboard gleamed against the sun, it had been lovingly polished, and a dancing monkey fixed on top moved crazily from side to side when he drove over any bumps. She could see from the driver details fixed to the back of the front seat that his name was Mulli. Curious about his passenger, he had asked in heavily broken English many questions about her thoughts about the town, why she was in India and if she could speak any Tamil.

Prema had taught her some simple Tamil phrases and she decided to reply to the driver, asking how he was.

"*Eppadi Irrukirai?*"

Mulli was impressed. "Very good ma'am!" he replied, smiling broadly at her through the rearview mirror.

He helped her unload her suitcase from the boot, beaming enthusiastically at the sight of the extra hundred rupee notes she placed in his hand.

"Ma'am, if you need me, just call." The small business card he handed her was imprinted with his name and mobile number. "All the best, goodbye."

Kerensa walked past the gushing fountain at the entrance straight to the front desk. It was 2.15pm. The young receptionist, Calvin, was deep in conversation on the phone. When he saw Kerensa he hurriedly ended the call.

"Hello Madam!" he looked genuinely pleased to see her. "How have you been? Ms. Vivien is waiting to see you when you are ready, she would like to meet with you privately in the lounge at 4.30pm this afternoon."

As she turned the key for her door, she felt a sudden surge of excitement at the thought of being back in her comfortable, spacious room. The bed had been turned down beautifully, clean white linen sheets spread smoothly across the queen-sized frame. A large rectangular vase containing pure white Frangipanis adorned her bedside table, their fragrance filling the room. A solitary truffle chocolate, wrapped in delicate pink paper with a white bow, had been placed thoughtfully on her pillow, along with a card that said, 'welcome back.' Warm sunlight filtered through the window creating myriad patterns on the neatly pressed white bedspread.

Tiredness overcame Kerensa suddenly the exhaustion of the past few weeks taking its toll. She kicked off her sandals and slipping between the cool sheets fell into a deep sleep.

***

Something woke her. She wasn't sure if it was a guest laughing in the corridor or a figment of her imagination. The bedside clock read 4:20pm. The blinds near her bed were partially lowered, obliterating the direct rays so the room was dark.

Remembering the meeting with Vivien, she knew she didn't have much time. She had a quick shower and changed into pressed clothes. Pulling on her favourite soft peach linen sundress, teamed up with white wedge sandals, Kerensa always felt comfortable when she put it on. Tying her hair up hurriedly into a neat bun with a light dab of crimson lipstick on her face, she was ready to go down.

The guesthouse lounge situated next to the Underground bar was a place for guests to relax and unwind. It had been tastefully decorated in soothing shades of cream and chocolate with Monet reprints adorned the walls and the contemporary white sofas were a centerpiece in the room.

Vivien sat on a single armchair by the window and stood up to welcome Kerensa when she entered the room. Her eyes were crumpled with tears. She reached forward and put her arms around Kerensa, squeezing tightly.

"Kerensa, please sit down with me."

The transformation in Vivien was shocking. Suddenly, she looked aged with dark circles wrapped around her sunken eyes and small lines visibly etched around her tightly pursed mouth.

"Vivien, are you okay?" Kerensa felt uneasy seeing Vivien upset.

Vivien looked at her unsteadily for a moment as she stifled a sob. "I know you liked my son, Kerensa, but I am sorry to tell you he is no more."

Kerensa felt her heart lurch, what was the woman saying?

"Vivien, I don't understand...?" Her face went white as she looked at Vivien with shock.

The older woman looked at her forlornly. "Kerensa, Samuel has been missing for some days now. I know you both really liked each other, so wanted to tell you personally." She looked down at her hands, unstaring.

"He left a note, and police have found his clothing washed up on the beach. They are waiting to find his body to confirm he is dead."

No, it couldn't be true. Not Samuel.

They had not known each other long, but it felt like a lifetime. She had dated on and off, but with Samuel it felt totally different. Almost what could be termed a soulmate connection, it had felt so powerful and intense.

And now, he was dead.

Kerensa felt devastation engulf her. The older woman was staring at her with moist tearful eyes.

"Vivien, I don't know what to say. I feel such utter shock, I really cared about Samuel and can't believe it. I am terribly sorry and hope you are doing okay?"

"Kerensa, I have been wanting to say to you that I am genuinely sorry that I told you misinformation, I should not have said that I filed the police report for your missing passport. I think I was just scared. There are a few things going on here and I just need to figure somethings out and then will confide in you," she looked genuinely crestfallen.

"Please don't worry, we can talk another time. This is so hard; I can't believe it about Samuel." Tears poured down Kerensa's face and Vivien rose from her seat, putting her arms around the girl.

Quickly muttering an apology, Kerensa ran from the lounge overcome with emotion.

It was in the corridor that the sobs emerged, and she tried to stifle them until she reached her room, falling on the bed where she burst into angry, hot tears.

Not only had she missed the chance to meet her father, but she had now also lost the first man she had truly had any feelings for.

CHAPTER

84

She woke early the next morning to the soothing sounds of crickets chirping rhythmically from somewhere in the distance. A loud cawing came from outside. Slipping out of bed, Kerensa quietly raised the blind to have a look. It was the same black crow as before perched on the railings, back once again. She had mentioned to Prema about the crow's visit on her arrival, and Prema explained that in South Indian folklore, the crow was considered a symbol of impending death and rebirth, if a crow greeted you it either meant someone you know was about to die or a deceased person had decided to pay a visit.

Remembering her words, Kerensa found herself thinking of Samuel. He had been so excited at the thought of seeing her again and her last memories of him were happy ones. She suddenly remembered that he had something preying on his mind that he wanted to share the last time she had seen him. Could it have been about his mother? Kerensa wholeheartedly wished she had taken more time to delve and ask some questions. There had been no apparent signs then that he was about to take his life but as she knew mental health was something invisible to the outside world and was easy to remain hidden.

She had barely known him but his touch on her skin had felt so right. There was a strong connection that went way beyond the physical. She felt as if she had known him all her life. Now, all that was left were sweet memories of their encounter and imaginings of what could have been.

She hadn't felt like eating breakfast and brought a large mug of steaming hot coffee back to her room. There were no signs of Vivien downstairs which had been unusual. Remembering Aruna had been at breakfast early most days, she was surprised to see her usual table was empty. Could she have left town, Kerensa wondered to herself.

Scrolling through her phone contacts, she found the number she knew she had to call. It was picked up quickly.

"Hello David, it's Kerensa."

It was a few moments before the reply came. "Kerensa, my goodness, I have been so worried about you! You were due to be back nearly two weeks ago. I had sent a few messages, but then your lawyer phoned me from Chennai and explained what happened. I am so sorry you had gone through this, are you okay?"

Kerensa had found seven texts and a voicemail from David waiting on her phone after coming out of prison. She knew he would have been unable to ask anyone in the guesthouse her whereabouts to maintain the level of confidentiality they had both agreed would work best in the investigation.

"David, so much has happened. To cut a long story short, I couldn't locate my father and when I tried to come back to Nagercoil, I was stopped at Chennai airport on the basis of having a counterfeit passport."

David's voice sounded shocked. "Kerensa, I remember you saying your passport had disappeared, and then returned. I think it must have been substituted then."

"I agree with you totally David, that's what my lawyer said probably happened. Apparently, there is a gang of forgers operating in the area in connection with the missing children?"

David took a breath. "Yes, and speaking of the missing children, while you were away I stayed there and did some serious digging around. I spent an hour talking privately to or rather putting pressure on the young guy at reception. I think his name was Vik. I explained the seriousness of the allegations about the file, and in no uncertain terms, threatened that if he were implicated in any way regarding the missing children, he would face a lengthy jail term. That seemed to do the trick." David chuckled to himself quietly as he continued.

"He admitted to seeing the file there but claims that he does not know who put it there. I don't believe that for an instant, there is a lot of covering up going on."

"David, Vivien confessed to my lawyer that she did not file the police report, however she promised me that it had been done," Kerensa said, feeling concerned. "Something just doesn't feel right."

"I know Kerensa," he replied. "Please stay away from Vivien, she is somehow involved in all this and I intend to find out how. Will end here, contact me anytime okay and stay safe. Bye for now."

After he hung up Kerensa thought about what they had talked about. She vowed to herself that she would stay clear of the guesthouse owner, at least for the time being.

The afternoon stretched in front of her and Kerensa was keen to do something a bit different to take her thoughts away from Samuel. On the spur of the moment, she decided to call Mulli, the taxi driver who had brought her from the airport the previous day.

"Hello madam, it is good to hear from you." He spoke loudly over the background noise of buses and cars hooting impatiently.

"Mulli are you free to pick me up soon from the guesthouse. I heard there are some good markets in town, could you take me to one please?"

"Of course, madam, I am at your service." He replied, enthusiastically. "Shall I come there at three pm, is that agreeable for you?"

"That would be perfect, thank you. I will meet you by the front entrance then."

The Golden Bazaar in Nagercoil was situated on the bustling MG road, famous for its wares. Small stalls stood proudly alongside designer outlets with sellers of clothes, toys, trinkets etc competing for the attention of sauntering passers-by, loudly shouting over each other in the hope of grabbing attention. It was popular with tourists and locals alike.

Mulli stopped the taxi on a side road next to the mall, and turned around to face Kerensa, his broad smile showing a set of very white pearly teeth.

"Madam, it gets very busy here and hard to find transport back; please allow me to wait for you, take your time."

Kerensa opened her purse and took out a handful of rupee notes.

"Thank you Mulli, I insist that you take this, please buy some food for yourself. I won't be longer than two hours."

Mulli examined the notes with excitement as he smiled at her gratefully, it was the largest tip for waiting that he had received. He folded the money carefully and slid it into his khaki shirt pocket. It would go nicely towards buying a sack of rice and portions of meat for his family.

"Yes ma'am, I will wait here for you."

The bazaar was an exciting place to be, full of noise and bustle. The first stall she passed was trading in exotic reptiles and the stall holder, a young boy with legs like sticks and greasy long hair that needed washing, begged her to come over. Before she could say anything, he placed a small lime coloured chameleon on her arm insisting that she take it for a 'very special price.' Kerensa shuddered, she had a deep-rooted fear of any scaly creatures particularly lizards. Seeing the look of horror on her face, the boy reached forward deftly removing the creature and moved towards a group of teenage boys, who looked at the creature with excitement as they boasted about who would hold it the longest.

There were jewellery stalls that caught her eye with their sparkling necklaces and shimmering trinkets on display. They were enticing and a crowd of women congregated around one in particular so Kerensa went over. It looked bigger than the others with a good choice and had a vast range of pretty metal bangles that caught the light as well as gorgeous necklace and earring sets in every hue imaginable. The women by the stall started pushing and jostling one another impatiently, vying to get a good place to make the best selection of items. Kerensa managed to manoeuvre her way through the crowd and pick some delicate, attractive bracelets and necklaces for mum and Emily, as well as smaller items for other colleagues.

The owner was an older woman wearing a deep green and red saree with at least five sparkling chains around her neck and had a bad-tempered scowl that dominated her heavily lined face. She looked irritated to see the crowd around her stall, despite the fact that business was booming. When Kerensa reached forward to give her the trinkets she wanted to buy, the woman snatched them without a word and separated them into tiny bags made out of old newspaper. They were a bargain price, each item no more than two pounds. Kerensa felt so pleased with herself.

After wandering around the stalls for a while she realised that nearly two hours had passed and that Mulli would be waiting. By the exit, a vendor was scooping out neat domes of different coloured ice cream into cones for a pair of school children and she chose a slim tall pistachio kulfi which looked like it was ready to melt in the heat.

On arriving back in her room, Kerensa noticed a small white box with a pink bow had been placed on her bed. A handwritten card had been stuck to the top, it was from Vivien who said that she had found the box in Samuel's cupboard and he had bought it as a gift for her. Inside was a beautiful baby pink *salwar kameez,* the traditional Indian outfit consisting of loose top, and trousers and the size was perfect. It was made from pure silk and had delicate white embroidery in the front. A note was at the bottom of the box which simply read - *Kerensa, you mean so much to me, can't wait to see you again, love Samuel.*

She felt like crying, it was too much.

As she walked near the door, she noticed that a note had been slipped under. It was from Aruna requesting that she came to have dinner with her at 9pm.

She was rather looking forward to seeing her interesting friend and wearing the outfit Samuel gave her, made her way to the suite and knocked loudly on the door.

After a few moments, Aruna came to the door.

"Hello Kerensa.' She looked pleased to see her. 'You look beautiful wearing an Indian dress!"

The sofa was comfortable and Kerensa found herself stretching out. Aruna passed her a small bowl containing shiny green olives.

"Aruna, I have had such difficult few weeks." Kerensa sat up and reached for the bowl as she continued. "I didn't mention before, but I am in India searching for my father, that is the reason I went to Chennai. On the way back, I was stopped at the airport for having a counterfeit passport. They put me in jail for over two weeks, it was terrible."

Aruna looked at her with concern. "I am so sorry to hear this, how terrible. How do you think this happened?" Her tone was nonchalant.

Kerensa lowered her voice conspiratorially as she leaned towards the older woman.

"Please keep this to yourself but I think Vivien had something to do with it. I have a friend who has been doing some digging around. I actually found a file at the front desk, which seems to have disappeared, it contained details of the local missing children."

Aruna stared at Kerensa silently, her expression had turned cold, inscrutable.

"I see. What is the name of your friend, may I ask?"

Kerensa looked apologetic. "Sorry Aruna, I am unable to say, he swore me to silence."

Without a word, Aruna went to a table by the window and turning her back to Kerensa proceeded to pour out something from a bottle, mixing it vigorously with a thin stirrer.

"I am so sorry I didn't offer you a drink. Do try this dear I think you will like it, it's an Indian beverage."

The glass handed by Aruna contained a small amount of a clear peach coloured liquid to which some cubes of ice had been added. Kerensa took a sip, it tasted like rosewater and had a delicious aftertaste. She quickly finished the glass.

"I think you will feel much better now," Aruna looked at her, smiling. "Don't fight it Kerensa."

What did she mean? Kerensa suddenly felt her head spin, and everything around her seemed hazy. As she struggled to stand up, she could see Aruna standing still, observing her silently without saying a word.

Why wasn't she coming to help her? The thought raced through Kerensa's mind as she fell crashing soundlessly to the floor.

CHAPTER

85

The worn stone floor beneath felt cold. Slowly opening her eyes Kerensa found herself gasping for breath, struggling beyond the eerie darkness. The nauseating chemical smell of bleach penetrated the air.

Kerensa lifted her head, and it was then that the pain hit her. Sharp and hard, coming from somewhere at the back of her head. She grimaced, as she tried to sit up slowly. Her bones ached, as though she was in the aftermath of a road accident. Where was she? The last thing she remembered was taking a drink from Aruna and then…nothing.

As she slowly stood up, her eyes became acclimatised to the blackness - what appeared to be the hazy outlines of a small table and a low bed in the corner of the room became clearer. The room was tiny from what she could make out. A small skylight was situated high up on the wall, out of reach.

The painful, dull ache emitted from somewhere near her right palm. She felt her fingers slowly, one by one. A piece of cloth had been tied neatly around the area where her index fingertip used to be. It had been removed cleanly at the joint.

The scream came from inside Kerensa and exploded into the darkness within the room. She gently touched the tender bandaged area, almost in disbelief, the intensity of the soreness made her cry out with pain.

Groping around carefully, she found what appeared to be a wall and leaned against it, her legs propped up against her chest. The severe ache from her hand was agonising.

Light slowly filtered in through the tiny window, as the first early rays of sun made an appearance. She found herself dozing off fitfully, in a semi-conscious state from exhaustion and pain.

She woke to the sound of a bolt moving loudly side to side. It was the door being opened. Fearful, not knowing what to expect she moved to the darkest corner of the room, whimpering quietly in fear.

The fluorescent light above suddenly came on, illuminating every inch of the tiny space.

Aruna walked in with a largely built, balding man who had a menacing look on his face and shut the door firmly behind her. The man remained by the door with his arms crossed, as though guarding it. Aruna looked at Kerensa coldly.

"I am sorry it has come to this Kerensa. I really enjoyed our chats, but unfortunately you were going too deep into our business. This is something that I have painstakingly built up and I can't allow for it to come crashing down."

Kerensa looked up at her with anger in her eyes. "How could you do this? Aruna, I trusted you and thought you were my friend," her voice rose hysterically. "And why would you take my fingertip off. What's bloody wrong with you?" She started crying.

Aruna answered in a cold, measured tone.

"Listen Kerensa for what it's worth, I really enjoyed the times we spent together. However, I have spent years crafting an underground empire, working all hours recruiting the right calibre of employees and building something up that is really working. I don't need foolish people to spoil everything I have worked hard for."

She continued, "Look I am sorry about your finger, but you needed to see that I am not a person to be trifled with. My assistant Vellu here will bring you some painkillers and also food in a little while. We have left a bucket in the corner if you need the toilet, and I will be back later."

Kerensa felt herself getting hot. She could not believe that she had trusted Aruna so implicitly without seeing any signs of her true nature.

"How could you do this? What sort of immoral person could kidnap innocent children and ruin their lives? Don't you have any conscience or shame Aruna?" She spat the words out.

Aruna stood up, and walked to the middle of the room, turning around to face Kerensa.

"I am proud of what I have achieved over the years. You may not agree, but I am offering a service to the community by dispatching children to where there is need."

"I have at the moment thirty-four children here I believe and some of them are ready to go to new places, homes in different countries. You will remain here until I decide what to do with you. This place is in the middle of nowhere, away from everything. Don't think for a moment of running Kerensa, because there is nowhere to go."

She broke into a maniacal laugh that made Kerensa even more angry.

"I can't believe I was suspicious of Vivien when all along it was you!"

Aruna had a malicious grin which she did not bother to conceal.

"Yes, Kerensa. Vivien was just my puppet, she organised for your passport to be taken but I am the one who masterminded that." She sounded proud as she described herself.

Kerensa grimaced in pain but there was a question she needed to ask. "What about Samuel? Did he know anything about what was going on?"

Aruna rolled her eyes. "That idiot boy. He poked his nose in too often where he shouldn't have, that was his downfall. He was warned by Vivien but still didn't listen. He brought it on himself."

Seeing Kerensa's distraught face Aruna continued bluntly. "I know you liked him, and Vivien told me that he was very keen on you too, so it is a real shame about the way things have gone. If all of you had minded your own business, none of this would have happened."

"Anyway, this is enough for the morning. I can see you are in pain, Vellu will bring some tablets and also something for you to eat Kerensa. I am not totally heartless."

She quickly turned and left the room without a backward glance followed by the tall guard, who bolted the door loudly behind him.

CHAPTER

86

It wasn't until the afternoon that she was finally able to have a good look around her room.

After Aruna's visit in the morning, the burly dark-skinned guard Vellu came back with a small blue packet containing a foil strip of six over-the-counter tablets. They were tiny, almost bead like, and Kerensa wondered at their effectiveness.

Breakfast consisted of a blackened slice of toast, rough cut into two which had been slathered unevenly with something that looked like jam but was an unusual dark brown colour and contained small lumps. A small plastic mug containing some watery coffee accompanied it.

Kerensa wasn't sure whether she should eat the unappetizing food but the throbbing pain coming from her right hand reminded her that she needed to take tablets quickly after consuming food. She was already starting to feel feverish and shivery and from the persistent throbbing in her head, she realized she may have been thrown to the floor. She took a bite of the toast and found to her horror that the bread used was mouldy, tiny green circles were starting to form on the underside of the toast. The jam-like topping was sour and possibly was an Indian fruit, but she couldn't be sure. With great difficulty she took a few bites and tried not to think too hard about what she was eating.

Reaching for the tablets, she pushed two out of the stiff foil covering and swallowed them with a mouthful of the tasteless coffee. By this point, her hand was shaking as the fever was starting to take hold. They took effect quickly and Kerensa could feel drowsiness overwhelm her. Making her way to the low bed, she collapsed onto it and fell into a deep sleep.

When she woke, she was unsure of the time but assumed it was early afternoon as the room was filled with sunshine filtering through the tiny skylight above. She looked around and saw how small the area was, like a box room. A large Indian flag had been pinned up behind the door almost as an afterthought. Apart from the narrow, low bed there was a wooden crate next to it that had been turned upside down to serve as a makeshift table. A small bucket lay in the corner to use as a toilet with another bucket nearby filled to the brim with water. A rusty jug lay floating in it. After her experience in the prison, Kerensa had become used to cleaning herself Indian style using water, items like toilet paper were unattainable luxuries.

She felt much better after sleeping and her fever seemed to have reduced greatly. Trying not to think about her missing fingertip, Kerensa mentally willed herself to stay positive. Surely someone would realise she was missing and come for her? The problem was no-one knew she was in this forlorn place.

The day dragged on, interrupted by only Vellu coming to bring her food or to remove the tray after she had eaten. She slept fitfully on and off and felt her fever rising and falling over the course of the day. Once when Vellu kept the door open as he brought in the food, she could see her room was at the end of a long, dingy corridor, off which were a large number of identical doors. She wondered if they were where the children were held and decided to ask Vellu.

"I cannot answer your question, just eat your food, I will come back in an hour to collect the tray," he answered curtly as he turned and closed the door abruptly. As he went, she noticed he had a large bunch of keys fastened to his waist. She quickly averted her eyes as she didn't want him to see that she had noticed them.

Her fingertip had started to become very painful, and she realized that it needed to be splinted and rebandaged in order for it to heal effectively. Vellu gruffly agreed to bring a fresh bandage and small piece of bark, and Kerensa set about cleaning the open wound first with water taken from a small vessel in the corner of the room and set the splint in place before wrapping the bandage around tightly. The pain coming from the area was excruciating but she continued to take the tablets to fight any infection as much as possible.

Three days had passed, and there was no sign of Aruna. Kerensa was mortified that she could have fallen for the woman's lies, believing her when she said that her business was not worth discussing, and even going to have dinner and share jokes with someone who was intrinsically evil. What else could somebody be, who took pride in snatching small children, and selling them in an underground market for large sums of money?

She looked at her outfit, she was still wearing the pink *salwar kameez* that Samuel had got for her, except now it was crumpled and filthy.

It was later that afternoon that Aruna finally came. The door unbolted loudly in familiar fashion. She was clutching the shoulders of a small, frightened little girl whom she pushed into the room. The girl looked petrified as she stared at Kerensa frozen, with doe-like eyes.

"This is Preeti, she will be joining you for a few days because we need her room for a new child arriving shortly. You can keep each other company until we decide what to do with you."

Kerensa smiled at the child reassuringly and patted the bed for her to sit down. She glared at Aruna.

"You need to let us go Aruna. This is not a joke anymore. I...I had informed the police and they will come looking for me, so you had better release us."

Her threat just made Aruna laugh, as she threw back her head and chuckled wildly.

"That's a good try, I have to hand it to you Kerensa. Unfortunately, this place is miles away from anywhere, so they won't be able to find you, even if they tried. And you may not have to worry much longer about them finding you anyway."

Her voice trailed off as she turned and left the room, locking the door behind her.

Kerensa felt alarmed, it felt like a direct veiled threat and they just had to get out of the place as soon as possible.

The little girl sat quietly at the end of the bed and stared at Kerensa curiously. She was undernourished and frail with arms that closely resembled sticks.

"What's your name sweetheart?" Kerensa asked gently.

"My name is Preeti, *akka*." She whispered. Kerensa remembered Prema teaching her that akka was a term used to respectfully refer to someone as 'older sister.'

"That's such a lovely name Preeti!" Kerensa smiled warmly at the little girl, who started to open up and began explaining how she was taken from outside her school weeks before, in front of her father who had tried to chase her kidnappers and that she had turned six years old a few weeks after she had been captured.

"Listen, Preeti, we have to get out of here, do you understand?" The little girl nodded in agreement.

"*Akka*, I want to leave but am scared. What if that big man catches us?"

She gave Kerensa a worried look and proceeded to put both thumbs in her mouth, sucking on them comfortingly. Kerensa felt shocked, it was something that she had done too when she was younger, something that used to annoy her mother no end. She had never met anyone else who had the same habit until now.

"Preeti, he won't, don't worry okay? I will look after you." She held her arms open and beckoned the little girl to come closer as she enveloped her closely in a reassuring, tight hug. She suddenly felt protective. Gently stroking her hair, she told Preeti about the plan they would carry out later that evening.

Vellu had a long evening stretching ahead of him. The other guard who was supposed to be on duty with him had an emergency at home so

Vellu would be doing many more extra hours. He was tired but once he had taken the dinner tray to the foreign girl and the small one, he decided he would treat himself to a smoke outside. He suddenly cheered up at the thought. There had to be some pleasures for doing such a thankless job, he thought to himself.

When the sound came of the bolt opening, Kerensa gestured to Preeti to get ready. The little girl sat on the bed pretending to cry loudly. Vellu paused when he entered, door wide open looking to see where Kerensa was.

As he put his head around the door, Kerensa hit him as hard as she could with the metal slop bucket. With a loud groan he fell heavily to the stone floor. Quickly removing the cloth flag from behind the door she wrapped it tightly around his mouth. Preeti deftly removed the bedsheet and together, they tied his hands tightly behind his back.

A mobile phone was sticking out of his pocket, Kerensa grabbed it and removed the bunch of keys from around his waist. Beckoning Preeti they locked the door securely behind them, leaving the motionless guard shackled on the floor.

Holding Preeti's hand they quietly tiptoed down the dimly lit hallway. There were no signs of any other guards but as they passed the locked doors, they could hear occasional sounds of crying coming from within some of the room. Kerensa knew that it would not be possible to take any other children yet only once they had reached safety, they would ensure that the police came to release everyone.

The huge door at the other end of the corridor was bolted securely. A box containing metal torches was situated next to the door. Preeti put her hand in and removed two. Kerensa fumbled through the keys, trying them one by one, to hopefully find the right one to open it. After a few tries, the lock gave a 'click' and she slowly turned the heavy handle.

The light breeze from outside gently blew over them, almost like a welcome. Looking at each other excitedly, they clutched hands, walking out into the night and into their first taste of freedom.

CHAPTER

87

The fear of the unknown can be the scariest thing of all.

Stepping out through the door into darkness the two girls held hands and ventured slowly out into the courtyard. A dim light hung from the side of the wall, serving little purpose except to gather fireflies around. Her heart was pounding with fear but Kerensa was trying to remain strong for little Preeti.

Past the courtyard lay an open grassy space surrounded by a wire boundary fence. A small cabin was located just by the fence and a man was standing outside smoking, the red embers of his cigarette lighting up the surrounding darkness. He had his back to the girls and over his shoulder was a long, black rifle.

The girls crouched behind a waste bin and waited. Kerensa squeezed Preeti's hand comfortingly. After what seemed like forever the man threw his stub onto the ground, stamping it hard with his heel before going inside the cabin.

This was their chance. They quietly walked towards the large entrance gate which was locked. Advising Preeti to keep a lookout, Kerensa tried different keys from the bunch, but none of them fitted. The solid metal gate was too big to be broken down. Preeti looked at her despairingly. Kerensa had to think fast, the man could step out at any moment.

The only illumination in the immediate area came from the warehouse and cabin beyond the fence, lay utter darkness. It was frightening to think what lay there but the girls had no choice. Aruna was not someone to mess with and Kerensa knew that she had no intention of letting them go.

Placing her finger to her lips, Kerensa warned Preeti to remain silent, urging her to follow. The only possible way to escape would be if there were any breaks or holes in the wire so they walked slowly around, pushing the fence to check if there were any gaps.

Suddenly, a dog started barking loudly inside the cabin. They could hear the man ordering it to be quiet, but the ferocious barking continued. The man opened the cabin door and stood by the entrance, looking around.

The girls froze.

Thankfully, the area had no lighting overhead, so it was relatively dark. He stood outside for a few minutes peering into the darkness outside the fence, then shrugged his shoulders as he went inside and closed the door.

They quickly continued walking around the wire fence, Kerensa knew they had to find an exit soon because it could be anytime that the man would realise that the guard, Vellu, had not made an appearance in the night.

Suddenly, Preeti called out urgently. "*Akka!*" She had found a broken part of the wire in a corner attached to a boundary post. Kerensa used her might to pull as much wire out as possible, finally creating a hole that could be big enough for them to crawl through.

Helping Preeti through first, Kerensa crawled through with difficulty but managed to come through to the other side. Preeti handed Kerensa another torch and looking back to check no-one was around they both switched them on. The surrounding area was barren wastelend stretching out for miles. Large patches of tall wild grass existed amongst the desolate, stony areas. In the far distance, Kerensa could make out the hazy silhouette of what appeared to be coconut palms. If they made their way towards them it could lead to a road, or back to town, Kerensa thought to herself.

They flashed their lights and could see a rough, dirt covered path leading through the tall, slender grass. They looked at each other hopefully and taking Preeti's hand, Kerensa took the lead. The sound of chirping night crickets surrounded them. In the distance, an animal howled wildly. Kerensa could feel Preeti's fear and squeezed her hand a few times to reassure her that everything would be okay.

Remembering the guard's phone, Kerensa quickly switched it on but was dismayed to find out there was no reception. They had ventured too far from the building. She could see the time, it read 9.15pm. The only light came from their torches and phone. Beyond the meagre illumination stood a pitch-black darkness and utter silence. It felt unnerving but there was no choice, if they wanted to avoid being caught, they had to keep walking.

For over twenty minutes, they continued along the path but Kerensa could feel Preeti slowing down. "Akka, I feel so tired," she sighed and suddenly sat down on the gravel her thin legs crossed.

Kerensa had to think quickly. There was still a lot of terrain to cover and as soon as it was discovered that they had gone missing Aruna would send out a search party, there could be no doubt about that.

"Preeti, come on my back I will carry you for some time." The little girl laughed with excitement and as Kerensa crouched down, she jumped on her back, holding tightly around her neck. Thankfully, she was extremely light.

"Hold up your torch so I can see when I walk Preeti." Kerensa instructed as she continued along the path. Her right hand was starting to painfully ache again as she tried to brush it to the back of her mind. They started to sing nursery rhymes ranging from Humpty Dumpty to Jack and Jill to make the time go quicker, and to take their minds off how much further they had to walk. After nearly two hours they finally reached the edge of the wasteland near a huddle of tall coconut palms.

Kerensa set Preeti down from her back, exhausted. She didn't know how much further she could go, her hand was excruciating and throbbing with pain. She was sure that an infection was setting in and she had no tablets to take.

They stopped for a short break, both sitting down at the base of a palm tree as they shut their eyes, exhausted. "Preeti, you cannot fall asleep okay? Kerensa felt worried, seeing the girl lean forward over her bent knees, she looked like she could drift off any moment. They had to keep moving but it felt almost impossible with the exhaustion they were both experiencing. Kerensa decided that they would rest for just ten minutes, and then continue.

Nudging the tired child awake, they both rose to their feet and continued through the grove. The ground was uneven and rocky, and they tried to tread as carefully as possible. They finally reached the edge of a paddy-field which appeared ominous and mysterious in the darkness. It seemed to stretch for acres and acres as far as the eye could see. A small, raised path made from soil ran by the edge and they followed it slowly, step by step. They were mindful of the dangers of falling into the murky water.

At the end of the paddy field, a cement road lay directly in front of them both Kerensa and Preeti looked at each other excitedly.

At last.

Kerensa suddenly noticed a white fiat car parked by the side of the road, under a streetlamp, and her heart leapt. Someone to help.

Holding Preeti's hand, they tentatively approached the car and noticed a woman with their back to them, speaking animatedly on the phone. On getting closer, Kerensa recognised her and gasped excitedly.

"Latha, is that you? Oh, thank goodness!"

Latha looked at them, one to another, in utter shock. "Kerensa, it's you! What happened? You are walking out here in the middle of the night, are you okay?"

After introducing her to a sleepy Preeti, Kerensa began narrating the events of the past few days. Latha listened quietly as Kerensa described what she had found and Aruna's involvement in the underground network.

Latha was silent for a moment before she spoke sombrely. "It seems like you know quite a lot about these evil people Kerensa. No wonder they had kept you captive. Don't worry, come with me and I will take you both to the police straight away."

She opened the door for Preeti to get in the back and then Kerensa joined her at the front of the car.

"Listen Kerensa it's a bit of a trek from here, so just close your eyes and sleep if you want okay. You both must be exhausted."

"Thanks, Latha," she replied, "but just out of curiosity, what were you doing out here in the middle of nowhere?"

Latha looked startled by the question and stared straight ahead.

"I…I had an argument with my boyfriend if you must know. I drove out to get some air as I normally do when we argue. That was him I was talking to when you came up, by the way," she added, starting the engine.

Kerensa felt bad for asking. "Really sorry to hear that Latha, hope everything sorts out for you."

Latha looked at her for a few seconds, smiling slowly.

"Kerensa, don't worry about me. Just close your eyes now and relax, okay. I will wake you when we reach the station."

At the back of the car, Preeti leaning against the window falling asleep. Kerensa settled comfortably into the seat and closed her eyes, relieved to have found someone they could trust.

It was the sudden jolt of the car stopping that woke her. In the back, Preeti was stirring.

Kerensa looked out and wondered why the place looked familiar.

To her absolute horror, she realised that they were in front of the building where they had been held captive. And marching towards them, a furious look on her face, was Aruna.

CHAPTER

88

Kerensa wanted to scream loudly.

'What the hell...Latha?' She could not even register what was happening, it was all too much. Now, betrayed, by someone who had invited her out for lunch, they had even cracked jokes together. The second betrayal, in just a few long days, was beyond any words imaginable.

In the back seat, Preeti started sobbing uncontrollably.

Aruna calmly opened the driver side door and Latha stepped out, without so much as a backward glance. She went straight up to Aruna and kissed her cheek affectionately. Latha pushed up her sleeves to reveal a tattoo of a snake that seemed to cause Preeti more distress, as the child put her arms around Kerensa and whimpered loudly.

Behind Aruna stood two tall, well-built men one of which Kerensa recognised as the guard from the cabin. Both of them wore stern faces and carried rifles. A shorter man with a balding head and glasses stood next to Aruna, his expression nonplussed.

The two guards moved forward to open the doors for Kerensa and Preeti, who slowly stepped outside the vehicle. Preeti instinctively moved towards Kerensa and clasped her hand tightly, burying her head in Kerensa's arm as she continued sobbing pitifully.

"Well, well, what do we have here?" Aruna's voice was caustic as she glared at Kerensa and Preeti, looking from one to the other. She muttered in Tamil to one of the men who promptly left and went inside the main building.

Kerensa glared at both women angrily. 'Latha, how could you? I thought you were someone I could trust we even went for lunch together. You and Aruna are liars of the worst kind."

Latha smirked. "I enjoyed our short time together but forgot to mention that I am very much with Aruna who is, in fact, my mum's cousin. We reconnected when she returned from the US and when she offered me a position in her business, I jumped at the chance. My boyfriend, Gopal is in the police force and doesn't suspect a thing. Now, I am earning more than ten times the normal salary of a girl my age in India." She looked lovingly at the older woman, with gratitude.

"You are disgusting!" Kerensa screamed, gripping Preeti's hand firmly. "Taking little children away from their families and then selling them to others like they are cattle. God will punish evil people like you and believe me there's a special place in hell waiting for you."

Kerensa's words seemed to amuse Aruna, who burst into insane laughter." I appreciate your thoughts, but he most certainly hasn't punished us yet."

The balding man burst into laughter too. Kerensa glared at him, wondering what part he played in everything.

The guard returned from the building prodding a manacled, bearded man walking slowly a few steps in front of him, head bowed. Kerensa looked at him then looked again. Why did he look so familiar?

With a cry she realised who it was. Samuel.

He was alive.

Samuel looked up in sheer surprise. "Kerensa?"

It was all too much. Hugging Preeti close Kerensa burst into emotional tears. The man she had feelings for, whom she thought was dead, was actually alive.

"We had to silence him." Aruna said ruthlessly. "He knew too much and couldn't be trusted. By faking his suicide, there would be no probing

or questions. But there is no further need for him or for either of you."
She looked pointedly at Kerensa and Preeti before turning to the balding
man next to her.

"Navin, will you do the needful?"

Navin reached into his pocket pulling out a revolver. He pointed it
at Kerensa, aiming it directly at her head.

Preeti screamed loudly and buried her head in Kerensa's waist.
Samuel uttered a loud scream as he lurched forward. "No!" came his
desperate cry.

There was the sound of a loud blast and suddenly a strangled noise.
Navin staggered backwards clutching his stomach. A deep crimson stain
was visible on the centre of his white shirt, which was spreading out-
wards, getting bigger and bigger. He fell to the floor, screaming as he
writhed in agony.

Aruna looked shocked for a moment, before pointing angrily to a
silhouette crouching behind a waste bin. One of the guards went over
to the bin, rifle cocked and dragged over out an older man, bringing
him to Aruna.

It was David.

Seizing the opportunity with the distraction, Samuel moved towards
Kerensa, throwing his manacled arms around her and the frightened child.
David looked straight at Kerensa with concern, before facing Aruna.

"Give yourself up Aruna the game is over, there's nowhere to hide.
Vivien confessed everything, told me the location of this place. The police are on their way here."

Aruna screamed and grabbed the shotgun which lay on the ground
near a lifeless Navin. In the chaos, Latha turned, and started running
towards the building. Aruna aimed and shot her in the back, she fell to
the ground.

"I cannot have my empire falling!" Aruna screamed maniacally, her
eyes unrecognisably wild and unfocussed.

"This is all your fault." She screamed at David as she reached for her gun, shooting him at close range. He collapsed in a heap, as a pool of blood emitted from the wound on his chest.

Kerensa and Samuel looked on in horror. Kerensa pulled Preeti closer.

Just then, a bright spotlight came on from the distance, aiming directly at Aruna, and a loud voice boomed across the chaos.

"This is the police. You have nowhere to go, throw down your weapon and stand with your hands up, where we can see them. If you resist, we will not hesitate to shoot."

Aruna tossed the gun angrily to the ground, swearing in frustration and put her hands up in the air. Two policemen immediately brought handcuffs, clamping them around the defiant, angry woman as they led her away.

An officer went over to David, where he lay motionless on the ground, checking his pulse. "He's alive," he shouted, and more officers came over, surrounding their fallen colleague. A few policemen went running into the building and helped escort more bewildered children out into the courtyard.

In the midst of the chaos, Kerensa continued to stroke the little girl's hair, who had her arms wrapped tight around her waist. Preeti suddenly looked up and gave Kerensa a beautiful smile of contentment. The horror of her ordeal was finally over.

As Samuel pulled her close, his voice lowered to a whisper as he muttered to Kerensa, "I love you and am never letting you go again."

CHAPTER

89

It was the vibrant and striking arrangement of flowers that caught Kerensa's eye first, in colours to weave dreams on - subtle shades of purple, white, pink and yellow, with some tight buds and moist flames of soft, silk-like petals that delicately fanned out of the glass base, filling the stark room with their magical, intoxicating scent. They were from Samuel who would be visiting her that evening, promised the nurse as she brought over the breakfast tray. She was firm and insistent that Kerensa needed to take it easy and rest in the meanwhile.

She'd had a high fever throughout the night and a different nurse had been on duty at the time whose name badge read 'Diya.' She looked about the same age as Kerensa and had long, shiny black hair neatly curled up and stuffed into her starched cap. She had an efficient air about her and brought damp white towels at regular intervals, damping down Kerensa to cool her down, whilst humming quietly under her breath. The chalky white pills Kerensa had been given tasted foul but did the job of reducing the fever and any possible infection.

Doctor Murthy, a swarthy man who had examined her the previous day, recommended immediate re-grafting surgery to close the wound on her finger which had been a success. Her flight back home was four days away and she would begin rehab once she returned to the UK.

So much had happened over the past days, almost impossible to fathom. Aruna had been arrested and would get her full punishment, Kerensa was assured by Constable Gopal. He had been one of the first on the scene at the shootout and sat slumped by his girlfriend, Latha's body for a long time, in a shocked state, unable to digest that she had secretly been a part of the underground gang.

Kerensa had spoken to mum and Matt early that morning and they were eagerly counting the days until she landed back home. When Kerensa spoke about being unable to locate Kaian, she could feel her voice breaking with emotion. Matt simply told her that they had managed so far without him and that they had a great life ahead to look forward to as a family, so not to worry. Kerensa could have hugged him at that moment.

It was the same nurse who popped her head around the curtain no more than two hours later. The strong pills were making Kerensa feel mildly hallucinated and drowsy, almost like she'd entered an alternate reality.

"Miss, can you see a special visitor, for just a few moments?"

Before she could answer Preeti appeared at Kerensa's side, a big Cheshire-cat like smile written across her tiny face. The nurse gave the little girl a tap on the shoulder, before adding sternly, "no more than five minutes, mind."

"Hello *akka!*" Preeti started jumping up and down, beaming excitedly. "How are you? My mummy is here and wants to talk to you."

Kerensa looked at the girl with deep affection - they had been thrown together in such dire circumstances, however, out of the mire had emerged a sweet bond between the two of them.

"It's so good to see you Preeti, your mummy and daddy must be so happy to see you again."

"Yes, but my daddy is here in this hospital. He is resting but mummy is keen to chat to you." Preeti disappeared and came back holding the hand of a woman. She was not tall, her frame was on the larger side with dark, pock-marked skin and she had long, oily hair almost down to her waist, pulled behind into a neat plait. A cascade of small white Jasmine flowers pinned tight behind her head exuded a heavenly sweet smell and the bright orange saree she wore lay crisp against her skin, like a cascade of flames against a dark night.

She flashed Kerensa a grateful smile and spoke in broken English. "Hello, thank you so much for helping find our daughter. These gifts are for you. I hope you feel much better soon." Removing two small red boxes from a bamboo bag in her hand she placed them on the table next to the bed. They had the words 'Cakebox bakery' imprinted in bold letters with a small picture of an elephant on the corner. She placed a sealed envelope on top with the words 'contact details' neatly handwritten on the front.

"Please take care. These are our details, once you feel better please stay in touch. Preeti likes you so much and hasn't stopped talking about you!" She looked down at her daughter affectionately, who was beaming at Kerensa as she continued to jump up and down excitedly. "My husband who is recovering from a coma here in hospital, wants to say a quick thank you to you too. One moment please, he is just coming."

She disappeared behind the curtain. Kerensa could hear a murmuring of voices speaking in Tamil before the woman and Preeti re-appeared with a man by their side.

He was tall, with speckled black and white hair and heavily bearded. His hospital gown was a faded shade of blue and he had an air of tiredness about him.

Kaian looked startled when his eyes fell on Kerensa. The pretty, frail girl lying on the bed, her dark hair in tumbled curls would be similar to how his daughter would look now, he thought emotionally to himself.

He spoke slowly with great effort, in perfect English.

"Hello, thank you so much for bringing our precious daughter back to us. She means the world. I am finding it tiring to speak, but my wife has left you our contact details, please get in touch once you reach England okay. All the best to you."

Kerensa looked at him and felt her heart leap, she didn't know why.

His large brown eyes had looked at her intently, almost knowingly with subtle signs of recognition, but she knew the aftereffects of the medication were playing tricks on her. The air of familiarity about him was something, however, she couldn't quite pinpoint. Almost as though she had known this bearded stranger in another life.

His wife, sensing his tiredness, gently pushed him away to go back to his own bed. He gave Kerensa a lingering wave of goodbye, almost as though he were reluctant to leave, and shuffled back behind the curtain and out of the door.

Kerensa could not understand the emotion she was feeling when the man left, it was almost a deep sense of loss as though an intense, profound connection buried inside had been severed.

As Preeti and her mother left the room giving a final wave, a forlorn Kerensa lay motionless staring up at the ceiling, wondering why she was suddenly feeling so lost and overwhelmed with crippling grief.

CHAPTER

90

The filter coffee was rather bitter so after taking a quick sip, she pulled the tray table down in front and balanced the cup precariously within the indented area.

Kerensa could not believe she was finally airborne, enroute to Heathrow. Finally going home. The wispy transparent clouds floating outside masked the murkiness of the endless ocean that lay beneath. Spots of incandescent sunshine filtered through the clouds, as they bounced off the glass in blinding radiance, dazzling her eyes.

Samuel had come to say goodbye at the airport. His hug was so tight as he covered her mouth with slurpy kisses, she felt as though she could not breathe, and she laughingly pushed him away. It felt like almost a lifetime since he first met her when she had landed in India, full of excitement and hope at tracking down her father. She finally accepted that meeting her father Kaian was simply not meant to be.

After Vivien's arrest for her part in aiding the trafficking gang, Samuel was in sole charge of the guesthouse. His enthusiasm ensured he would do an excellent job in the day to day running of the place.

She promised that she would return to him as soon as possible, dreading being apart from the man she had deep feelings for. He, in turn, had promised Kerensa that she would have the Executive suite when she came back and as he held her close, at the departure gates, tears cascaded down his cheeks as he almost refused to let her go. After a last kiss, she scanned her passport at the e-gates and turned to give Samuel a last emotional wave.

The plane was surprisingly empty and would be breaking the journey shortly in Dubai for a few hours.

At the end of the row, an older woman with short, silver hair and clinking turquoise metal bangles that perfectly matched her soft, chiffon sari, gave a loud, unladylike yawn. She then reached into her handbag, pulling out a newspaper which she threw on the seat in between them, and left to use the bathroom. Kerensa glanced at the paper curiously.

Entitled the 'Daily Chronicle,' near the top was a picture of a smiling Preeti, standing in front of her beaming parents.

The bold headline above the photo read as follows: **Senior Chronicle journalist, Kaian Achari, re-united with his missing daughter Preeti.**

Her heart lurched as she grabbed the newspaper, opening it carefully onto the tray table, whilst holding the hot paper cup in her spare hand.

She could not believe what she was reading.

Suddenly remembering the envelope given by Preeti's mother, she pulled it quickly out of her handbag, hands shaking uncontrollably as she hurriedly tore one side open. A single sheet of white paper had been neatly folded inside.

Next to the phone number and email address lay the neatly written words: with love, Kaian, Jingles and Preeti Achari.

Kerensa did not feel the burning liquid as it spilt heavily across her jeans, dripping noisily onto the carpet below.

It was him.

Her search was over.

EPILOGUE

W ords could not describe the feeling when Preeti fell into my arms once again. My beautiful, smiling princess. After two long months of hell, she is back with us, just as though she has never been away.

I am back at work finally, on the frontline for the Chronicle. My first article, aptly so, is about the trafficking gang that operated locally led by Aruna Pillai, formerly from this town. She is a ruthless woman, but every ruthless woman has a story.

It turned out that Aruna was the girl with the staring eyes, that I remembered from my childhood at Old Pound street. I conducted an informal interview with our neighbour, Mrs Kumar, our elderly neighbour who just loved to talk. I found out about Aruna's sad childhood that probably had a part to play in the woman she turned into. She is in jail for a very long time and will never see the light of day again.

Seeing the British girl who rescued Preeti brought back memories of my sweet daughter Kerensa. She would probably look similar, with dark hair and golden skin. I never got to ask the girl's name and I absolutely wish I had.

She has our email address and hopefully she will write, so we can get to know her more, and thank her properly. I felt so sorry for her, losing her fingertip in such a terrible manner, but I can see she is a fighter.

Wait.

I am at my desk and an email alert has suddenly popped up. There is a new message in my inbox, it has a UK email address and is marked 'urgent'. It could be from her.

I will open it as soon as I finish my cup of sweet milky tea made for me by my loyal wife Jingles which is of course, as always, accompanied on the side by a crisp, swirly orange *jelabi*.

The End.

Printed in Great Britain
by Amazon

62982104R00173